Ramped Up Love

T. A. SMITH

Published by T. A. SMITH, 2023.

RAMPED UP LOVE

First edition. May 4, 2023.

Copyright © 2023 T. A. SMITH.

ISBN: 979-8223688914

Written by T. A. SMITH.

RAMPED UP LOVE

I owe thanks to my Husband for always supporting me and the endless coffee he supplied while I write. Also, my children who made me want to prove that a dream is worth chasing and that anything is achievable no matter what your background.

Thanks also to my dear friend and critic Lesley, without her reading my books and giving me honest feedback and support, and telling me to "hurry up, I need to know what happens" I would have never gone ahead with getting any of my writing published. Also, my eldest daughter Bethan for helping with the actual publishing.

CHAPTER 1
T.J AKA TIFFANY JADE

So here I am standing outside what is soon to be my new place of work, my bag slung over my shoulder. I had to get this placement on my own as my college tutor hadn't been successful in getting me a placement, probably because he let on that I was female. I got lucky with this job; I didn't use my full name for a start. Something about being a female mechanic that not a lot of garages in my hometown like, so instead of filling the C.V out using Tiffany Jade Govern, I used my initials T.J. The boss of this place, Frank McIntyre owns and runs it, he didn't even ask for an interview he just asked for a letter of recommendation from my college tutor. We had emailed and text a few times to sort out start dates and college information. I had to beg my tutor not to give out my full name or that I was a girl. He warned me that doing so was deceitful and against his ethics, I pointed out that in mechanics ethics is bullshit. College, yeah, that was another big deal, ever tried being the only female student in a male dominated class? Nope thought not. I had to put up with a lot of sexist remarks and comments, but you have to expect that in this trade, in case you hadn't figured it out yet I'm one of the 200 female mechanics in the U.K compared to the 500,000 male mechanics. Like I said it's a male dominated trade. Yeah, so what? I'm a girl, I can do this shit and have been for years now, in my own time after school, and studying, anything to get away from the bullies in the care home. I'm not a tomboy though in fact far from it. I like dressing up, make-up and heels, I like baking and shit too, but cars especially the older models are where my heart lies. Nothing beats the feeling of fixing something that should be scrapped and then hearing that engine roar to life after. I'm rambling again, another thing I do a lot when I'm nervous. So, as I was saying I got this job purely on merit and my C.V plus the belief that I'm male, shit what do I do now?

Frank thinks I'm a guy, boy is he in for a shock when he realises, I'm a chick. Well here goes nothing I guess, wish me luck.

I pull the door open and the little old-style bell hanging over it gives a little melodic ding a ling, making me chuckle.

"Hi, can I help you?" some guy with blonde shaved hair asks me.

"Hi yeah, I'm here to see Frank McIntyre".

"FRANK" the blonde guy shouts

"YEAH" some voice gruffly shouts back from the main ramps.

"SOMEONE HERE TO SEE YOU"

"WHO?"

"Sorry love, can I have your name please?" asks blonde guy.

I muster up all my courage and go for broke as I shout.

"T.J SIR" the silence was deafening as everyone stopped what they were doing, someone even dropped a spanner on the floor.

I fidgeted on my feet as the blonde guy sucked in a breath and scratched his head.

"Well, shit this I wasn't expecting, so you're the new guy?" blonde guy looked at me with a smile.

"New chick I'd say" I held my hand out for him to shake, he took it then kissed it, like what the fuck, this isn't some Mills and Boon romance drama.

"Names, Cole and this is my twin brother Mitch" as he said that another blonde guy walked into the office area, his hair was longer, neatly trimmed and with a quiff. They both looked to be in their mid-twenties, and both had that loveable rogue look about them. Mitch had a tattoo on his shoulder just peeking out from his t-shirt, muscles that rippled as he moved his arms. Cole had a full sleeve of tattoos, mainly skulls and dragons, he also had muscles that rippled. Guess these brothers worked out a lot.

"So, is this the new dude then?" Mitch asked as he walked over with a 'fuck me 'grin on his face.

"The dude is a chick, fuck bro I thought you learnt to tell the difference in pre-school" Cole smirked.

"Fuck you dude" Mitch punched his twin in the arm.

"Boy's, work now... That Golf needs an oil change Cole and you Mitch get that shitty Renault out of my garage asap" This dude must be Frank, Tall, muscly about forty-five bold and tattooed heavily.

"So, you lied about who you are? Not a good start. I don't like liars" Frank glared at me with obvious anger at being deceived in his eyes.

"Excuse me sir but at what point did I lie?"

"OOOOSSH" the twins both said as they walked out the office, Mitch shook his head and Cole gave me a sympathetic look and waved bye to me.

"Well, you sure as fuck aint no fella, are you?"

"Nope, and I don't believe that at any point during our emails and texts that you ever asked if I was male or female. I can double check but I'm fairly certain. So again, at what point did I lie?" where the fuck did my courage suddenly come from? Who was I answering back at my new employer, and the shortest job ever, no way was he going to keep me on now. I mean I lied about what I was to him, and now I'm back talking to him. Shut up Tiffany, I tell myself.

"Touché, so what's a girl like you doing working as a grease monkey?" Frank wiped his hands on a rag and leaned on the countertop, his demeanour softening slightly.

"What can I say? Cars are fascinating, the engine structure and how they run and sound, a healthy car especially an old style V8 is music were as a sick spluttering car running on only two cylinders is not a nice sound at all, oh by the way I'd say that Renault that's just started up, yeah sounds like it's only firing on three, check the compression on the plugs and maybe change them out for newer higher spec ones" I dropped my bag to the floor as I leaned over the counter to look into the garage.

"Not bad, I'll give you a month's trial, be warned the twins are very dirty minded, they mean no harm, but their brains are in their ball sacks" Frank leaned over and shook my hand.

"Thank you, you won't regret it".

"I better not, anyway what does T.J stand for?"

"Tiffany Jade sir"

"Call me Frank, I'm not a schoolteacher or that fella from that film all the girls are going crazy over" his comment made me laugh, like full on laugh out loud laugh.

"So, you got sense of humour then, that will be good, let's see how you cope with the boy's banter over this month, they may break you, and make you quit" Frank winked at me.

"Not a chance Frank, I can give as good as I get".

"Now that I'd pay to see, those boys need a run for their money".

"Hey Cole, make us a brew will ya, splash of milk and two sugars, try to leave out the dash of engine oil" I shout into the garage.

"Make your own fucking tea" Cole shouted back.

"Just make the damn brew" someone else shouted.

"I'm going to love this," Frank smiled as he led me away to the locker room. For a small business this place was top notch, lockers, staff room and a kitchen. They even had a shower room; Frank did say it was put in as Mitch kept having small oil explosions and had to go home to change one too many times. After the quick tour Frank left me alone in the garage with the twins.

"Next time you make the fucking tea, tea maid is not in my job description. Do I look like a fucking tea lady" Cole passed me a mug of the milkiest tea I had ever seen.

"What the fuck is this? I asked for a tea not a fucking warm mug of watered-down milk" I threw the tea into the sink and walked over to yard were the cars waiting to be sorted were parked. The other thing I liked about this garage, all the cars were pre 2000 and they were fucking amazing. I love classic cars. Frank had given me a set of keys and told me the car in question needed a full service done. I knew he was testing my car finding skills as well as my mechanical skills. Seriously if he was shocked at me being a girl then this was going to blow his mind when I finish the job, I quickly found the Ford Escort mark 3 and drove her into my workspace in the garage, I didn't have a licence so I knew this was the most driving I would get to do. Ok, ok I hear you asking why I don't have a licence yet I'm a mechanic. Firstly, I'm only 17. Secondly, I don't have an actual address to send a licence to, yep, I'm homeless. I did have a sort of home if you can call it that, but I left, I'd had enough, and it was overcrowded so I lied to my care worker Pam about staying with a friend and left. Sorry let me back track here as you're probably confused. I'm a care home brat and have been since age 14. Actually my 14th birthday to be exact, my mum was killed on a night out in a mugging gone wrong, she got stabbed and the injury was so bad she didn't make it to the hospital. Dad, well he tried so hard but eventually he couldn't deal with his guilt, he blamed himself and kept saying he should've protected her better, I never blamed him, I knew how much he loved her and would've died for her. Guess that's why he felt so bad as she died not him, he got injured too but not as seriously as mum. Anyway, a month after her funeral I came home to find him hanging from the banister railing in the entrance way to the house. A few hours later the police officer took me to the care home and that was the day I lost my friends too. Who wants to hang out with the kid who lives in a care home and has no parents? No one that's who. I was bullied in school and at the home. Turning 17 meant you had two choices in a care home, either go to the centre and live there where you get your own room but share a kitchen living area and bathroom, they help you manage your finances and stuff ready for the big wide world, or you ship out completely, me I chose to ship out. I enrolled at college doing a three-year mechanic's course with apprenticeship. My GCSE grades were so good that I skipped the first year and went straight into year 2. Guess locking myself in my room and studying paid off. So that's what has led me here, I used the local library to get my C.V and emails set up and do my studying for college, I had enough money from my parents' insurance to pay for a hotel for a bit, so I wasn't destitute or on the streets, well not yet anyway, but I still classed as homeless in some circles. I just needed to keep up my act and hope no one ever found out. I knew the money was running low, Dad spent a lot of mum's money on booze and her funeral then I had to pay off debts and a funeral for him with his money so there wasn't a lot left. Oh yeah that saying that your debts die with you. Yeah, it's bollocks, they don't, they get handed down to the person named on your life insurance documents and the money gets taken from that. I'm rambling yet again, bad habits die hard, I guess. So now you know, I'm an orphan mother murdered, and her killer is still out there somewhere, and my father committed suicide, and to top it all off I may be living on the streets in a week or two when the money finally runs out. I need this job at the garage more than anything else, this job could be the start of me actually getting on my feet and having some resemblance of a normal life and maybe even a place to call home again. Even the college isn't aware of just how dire my living situation is, and as for my care worker, yeah, she just rings me up to check on me and that's it.

"He deliberately makes the drinks bad, so you don't ask him to do it again" Mitch shouted over to me.

"Maybe we should make him do the drinks all the time until he gets it right, maybe he just needs the practice" I shouted back.

I heard a chuckle from both Cole and Mitch and Cole gave me a big grin and winked. Mitch shook his head and headed off to his car while Cole stood and just watched me for a while.

"Cole, stop gawking and get to work" Frank shouted.

"On it" Cole shouted back and walked over to his own bay to start working on a Ford Fiesta.

CHAPTER 2
TRAVIS P.O.V

Frank called us all into the office first thing this morning, great stuck in a meeting with Tweedle dumb and Tweedle dumbass the twins. These guys were always fucking about, I have no idea why my uncle stills keep them on. Yeah, yeah ok it's because they are good at their job. My uncle only deals with cars predated in the 90s in his garage, he prefers the idea of proper work, not just plugging in a computer to the car's ECU and pressing a few keys. No sir my uncle Frank likes it old school dirty oily and greasy as fuck. Gotta admit, it's my thing too, the older the car the better in my view, older cars have more style, and they have their own personality too, no wonder people named cars more back in the day.

"So, what's the meeting for? It's too early in the year to be about a Christmas works party" Cole chuckled as he sat backwards on the dining chair in our staff room.

"What Christmas party?" Tweedle dumbass or Mitch as he is known swaggered into the room dropping his bag in his locker.

"The one you weren't invited too" That's Cole's reply.

"Fuck you" and the bickering started, see why I call them Tweddle dumb and Tweedle dumb ass?

"Sit the fuck down" Frank walked into the room "Travis get your god damn feet of the fucking table" He roughly shoves my size 10s onto the floor.

"What the fuck man?" I snap at him.

"Don't start Trav, you can do what the fuck you want in your apartment but in here I like my table I eat from to not have fuck knows what on it from your feet"

"Whatever" I slouch back in my chair, I'm fucking shattered and can't be doing with his shit today. He knows I've had it rough these past three years after witnessing that brutal mugging in town. They never did catch the bastard that killed that woman. I hope she didn't have any kids at home. It's the anniversary coming up next week too. I always put a flower on the wall by the place where she died. I was walking back from a band meet when I heard shouting, being in a rough part of town I knew not to get involved so I stepped into the shadows and watched, I wasn't expecting the bastard to pull a knife much less use it. The poor couple never saw it coming. The bloke tried to protect his wife, but it wasn't enough, he suffered injuries too, the paramedics said if it wasn't for my quick actions then they both would've died that night. Though choosing who to treat first on the side of a road in a dark alley, it was obvious that she wouldn't make it with the amount of blood she had already lost, in fact I thought she was already dead which is why I chose to try and save the man's life instead of hers. He kept drifting in and out of consciousness but when he was lucid, he kept asking for his wife and if she was, ok? I lied and said she was doing just fine. He lived but she died shortly after the ambulance arrived, they said they couldn't do anything to save her as she had already lost far too much blood. So, I saved a man, but I couldn't save the woman. That sucked.

"Right, we have a new guy starting today, his name is T.J, a college student on an apprenticeship with us. Don't screw around with him. "

"Great another fuck turd" I stood up and stormed out slamming the door behind me.

"What's his problem?" I heard Cole shout.

My problem was, I couldn't be dealing with shitty college boys, hormones and bitching about what chick they want to bang, fuck it's bad enough listening to the twins going on about their latest conquest at the weekend and now Frank adds another twit to the mix. Don't get me wrong I love women and I get my fair share, but I don't boast about it. It's degrading to the poor girl and not to mention wrong on so many levels. Keep it in your pants and keep it secret. Fuck if they knew what I get up to I'd probably scar them for life.

So, T.J a new college brat, great, and what the fuck sort of name is T.J? must be short for something. Maybe he will quit after a few days of putting up with me. The last guy did, he said I was too blunt and rude as well as intimidating. The guy fucking pissed me off, so I hung him from the ramps by shoving a broom handle through his sleeves and hooking it on the ends of the ramp. Guess I went too far. I chuckle darkly to myself at the memory.

So, I'm a moody bastard but you would be too seeing shit I had. I'm a fucked up 23-year-old man with sexual desires and habits that would make most men blush and women run for the hills screaming, well some of the women run to my bed begging for me and then run for the hills calling me a sex fiend. Some only make it as far as my bedroom door and see my display before they make up lame excuses to leave. I always hand them their coats and kiss them goodbye, no hard feelings my kink isn't for everyone. I've had the few try it thinking it would be fun and then beg me to stop and they leave after I talk to them and soothe them, I'm not one to let a woman go home distraught and upset.

I'm so caught up in my work, trying to fix this old school Audi Quattro, the owner tried to drive it with a blown gasket, that left me with a shit tonne of work to do. But a car like this was so worth the time and attention, she was a beauty. anyway, I was so caught up I didn't notice the bell ring, I heard Cole shout Frank and listened in on the conversation, when I heard her voice shout Frank.

"IT'S T.J SIR."

I dropped my spanner on my foot, thank fuck for steel toe capped boots. What the actual fuck? I thought Frank said we were getting a guy. That voice is definitely not a guy. That voice was soft, sweet and alluring. I took a quick peek towards the office and fuck if my cock didn't get instantly hard. She was perfect, so fucking perfect, curvy ass big tits and tiny waist. Her yet black hair pulled back into a braid. A college student though? Seriously, that meant she was young and certainly too innocent for me. I'd have to just stay away and make her hate me so she would stay away too. I'm to fucked up for someone that innocent. And not to blow my own trumpet but girls can't stay away from me. Then I heard her laugh, like a proper laugh and it was the most beautiful sound after a V8 roaring to life I had ever heard. This was going to be hard, harder than my cock is right now and that's pretty damn hard.

Then she practically ordered Cole to make her a cup of tea, fuck if that didn't make me smirk, having her around here was going to be both fun and challenging. life was going to get just a little bit insane now. I needed to get out of here and fast, my little well not so little friend now needed to be attended to.

"Frank, I'm off on a parts run, do you need anything picking up?"

"Grab the butties from Paula's pantry for lunch, they should be ready by the time you've got the parts."

"Right will do".

I threw my spanner into my toolbox and headed into the yard hopping into the works van. Piece of shit vehicle, Volkswagen caddy van still all original, if it was up to me, I'd lower it and whack on some sweet tyres and deep-dish alloys, black out the windows and give it a wicked paint job. Nope not Frank he's a 'keep it original guy.' Now for my place and a cold shower.

CHAPTER 3
T.J AKA TIFFANY

I spotted the mystery man behind that fuck me voice getting into what Cole called the shag van or work turd, this man was sex on legs from what I could tell. Shoulder length black hair tied into a loose ponytail and is that a nose ring? muscly arms and broad shoulders. His work boiler suit pulled down to the waist with the sleeves tied around his waist, his t-shirt sleeves cut off giving him a bad boy ripped vest look. Bad boy rock star vibe, one I should stay away from., but my body has other ideas as I feel a tingling achy sensation between my legs, holy hell this guy is going to be the end of me, I need to stay away from him if I'm going to survive. I'm a good girl with twelve GCSEs to my name. I did eight when I was fifteen and got A star in them all, also have three A levels. Being stuck in a kid's home locking yourself in your room really does pay off in your education. When my parents died, I threw myself into schoolwork and studying alongside working on beat up cars, seeing as my friends deserted me and the kids in the home were bullies. I suffered a broken nose one day when another girl accused me off looking at her fuck ugly boyfriend. Yeah, kids in care can be screwed up, but what do you expect when they are misunderstood most of the time. Not all care kids are nasty drug taking scum bags, some are like me, orphaned, or parents can't cope due to health issues. People should really get the back stories first before judging these kids. Give a dog a bad name and you get a bad breed. The same thing applies with kids like me. Anyway, rambling again, like I said mystery man is a bad boy and I'm staying away even if he is incredibly gorgeous and his voice is so sexy, that it sets my heart racing at 100 miles an hour.

Shaking my head, I quickly parked the car over in my spot that Frank had pointed out to me earlier. With a quick tug by the steering wheel, I popped the hood, took my three seconds to lift the hood fully, I could feel eyes on me from Cole and Mitch. Ah screw them

I'll show them I can do just as good a job as them. I gave a loud whistle and looked at Cole.

"Hey, dipstick, Where's the garage tools? "

"That, grey toolbox by that wall" Cole answered.

" Dude, she called you a dipstick and you said nothing, what the hell is wrong with you?"

"Fuck you Mitch, this chick can call me her dipstick all she wants as we all know she will try it soon enough" Cole cupped his man parts in his hand and thrust his hips towards me.

"Nope not a chance in hell, besides dipsticks are too skinny for my liking" I rolled my eyes at him as I grabbed the tools needed.

"Roasted" Mitch roared with laughter at his brother.

I got on with my job, my service on this ford escort mark 3 would not be as quick as I thought as several bolts were seized and needed a bit of persuasion to get it off. I didn't realise I was grunting and groaning until I heard that Mitch behind me

"You know if you want to make noises like that, I can show you a better much more fun way of making them".

"Fuck off Mitch"

"No can do, its lunch break and your food is in the kitchen, Frank insists on at least half hour a day with all of us bonding"

"Great, so not only do I work with you monkeys I also have to watch you eat, I'd rather do my A level maths exam again"

"Get your tits out your knickers and come eat will ya, besides you haven't met Trav yet".

"Whatever" I dropped the spanner onto the bench and followed Mitch to the kitchen while wiping my hands in the rag I had hanging from my belt loop, on my work trousers.

"Travis get your filthy feet off the table, how many times do I have to tell you" I heard Frank yell at someone I assume is called Travis, that must be mystery rock star bad boy vibes then.

"T.J, there you are, this is my nephew Travis" Frank introduced us.

"Hey," I held out my hand and got nothing, he straight up blanked me. Not that I'm not used to it, but this was out of order.

"I said Hey" I tried again.

"Yep, I heard you the first time, what do you want a gold star for your first word?"

"Someone on their period" I snapped back earning an "oooohhhhhsssshhhhh" from the twins.

"Last I checked us guys don't need to waste time on bathroom breaks with those trivial issues".

"Wow, you're some piece of work, tell me how long did your last shag last? Three seconds, because that's how long you had my attention for "

Frank had pulled up a chair by now with an amused look on his face, judging from the look on the twins faces I'd say this is a first for Frank.

"Funny, I could've sworn I saw you gawping at me earlier in the yard, I counted at least what five minutes at least "

"Not at you, I was gawping at the fine piece of art outside that I believe is a ford capri, I wouldn't waste my time with looking at Mick Jagger's offspring thank you".

"ouch" both twins said together.

"Fuck off, whore if I was Jaggers offspring do you think I'd waste my time looking at you?"

"oohh so you admit looking at me? "I rolled my eyes at him and pushed his feet off the chair and sat down glaring at him. How is a dick like him so fucking hot?

"I never said that you know what fuck you, I got work to do" he stood up pushing his chair back and glared at me.

"You wish you were fucking her; cos boy do I know I am right Mitch?"

"Yep" Mick mimicked moving his junk around in his trousers.

Travis gave both boys daggers and made a motion as if he was about to throw them a punch, as he stormed out towards the garage.

"Well, that was interesting, no one has ever back talked to our Travis" Frank handed me a sandwich.

"Something else interesting, this chick here said she has an A level" Mitch calmly said, even Travis stopped moving and turned to look at me.

"How old are you?" Travis asked me.

"I'm seventeen but I'll be eighteen next week, why?"

"Bit young to have an A level already and be in college on a year 2 placement".

"I did most of the twelve GCSE's I have at an A star grade when I was just fifteen the rest I did six months later, I also have three A levels again at a grade A. I studied instead of goofing about".

"Twelve GCSE's, what the fuck bro she got more than us put together" Cole squeaked.

"Yeah twelve, Maths, English lit and language, History, Geography, Biology, Chemistry, Spanish, P.E, Home economics, and Music and art and design.

"Nerd" Cole spat out earning a look from Frank who was now leaning on his elbows set on the table.

"So, we got a brain box working with us? Must say I'm impressed, what A levels you got?"

"Maths, English Lit and Geography"

"That's one heck of an academic achievement before the age of eighteen. And you choose mechanics? Well, I'll be damned" Frank looked well and truly proud, the look you'd expect a proud father to have with his daughter, the look I never got.

"Mechanics isn't the only course I'm doing" I admitted as I pulled my crust from my sandwich.

"What?" four voices said at the same time.

"I'm doing two, night courses as well, one in adult drawing and another in cake baking and decorating".

"I heard cakes" the twins chirped.

"You would" Travis rolled his eyes at them and went back into the garage.

"Your parents must be proud" Frank said as he stood up and patted my back.

"Yeah, real proud" I said loud enough for him to hear but quietly "if they were alive" I grabbed a bottle of water and went back to my task of a service on this escort. It needs oil filter and oil change, air filter change, spark plugs, plus cam belt change as requested by the customer. Three hours later and I'm wiping the car down and closing the bonnet down, job done.

"Finished already T.J?"

"Yep, wanna check it over Cole?"

"I'll check you over if you want".

"Who's checking who over?" Mitch popped his head up.

"The doctor, he's coming to check over your std's in half an hour, said if he leaves it any later your dick might drop off" I retorted, I heard a small huff type stifled giggle from Travis, so he does have a sense of humour then.

"So earlier you said it's your eighteenth next week, what have you planned? Night with the girls or out with the parents?" Mitch slung an arm over my shoulder.

"Nope, I'm having a quiet night in" I didn't want to tell them I had no friends or parents to celebrate with, I couldn't bear the pity looks I'd get. Which reminds me I need next Thursday off work.

"Frank, I forgot to mention I need next Thursday off please?"

"And we all need Friday off as well" Cole added.

"Sorry, Travis has next Thursday booked already and I got cars booked in, but yeah as we are taking our girl out Thursday night you all get Friday off".

"Yes" the twin's fist bumped.

"Frank please, I need it off, I have to go see my parents".

"See them after work, I'm sure they won't mind".

"No course they won't" I jump into the escort ready to take her back into the yard "They won't mind cos they are dead, and my birthday is the anniversary so why should they mind. Not like they can go anywhere either." I mutter to myself trying not to cry. I didn't realise Travis was getting a cloth from the rag bag next to my bay and had heard me.

"Frank, give Tiff my day off I'll work instead" he hollered at Frank making me jump then eye him suspiciously. Did he hear me?

"You sure Trav, you've taken this day off every year for the last 3 years now, you know I know why? right"?

"Yeah, I'm sure" Travis hung his head and walked off.

"What if you both work till lunch then take off?" Frank suggested.

"Yeah, that will do me fine" I thanked Frank.

"Yeah, thanks man" Travis went back to his work.

I don't think he heard me, as he didn't give me any weird pity looks or say anything. Maybe he was just trying to be nice.

"So, what's the plan for the girl's birthday then?" Mitch shouted across the shop floor.

"Well, I think Indian meal then hit the bars? She is eighteen after all, first legal drink and all that" Frank replied.

"Hell yeah, what about a strip joint? You know that new one has guys and girls in it?" Mitch suggested.

"You'd know all about the guys wouldn't you Tweedle dumbass" Travis mocked him.

"Well, you'd know all about the girls, and know all of them too" snapped back Mitch.

"Eww gross" I said it before I realised it.

"Ahh cupcake don't mock what you don't know, I bet you haven't even had a first kiss have you?" Travis was standing right next to me now leaning too close. I blushed at his words making him smirk, he fucking smirked and then winked at me "didn't think so, too fucking pure".

"Wait, you've never kissed anyone?" Cole looked at me with surprise.

"Dipstick, she spent her teenage years studying what did you think? Don't tell me you thought she was just like all those other schoolgirls, dropping their knickers at any boy?" Travis threw a dirty rag at Cole. I wanted to disappear into the wall, or have the ground open up and swallow me. Then I remembered I have a car to move, so that's what I did.

CHAPTER 4

TRAVIS P.O.V

I know I was an asshole to her at lunch but that was my plan. But getting a proper look at her made it so much harder, and I'm not talking about just my dick, even though that was definitely getting hard looking at her. She is just so perfect and fucking gorgeous, I honestly have never felt like this about any girl I've ever been with. I feel like I need to protect her from everyone and look after her. What the fuck is wrong with me? I want to ask her out and take her to the club and maybe meet my band mates and I've never wanted to do that with anyone before. I've only known her a few hours and already she has gotten under my skin and into my head, I literally can't stop thinking about her.

I gave her attitude at lunch, and she matched me at every turn. No one and I mean no one have ever dared sass me like she did, and I'd be lying if I said it didn't turn me on a bit, that and the thoughts of how I could make her squirm from punishing her for the way she talked back at me. I was ready to get back to work when I heard Mitch say she had an A level. The fuck? An A level at her age and in college, maybe I got her age wrong, I had to know so I asked her.

"How old are you?"

Then she said it she is seventeen but eighteen next week, still so young to have an A level, then she surprised us all, she got twelve fucking GCSE and three A levels, and she is just seventeen, my jaw nearly hit the floor, I kept my cool though. She was one hell of a sexy nerd. My sexy nerd, where the fuck did that come from? She isn't mine, well not yet anyway. The more I learnt about her the more I wanted her, and I wanted her so fucking bad.

As if her academic grades weren't enough, she then tells us she is doing another two courses as well as the mechanics one, like does this girl have a home to go to? Actually, looking at her, maybe that's closer to the truth, her work trousers looked too big for her and the belt holding them up had seen better days. I am going to make it my mission to find out as much as possible about our Tiff.

What got me even more determined to find out more about her was when she asked Frank for next Thursday off, guessing that must be her birthday then. As she said earlier that she was 18 next week. When Frank told her that was my day off so she would have to work I saw genuine hurt and torment flash across her face, the look was gone so quick I could've imagined it but I trust my gut on this one and I stepped closer to her quietly so she wouldn't hear or see me. Sure enough, as I looked closer, I could see her eyes looking watery and she sniffed as if she was trying to stop herself crying. I'd be a complete bastard if I didn't do or say anything to Frank. She didn't see me standing next to the ragbag set in her bay. But I heard her. The anniversary of what I witnessed is her birthday and also her parents are dead. That's a coincidence, right? What are the chances of the woman I saw die and Tiff's parents die on the same day? Yeah, it's just a coincidence, has to be. What a shit birthday though, sharing it with your parent's death. I'm taking her to get a tattoo in their memory on Friday, Skeet will fit her in, he always does when I call in. I'll just nab her sketch pad I saw in her bag and design something for her from what I see in her drawings. What am I thinking? My head must be screwed thinking about taking Tiff to get a tattoo, shit is that what it feels like to actually care about someone you like? Shit, do I like her as in LIKE her? Yes, yes, I do, I fucking Like Tiff and I want to be with her. When I teased about her being a virgin and never even kissing a bloke, I wasn't expecting it to be true, I mean all girls have at least kissed a boy at some point in their teenage years right? Wrong, because apparently Tiff has never been kissed. To say I nearly blew my load at her flushed face and the knowledge that I was right would be a slight understatement. She is so pure, sweet and innocent despite having a mouth on her and some balls to sass back at us guys in this garage.

I know both Cole and Mitch are interested in her. Those twins do a tag thing where one of them does the dates and stuff and when it comes to the sex, they tell each other when and where, one fucks the girl while the other watches before taking his turn. I've even heard that they share girls at the same time on occasion. They never see a girl more than once though as they claim to not be ready to settle with a long-term relationship yet. I'd give anything to find my soul mate and settle down. Could Tiff be that person? What the fuck am I on? I don't even know this girl and already my mind is thinking of being with her for life and my fucking dick is saying he wants to be in her now. Right now, all I know for sure is that I need to keep her away from the twins, Fuck I need to protect her from jerks like those twins and assholes like me.

"Trav, get in here now" My uncle calls me over to his office. He knows about mugging and shit. He's a great guy who took me in at age 15 when my parents moved to Australia, and I decided to rebel and stay behind. Frank is my mother's brother and was only too happy for me to stay with him. Now I'm 23 and a moody bastard. Originally, I was meant to move out to Australia when I finished school, but I begged my parents to let me stay, my life and friends are here. Hell my band is here. Yeah, I play drums in a band, and we get a few gigs.

"On my way old man" I shouted back at my uncle.

I walk into his office and kick my feet up onto his desk as I flop into the chair.

"Feet Travis"

Plopping my feet back down onto the floor I glare at my uncle.

"So, it's nearly the end of the day, what do you make of our new apprentice?" he asked me.

"She does a good job and gives the twins a good run for their money on the banter front. Why are you asking me?"

"I'm thinking of taking her on full time at the end of this month's trial. I think she has what it takes to work in this garage with you boys and our older cars. She won't need to attend college as much as she can work here and get her grades and stuff".

"Qualifications uncle, that's what they call it now. I think your right and she does have what it takes, but those qualifications will help her with the newer cars if she chooses to work in a more modern garage".

"True, but she told me she prefers older cars, and bringing them back to life again".

That piqued my interest, Tiff likes older cars and bringing them back to life, just like me.

"So, ask her then. What's the worst that could happen?"

"She could say no and leave me looking for someone else for months again".

"You won't know until you try Frank".

"You're right, I'll ask her."

I stood up and left to pack away my tools for the day. Frank called Tiff into his office. She was in there for a few minutes before coming out with her bag slung over her shoulder, I noticed Cole and Mitch hanging back watching her like wolves watching their prey. Good job this big bad wolf is watching the cubs to make sure they don't get their prey.

I watched as Cole jogged up beside Tiff and they talked. From where I was, I couldn't hear much but then I saw Tiff knee Cole in the nut sack. Ouch that had to hurt. Wonder what he said to deserve that. I walked closer as I fished my keys from my pocket and heard Mitch talking to Tiff, doing the usual tag team thing I'd seen countless times, Mitch covering for Cole and making out that Cole is a bit nervous around girls, practically begging for them to give Cole a second chance. These guys were priceless, most girls fell for it though and this worried me, I was just about to step in when Tiff shouted at Cole.

"Cole, coffee tomorrow morning at the small coffee shop just of the college campus, consider it a restart, as friends,"

I was so glad she added the 'as friends' bit. I was seriously worried she was going to say date. I need to step in and claim her as mine and soon, or at the very least warn the twins of her, she will be mine as soon as I can sort my shit out and start acting nice. Tiff deserves a nice boy not a moody bastard like me.

I watched as Cole and Mitch got into their car and drove away before I pulled my car up alongside the pavement by Tiff.

"Get in" I ordered her.

"Why should I?"

"Just get in and let me take you for a burger, as friends' ' I added them as friends but hoping she would get in the car and come with me.

"Nope"

"Just get in the car".

"I said no".

"Stop being stubborn and get in the fucking car".

"Fuck off Travis, I'm not taking orders from you".

"Tiff, please just get in the car so I can take you for a burger as friends at the end of a long day at work".

She paused and sighed before opening the door and getting into the passenger seat of my car.

"Fine, but I might bitch at you".

"Fine by me"

She pulled the seatbelt over her shoulder, and I watched as it rested in-between her perfect boobs separating them slightly. My dick was as usual being a dick and starting to throb as it hardened, this was going to be a long dinner.

CHAPTER 5
T.J AKA TIFFANY

After I'd finished up for the day Frank called me into his office.

"T.J you did really well today. I am actually impressed and if this month's trial goes well then, I'd like to employ you here at the garage. I'm hoping you can continue to stand up to the boys and take their banter. Travis is a moody bastard, but his heart is in the right place".

"Thanks Frank, the boys are just kids with raging hormones, nothing I can't handle" And I meant that. Growing up in care homes during your teenage years left you open to a lot of advances from sexually frustrated boys. And some of those boys didn't like to take 'NO' as an answer. Yeah, I had a few near rapes and sexual assaults but hey I survived.

"Tiff, can I call you that? Those boys will never grow up" Frank laughed.

"Tiff is fine. Boys will be boys. What is Travis' deal anyway?"

"Not my story to tell, sorry. All I will say is he saw some shit that no young man should ever see."

Cryptic clue there, and not much else to go on, guess I'll have to do some digging if I ever want to find out why Travis is such an arsehole. But do I really want to know?

"Well, I'll let you get of home, and I'll see you on Wednesday as I believe you have college tomorrow".

"Yeah, I'll be here Wednesday and Thursday all day and then I can do Friday afternoon if you want me in".

"Sounds good to me. Now go home and rest up, you did a lot of hard work today".

"See you soon Frank, and thanks for giving me a chance I really appreciate it".

I slung my bag over my shoulder and headed out the door with the little bell ringing as the door closed behind me.

"Hey, you want a ride?" Cole walked up beside me.

"No, I'm ok to walk thanks".

"It's no bother, I can drop you back home".

"I said no" I was starting to lose my shit with Cole as he put and arm around my shoulders pulling me into his side. I shrugged his arm off and turned to face him.

"Seriously, I don't feel like a young girl like you should walk home on her own".

"Look Cole, I know how to look after myself so just do yourself a favour and fuck off"

"I'm not saying you don't know how to look after yourself, I'm just saying I'd feel happier if I saw you home safe and sound."

"Oh, and I suppose it would make you even happier if I invited you in for a coffee and then we screwed as well" Yeah, I know his type.

"Well, now you say it" He didn't finish what he was saying as I brought my knee up to meet his groin before turning my back on him scrunched up and whimpering.

"I'm not a whore or a quick easy lay so fucking quit trying to get in my knickers" I shouted at him over my shoulder.

Mitch ran up and grabbed my arm, spinning me around to face him.

"Look my brother didn't mean any harm and he certainly didn't mean to make you feel like a cheap hook up. He likes you and he isn't very good at expressing himself. Guess only one twin gets the brains as well as the looks. If he offended you then at least give him a chance to put things right, and he totally deserved that kick in the nut sack".

"Mitch, I don't care if your brother is Paul Walker, I'm not interested in him or any other boy for that matter" Except my body is secretly craving Travis not that I'm going to tell them that or anyone else for that fact.

"Look, I get it Cole has been coming on a bit strong all day and I admit I've been flirting and stuff as well, we both like you but I'm stepping back for my brother. Just give him a chance, please" Mitch all but got down on his knees to beg me.

"Cole, coffee tomorrow morning at the small coffee shop just of the college campus, consider it a restart, as friends".

"Thanks T.J " Mitch stepped away and went back to his brother who was still holding his balls as he slowly walked towards their car.

I'd only walked a few steps when Travis pulled up to the pavement alongside me in his Volkswagen Golf GTI, he wound down the window and leaned over to talk to me.

"Get in" he ordered me, yep ordered.

"Why should I?" I snapped back at him.

"Just get in and let me take you for a burger, as friends" did he overhear the conversation with the twins?

"Nope" I blurted before I could stop myself. I wanted to get in his car and go anywhere with him, or at least my body did, my mind however was still in bitch mode.

"Just get in the car".

"I said no".

"Stop being so stubborn and get in the fucking car".

"Fuck off Travis, I'm not taking orders from you" although my body was loving this dominant bad boy ordering me around, what the fuck is wrong with me?

"Tiff, please just get in the car so I can take you for a burger as friends at the end of a long day at work".

I paused looking at him before I sighed and got into his car. I was well aware of his roaming eyes as I buckled up the seatbelt. The sexual tension in the car was palpable.

"Look I'm sorry if I was a bit of a dick at lunch time" he looked at me quickly before looking back towards the road.

"A bit of a dick? I'd say you were a major douchebag in all honesty".

"Douchebag huh? Guess it's about right. But I mean it, I'm sorry. I had no right to treat you like that".

"Wow the big bad boy actually apologises, this may have to go into some record book or something".

"You can keep a record book on my douche Ness if you want, tally up if the apologies match the snarky Ness".

"Keep sweet talking to me like that and I may have to put you into a little black book" Where did that come from? This isn't me.

"Now, I don't believe for one moment that you own a single black book yet alone a little one" he teased as he shot me a quick grin. Fuck if that grin didn't do things to my insides. Guess we could call it a panty melting grin.

"Guess you'll never know" I winked at him, like what is happening to me?

His fingers brushed against my knee with every gear change he made. And every touch sent electric shocks up my thighs and straight to that sweet spot.

Travis took me to a small burger joint just outside of town and even held the door open for me like a true gentleman. Ok what happened to the Travis from earlier? we took a booth in the corner of the restaurant and sat opposite each other.

"Order whatever you want, it's my treat" Travis handed me a menu and smiled his megawatt panty melting grin.

"Thanks, I'm not a big eater though" I tell him honestly.

"You'll get a bigger appetite working full time with us guys at the garage. Today wasn't too bad but we get a mad rush in early spring as everyone wants their cars done ready for the summer car shows they attend."

"Hi, can I take your order?" A skinny blonde girl with obvious fake tits asked Travis as she practically shoved her tits in Travis face,

"Banana and chocolate mix milkshake stacked up burger and fries and the banoffee pie please, plus whatever my date is ordering"

Travis ignored the blonde and shot me a quick wink and a look of desperation asking to play along.

"Thanks honey, I'll have the same please as it sounds as delicious as you are" I smiled goofily at Travis and made gooey eyes at him.

"So, you two on a first date then?" asked blonde bitch.

"Nope it's our one-year anniversary date" Travis shot back at her.

"Oh, really? Cos I've never seen you in here with her before" Blonde bitch stood with her hands on her hips glaring at me.

"Claire, how many times do I have to tell you I'm not interested in you and your fake arse tits? Now you know why, so just fetch us our order and leave us the fuck alone."

"Actually, can we have a different waitress please honey? I don't trust Claire not to spit in my food" I couldn't help myself, the glare she was giving me was making me feel uncomfortable.

"Why, you bitch" Claire lunged at me as she reached and grabbed my hair pulling it hard and me along with it. I crashed face first onto the floor at her feet.

"Claire" Travis warned her I stood up fists clenched. I'd met her before in care.

"That was a big mistake" I told her through clenched teeth.

"You're a big mistake, Travis will get tired of you soon enough and then you'll just be another stupid groupie bitch following him around in the hopes of getting another night with him, but it will be me in his bed not you" she mocked me. Groupie? What was he? Before I knew what was happening, she launched herself at me again and my fist came up and met with her jaw. She stumbled backwards as my other fist swung round and caught her in the ribs making her double over. As I was about to swing again, strong arms wrapped around my waist and pulled me away.

"Hey, let it go. She is trying to wind you up" Travis whispered in my ear, his breath sending shivers down my spine. My hands dropped to my sides, and I relaxed into Travis arms.

"Good girl" He whispered again, his lips brushing against my neck, I let out a small moan without realising it until I heard Travis chuckle against my neck.

"Come on let's get these burgers to go and I'll take you somewhere else to eat them. It was then I realised that an older scruffy man was pulling Claire into the kitchen area while a young dark skinned almost like a really good suntan man held out our food.

"Sorry about her Trav, you know what she's like".

"No worries, Brad, you at practice tomorrow?"

"Yeah, if I miss it then Clint will bite my head off," Brad laughed. "Hey, why don't you bring your girl with you?"

"I might just do that," Travis replied, looking at me as if for approval. Hell, why not, it's not like I have much else to do. Practice, that's like football or something isn't it?

"I'd like that" I found myself saying before realising that Brad referred to me as Travis girl and Travis didn't correct him.

Travis nodded at Brad and took the food from him before ushering me towards the door and his car.

"So, you play football then?" I asked him as he placed the food and drinks carefully in the car.

"Football? What makes you think that?" He asks me as we both get into the car and buckle up.

"Practice"

"No not football practice" he chuckled.

"So, what then?"

"Let me pick you up from college tomorrow night and I'll show you".

"Can't you just tell me?"

"Nope, because you'll laugh. I need to show you so you can believe it and experience how awesome we are".

"We?"

"Yeah, me and my friends"

"Wow, did I hear right? Travis has friends?"

"Hey just because I'm a moody bastard doesn't mean I don't have friends you know".

"Yeah, yeah" I laugh at him as he drives us to God knows where.

Turns out God knows where a small car park is next to a lake. There were a few picnic benches spotted at random intervals. Travis grabbed our food, and I grabbed the drinks following him to a bench that was right next to the edge of the lake. The full moon lit the area up and made the whole atmosphere sort of romantic and peaceful.

"That was some punch you gave Claire back there".

"Thanks, I think"

"Where did you learn to throw a fist like that? Most girls put their thumbs inside their fists but you, you knew what you were doing".

"You need to learn to fight right growing up in a care home" I blurted without thinking.

"Care home? Where's your parents?"

"Dead, mum was murdered, and dad couldn't cope with the guilt so killed himself not long after. I was 14 at the time so I went home. Nobody wants to foster or adopt a teenager with my baggage".

"Shit, I'm sorry about that".

"Don't be, and don't start with the pity either I hate all that pity shit. What happened, happened I dealt with it a long time ago".

"Fair does. Now about tomorrow, you never said yes".

"Seriously, you want me to go to this practice?"

"Yeah, actually I do".

"Ok, then yes"

"Great, I'll pick you up from college then at 5?"

"Make it 5:30 as I have a late class tomorrow".

"You know this will be the first time I've ever taken a girl to practise".

"I'm honoured"

"Chloe will be stoked to have company watching us practise".

"Chloe?"

"Yeah, she is Brad's girl".

"Cool, I shall look forward to it".

We ate the rest of our food in silence, occasionally looking up at each other. I admit I think I am totally into Travis and my body is most definitely into Travis the dirty depraved bitch is sending sexy images to my brain of fucking Travis on this picnic table. Yeah, I may not have kissed a guy but I'm sure as hell not innocent, I've watched porn on my phone and touched myself, admittedly I haven't orgasmed like I think you're supposed to but that's because the feelings scare me a bit.

"It's getting late, let me drop you off back at home" Travis held his hand out for me.

"It's ok just drop me of back at the garage and I'll walk from there".

"You sure? I don't mind dropping you of at home".

"It's fine, I actually enjoy the walk to my house from the garage. Besides it's only round the corner from there"

"If that's what you want. Can't say I'm happy about it but I won't push the matter".

"Appreciated" I smiled at him. I really don't want anyone to know I live at a hotel, well for now anyway but maybe next week I'll be homeless when the money finally runs out.

Travis, true to his word, drove me back to the garage and dropped me off with a promise to pick me up from college the next day.

CHAPTER 6

TRAVIS

I had a great time with Tiff tonight, well except for the little run in with Claire. But fuck did Tiff handle herself well. Seeing her swing her fist and land two punches was the biggest turn on I'd ever seen from a girl before. Yeah, I had to rearrange myself in a subtle way. Then calling her my girl to Brad, well he said she was 'my girl' and I didn't correct him. But even Tiff didn't put him straight on it. Then she agreed to come to practice with me tomorrow, when he suggested it, that was the icing on the cake. I'd never taken any girl with me to practise, ever. Ok so Tiff thinks that Practice is some sort of team sports thing, boy will she be surprised when I turn up at Clint's place and we start playing our instruments. Yeah, in case you hadn't already guessed I'm in a rock band and a bloody good one if I do say so myself.

I dropped Tiff off back at the garage against my better judgement, but I knew if I pushed it, she would just get mad and probably storm off anyway. When she said she was in a care home I knew she would either be living in one still or in one of those awful in-between centres, but then she said she lived a few roads down from the garage. That had me puzzled as there are no care run places near the garage. I planned to drop her off outside her front door but as you already know she didn't want that, which meant she was hiding something about where she lived. This was something I intended to find out about. I was hoping she wasn't living in one of those run-down apartments or worse still in some shady hotel. I would drop her off back at the garage then park up a few roads away and hopefully be able to follow her. That is my plan.

"Just drop me off here, I can walk the rest of the way" Tiff pointed to the side of the road.

"You sure? I don't mind dropping you off at home" I had to try just one last time.

"No here is just fine".

I pulled over to the pavement and watched as Tiff grabbed her bag from the footwell and climbed out of my car, she bent down and popped her head back in.

"Thanks for tonight, I really enjoyed myself".

"You're welcome, I enjoyed tonight too. I'll pick you up tomorrow evening" I gave her a smile as she nodded and closed the door. I drove off and parked up round the corner before hopping out the car and heading back in the direction of where I'd dropped her off. Sure enough, she was walking towards a side alley and kicking at a stone on the way. Her head hung low, and shoulders hunched up. Her whole body screamed that she was uncomfortable and scared. Hell, even I'd be scared walking down these side alleys at night on my own, especially after what I witnessed a few years back. Thinking about it had me wondering again if the couple I tried to help were Tiff's parents. The timing was perfect for it to be them.

Tiff headed down the alley and then turned right onto the main road at the other end of it. Shit she was heading towards the shady end of town, yeah, my uncle's garage was on the very edge of the shady end, it was cheap rent and the main route out of town towards the motorways, perfect for the older cars heading out for their shows. I stayed back in the shadows hoping that Tiff wouldn't see or hear me following her. She walked for another 10 minutes heading towards the shady hotels in the area, my heart was pounding and my mind reeling, why was she here? Looked like she lived in one of these hotels, and point proved when she walked into the smallest most run down hotel on the street. Shit this isn't good. Not good at all. Did this mean she had no home? How was she paying for this place? Obviously, she had little to no money to be staying here but even as run down as it is it still costs money. I needed to do a bit more digging on my girl and try to help her out without actually letting on that I know how she is living right now. Maybe I can get some more out of her tomorrow night or ask Clint to do some digging for me. His line of work meant he could access data that the general public couldn't, perks of working in the police department even if he wasn't a copper. Knowing she was somewhat safe for now I turned around and headed back towards my car, I grabbed my phone from my back pocket and called Clint.

"Hey bud, you free?" I asked when he answered.

"Yeah, why what's up?" Clint knew me too well. If I called on non-practice nights, then something was bothering me. Clint had been my rock after I witnessed the mugging. Without him I would've probably turned into an alcoholic, I came close to it a few times, and each time Clint found me and got me back on the straight and narrow. I'd be lost without him.

"I just need a few drinks with decent company" I told him truthfully.

"Meet me at Nancy's bar in thirty minutes" He hung up before I could reply.

Nancy's was a small pub in a secluded part of the town centre, not many people knew it was there as it was a bit of the treck from the usual pubs and clubs. It was also where we did most of our gigs. It also helped that Clint had a 'friends with benefits' relationship with the barmaid/manager Amber. She was fresh out of a long relationship and not ready to commit just yet, and Clint, yeah, he was just a fuck em and leave kind of guy, so the arrangement suited them both.

Walking into Nancy's bar it wasn't hard to spot Clint as he sat at the bar chatting away to Amber, his friends with benefits girl. She had bright pink hair, cut into a pixie cut I believe. The hair really suited her though, she was a dainty thing, small and petite but she had a charm about her that drew you in and you couldn't help but be happy around her. Something I really needed right now. The pub itself wasn't too small but was quaint with a stage in the far corner where us guys would play Wednesday nights and weekends. We always brought in quite a large crowd. More girls than guys, not my fault we are all good looking and irresistible.

"Trav, what's going on?" Clint asked as he patted my back while I sat down on the bar stool.

"Whisky?" Amber asked me as she pulled a glass down from the shelf above her head that ran around the top of the bar.

"Yeah, thanks Amb. Clint man, I think I'm working with the daughter of that couple".

"Shit, are you sure? "Clint looked at me with a worried look in his eyes "Is she the girl that Brad told me about earlier?"

"Yeah, but I'm not 100% sure yet. But she is living in one of those shady hotels on Oak way".

"Fuck man, why is she living in that dive?"

"Boys, I'll leave you to chat. I got customers to serve" Amber waved at us as she went back to work.

"She has been in the care system since she was 14 when her dad killed himself shortly after her mum was murdered. And the anniversary in next Thursday"

"Fuck, that's a huge coincidence, you really think it's her. How old is she?"

"She turns 18 next week, she looks so much like that woman that died".

"Fuck, I take it you haven't told her or asked her?"

"Nope, I can't think of how I can ever ask her about it".

"You have feelings for her, don't you? That's why you're bringing her over tomorrow night. Brad told me you were bringing a girl over".

"Yes, no, fuck I don't know, I think I do. She has got under my skin and the thought of her with anyone else makes me so fucking angry".

"Going to be hard holding it back with those twins around".

"She can handle them better than I can" I chuckle remembering how she sassed them earlier today.

"The girl got spirit then?"

"She punched Claire, twice".

"Now that I would've paid good money to see. That bitch needed a good smacking, thinking she fucking owns us".

"Tiff put her straight".

"Tiff huh? Is that her name?"

"It's Tiffany, she actually got the job using her initials T.J and making my uncle think she was a dude" I smirked at the memory and the look on my uncle's face when he heard her shout who she was.

"Bet your uncle wasn't happy about that, we all know how much he hates being lied to" Clint raised his glass and shook it at Amber motioning for a refill.

"That's just it, Tiff pointed out that she never lied because no one asked what sex she was."

"Fuck that girl has balls or a death wish".

Amber filled both our glasses again and leaned against the bar top.

"What girl?" She asked.

"Trav here has a girl working in the garage who can handle the twins and Frank by all accounts, oh and she punched Claire" Clint filled her in.

"She punched Claire?"

"Yep twice" I answered.

"Fuck that girl best be watching her back now, you know what Claire is like" Amber shook her head.

We all know what Claire is like, she cries rape and assault left right and centre when things don't go her way. It's one of the reasons the band and our girls stay clear and always tell Claire to fuck off.

"Brad witnessed the whole thing. It happened in the burger joint he works in, which just so happens to be where Claire works as well now" I told them and judging from the looks on their faces it was news to them that Claire was working in the same place as Brad.

"Brad needs a new job and fast" Clint said.

"I need a new barman, maybe you guys can convince him to work here instead" Amber offered as she walked back to serve more customers.

"I'll talk to Brad tomorrow," Clint called after her.

"So back to this Tiff, you said she was staying in the hotel on Oak way? What do you want from me?"

"I need you to find out as much as you can about Clint. I'm worried about her".

"I'll do what I can, but it might be hard as she is still a minor".

"Any info is better than none. I'll get her info from my uncle regarding address and bank details "

"I'll do what I can bro. I'll look forward to meeting her tomorrow night."

"Shit"

"What's up?"

"Cole is taking her for coffee tomorrow morning, you know what a sleaze he is".

"A date?" Clint looked just as worried as I was.

"She said as friends but you know what those twins are like"

"I'll ask Chance to accidentally on purpose knock into them or something so that Cole has to leave".

"Your cousin is still at college?"

"Nah, Chance is working in the coffee shop now and doing his photography in the evenings and weekends".

"Guess people don't want arty photos then?" I chuckled as I asked. I told Chance many times he was wasting his time doing a course on photography and arts, but he wouldn't listen.

"I think it's more that Chance isn't as good as he thinks he is," Clint laughed.

"Thanks for everything tonight, Clint, I best be off "

"See you tomorrow bro".

I waved at Amber as I left the pub and headed back to my apartment.

I'd text copies of Tiff's information in the morning and hopefully Clint will have something for me by lunchtime. I just hope Chance can pull something off tomorrow morning to save Tiff from those twins Cole and Mitch. Yeah, they come across as harmless and playful, but I know them all too well, hell I've been working with them for the past 5 years and even gone out for nights out with them and the band. They are players who prey on sweet innocent girls like Tiff. To them getting a virgin like her is like finding the holy grail is to Indiana Jones. They will worm their way into her life as boyfriends then use her and dump her when they have had their fill. Tiff deserves better than that. Maybe I should try to set them up with Claire, they would be a perfect match for each other and I'm sure she would get off on the whole sleeping with twin's thing they often pull-on girls.

CHAPTER 7

T.J AKA TIFF

I actually really enjoyed myself with Travis last night and surprisingly I'm looking forward to seeing him again tonight. I may have to ask him about the whole being 'his girl' thing. To be totally honest I wouldn't be against being his girl, the idea sort of makes me feel happy, like little butterflies in my stomach fluttering away. Not to mention the achy needy feeling he gives me in my most intimate area, yeah ok I mean my pussy. I need to stop thinking about Travis as I need to get ready to meet up with Cole this morning. Don't get me wrong Cole is a nice enough lad just not me type, he's too cocky and cheeky for my liking, he also gives me a stay away gut feeling, I always trust my gut on these feelings. Being in care and living around hormonal teenage boys has taught me a lot about who to trust and who to avoid, Cole fits the avoid category, Mitch is in the in-between line as I still can't quite figure him out, but he isn't sending off 'stay away' vibes just yet. I'm glad I asked Cole to meet me at the coffee shop as it's somewhere with other people around so I can wiggle away if needed. Checking my watch one more time I head out of my shabby hotel room and head down to the main foyer.

"Miss Govern, today is your last night, do you need to stay on, or will you be leaving us tomorrow morning?" Gary the hotel manager asked me with a sneer.

"Morning Gary, I might be stopping on for a couple more days, what's the bill for that?"

"Price has gone up. Fifty-five pound a night now"

"That's fine I'll pay for another 3 nights later on" really, it's not fine, that will be almost all my money gone. I know he's deliberately put the price up; he's suggested several times 'other ways' to pay. He really does give me the creeps.

"I'll put the bill through your door then".

"Yeah, thanks Gary" I wave at him as I step out onto the street and suck in a breath. I need to find a full-time paying job and quit college or find somewhere to stay that is free. Then the idea hit me, the garage, it has a couch I could sleep on and a shower to wash in. Question was how would I pull that off without the guys finding out? That would be a problem for later, but one I'm sure I can solve.

It took me 15 minutes to walk to the coffee shop on the college campus and sure enough Cole was standing outside waiting for me. He looked up and smiled at me as I approached him.

"Hey, you made it then?" he asked me.

"Yeah, shall we?" I motioned to the door.

"Yeah, after you" Cole opened the door and let me past him.

We sat at a table in the centre of the coffee shop as I didn't feel comfortable sitting in one of the booths that ran along the outer walls of the shop.

"What are you drinking? I'll get it, my treat" Cole handed me the menu.

"Just a latte please"

"Anything to eat?"

As much as I wanted to say yes having not eaten anything since the burger last night, I told Cole no.

"So, you got a boyfriend?" Cole asked me.

"No, you?"

"Funny, nope no boyfriend or girlfriend for that matter"

"I'm sure you'll find someone, one day" I replied knowing full well where this conversation was heading.

"Maybe I already have, and she just hasn't realised it yet" he winked at me.

"Look Cole, you're a nice enough bloke and all, but you're not for me".

"How do you know if you haven't tried?" he reached a hand across the table and grabbed my hand with his before stroking a thumb across my knuckles. I tried to pull my hand away, but his grip tightened.

"Cole, I said we are just friends, nothing more".

"Come on, I know you like me, all that flirting yesterday".

"That was not flirting, that was me giving back as good as I got with the banter at work".

"Call it what you want, I know you want me" again I tried to pull my hand away but this time he gripped it so hard his nails dug in.

"Cole let go of my hand. I looked around with my heart pounding and feeling slightly panicked. Just then a waiter brought out coffees over and tripped sending our drinks flying and pouring onto Cole's lap. Cole jumped up and glared at the waiter.

"Chance didn't know you worked here".

"Cole, yep work here and still do my artwork. Who's the girl?"

"This is my girlfriend T.J."

"Not your girlfriend Cole, and not your friend either now" I grabbed my bag and ran out of the coffee shop. How could I go back to work at the garage now after that?

"T.J wait up" I heard Cole call after me and I ignored him. Not that it did much good as he caught up to me and grabbed my arm at the elbow pulling me back into his chest.

"I said wait up" He glowered at me.

"Why? So, you can try to convince me to be your girl? News flash, I'm not your girl and never will be. And you can explain to Frank as to why I've already quit" I pulled my arm out of his grip only for him to push me against the wall and grip my face in his hand.

"You will not quit, and you will go on at least one date with me. Tonight"

"Can't do that as I already have plans".

"Cancel them and I'll pick you up".

"No and no" I pulled my knee up and caught his nut sack again making him double over giving me my exit. I ran around the corner of the building and straight into some firm arms.

"Whoa there, what's the hurry?" The guy from the coffee shop asked me. His dark eyes looked at me with a caring and worried look on his face.

"You, ok?" He asked me as he blew some of his dark hair out of his eyes.

"Yeah, no, no I'm not ok" tears swam in my eyes as I tried to fight them back.

"Come on, let me buy you that latte you never got, and I'll call whoever you want me to" he wrapped an arm around me, and I got the feeling of being safe with him. We walked back to the coffee shop in silence, me wiling the tears not to leak. Not like it was the first time I've ever been in that position before, but this was the first time I genuinely felt scared.

"Here sit yourself down while I fetch you that drink" The guy pulled a chair out for me.

"Thanks"

"It's T.J isn't it?"

"Yeah, and your?"

"Chance" He held his hand out for me to shake. What a gentleman. I took it and shook his hand gently, still shaking slightly from my unnerving encounter with Cole.

"I'll just go grab that latte, you best call someone to come fetch you, you look too shaken up to go into college today. And if I know Cole, he will hang around all day to get a chance of talking to you again".

"I don't have my phone on me" A lie as I don't actually own a phone, it's just another expense I can't afford at the moment. I used a pay as you go for a few months until it stopped working given it was as old as the ark.

"No worries, here use mine" He handed me his phone already on the keypad screen. The only number I knew was for the garage. Would anyone come for me? I sort of hoped Travis would. I put the numbers in but didn't dial it, why? Well, what would I say for a start? Cole said I was flirting with him, was I? Did I give him the come on? Was today my fault? God I'm such an idiot.

"You call anyone?" Chance asked as he placed the lattes on the table and sat down across from me.

"No, honestly I don't have anyone to call" I handed the phone back to him. He looked at the number I'd put in and pressed call.

"What are you doing?" I asked him with alarm.

"Making the call" He winked at me.

"Hi, yeah, I've got a young girl here, she gave me this number to call".

Chance answered the other end of the call.

"Yeah, she needs someone to come and collect her from the college campus coffee shop" a pause before Chance spoke again.

"Just a little incident with a young lad, no she is fine just a bit shaken up right now."

Chance hung up his call before answering a text message he'd received during his call to the garage.

"Someone will be here to pick you up in a few minutes. How about I keep you company while we wait?" he offered with a small friendly smile.

"It's fine, I'm sure you have work to do".

"T.J there you are" Cole's voice echoed across the coffee shop making me cringe. Chance stood up and walked towards him.

"Cole, I think it's best you leave, like right now" Chance told him.

"No, I don't think so, you only want me to leave so that you can swoop in and steal my girl again".

"I never stole your girl, Cole; she dumped you and went off with Marcus not me. Oh, and I do believe I heard T.J say she wasn't your girl" Chance stood his ground and pointed to the door.

"T.J, come on we need to go" Cole glared at me. My heart pounded in my ears and my chest went tight, the beginnings of a panic attack starting, this is not good. Cole pushed past Chance and headed towards me, my breathing became out of control as pain seized my chest and arms, panic consuming my whole body.

"Cole step away from her now"

"Fuck off Chance, she is my girl and I'm taking her home" His hand wrapped around my wrist sending my panic to even greater heights as I struggled to breath and the pain wrapped itself around my heart even tighter. I'm going to die right here in this coffee shop.

"Cole, you're scaring her, back off now before I have to call the police".

"She's fine" Was the last thing I heard as panic gripped me so tight, I blacked out.

"What the fuck happened?" Was that Travis?

"Cole happened, he wouldn't leave her alone and she panicked" I think it was Chance's voice I could hear as I slowly regained consciousness.

"That fucking prick, I'll fucking kill him".

"Trav calm down, last thing she needs is an angry Travis when she comes round".

"Chance what the fuck happened to make her panic with Cole? She was fine yesterday with him" Travis asked in a calm voice.

"Man, first he wouldn't let go of her hand in the shop even though she kept trying to pull away, then after I spilt coffee on him, she pulled away and told him she wasn't his girl or friend any more before running out of here".

"Smart girl."

"No not smart as Cole ran after her and she ran towards dead end alley Trav".

"She might not have realised where she was heading".

"You know its other nickname is rape alley, don't you?" Chance asked with a hint of anger and concern in his voice. My eyes are still unwilling to open.

"Fuck, he didn't though? I'll fucking kill him" I could feel the anger rolling of Travis.

"No, she kneed him in the balls and ran straight into me as I backed away to see where she went".

Wait, Chance followed me and saw what happened? Guess I should thank him.

"That's my girl," Travis chuckled, and I felt his knuckles gently brush across my face.

"Your girl? Does she know that yet?" Chance asked him.

"No"

"When are you going to tell her Trav?"

"He doesn't need to tell me" I mumble as I open my eyes and look into Travis blue eyes and see the dark mysterious brooding as well as the worry whirling in his eyes. The look of someone who has seen more than they should've done in their lives.

"Hey, are you feeling, ok?" Travis asks me as he helps me sit up. I'm lying on a small couch in what appears to be a staff room for the coffee shop given the small lockers and table along with the smell of fresh coffee grounds.

"Where's Cole?" I ask as panic starts to wrap around me again.

"Hey, deep breaths. Cole is gone, you're safe now" Travis sits next to me wrapping an arm around me in a possessive hug.

"I can't go back to the garage Travis" I look at him as tears well in my eyes.

"Yeah, you can, I'll sort Cole out and Frank won't have him back now after today anyway" Travis brushed my hair back behind my ear and smiled at me.

"What about Mitch?"

"Mitch can stay on provided he doesn't cause any issues" Travis gave Chance a look that said they knew more about the twins than I did.

"Come on let's get you home" Travis stood up pulling me up with him, his arm still wrapped around me.

"I can walk it's fine".

"Tiff, I'm taking you home no arguments."

"I don't want to go home" Really, I just didn't want Travis to see where I was living.

"Fine, then at least let me take you back to my apartment to rest".

I nodded my head knowing that I couldn't win this argument even if I tried.

"Catch you later" Chance waved at Travis as we left the coffee shop with Travis' arm still wrapped around my waist.

"Yeah, later bro. And thanks for giving me the call to pick her up".

"Anytime bro, although I didn't know she worked for you until you answered the phone at the garage, thought I recognised the number that T.J put in my phone".

"Let's hope Frank sorts, Cole out before I get my hands on him" Travis said as his muscles flexed from anger.

"I'm sure your uncle will have him strung up by now" Chance slapped Travis on the back and went back into the coffee shop.

"Come on Tiff, let's get you back to mine for a rest" Travis led me to his car and opened the door for me.

"You don't have to do this for me you know".

"I know, but I want to and besides you shouldn't be left on your own right now" He smiled at me again as he closed my car door and ran around to his side.

It didn't take long to get to Travis' apartment. He pulled up outside an old brick building with what looked like an old storage facility underneath it.

"Welcome to my place" Travis waved his hand at the building as he helped me out of the car.

"You live here?"

"Yeah, well upstairs, but yeah. It used to be a garage back in the day then someone converted it to a small holding facility, it's not very busy which is fine by me as it's quiet".

I followed Travis to a door at the side of the building. He quickly unlocked the door and helped me up the stairs to his apartment. It was an open design with a large room containing a plush black leather sunken couch that bent round in a U shape with a round glass coffee table in the middle. A large television was sunk into the wall and speakers dotted the bare brick walls around the entire room. A breakfast bar separated the kitchen from the living area, the maroon cupboards gleaming with the light shining in through the kitchen window. Black marble countertops that were surprisingly clear of any junk or mess lined the cupboards and walls in the kitchen. There were 3 black doors leading off from the living area.

"The 2 doors on the left are bedrooms, the other is the bathroom" Travis let go of my hand and walked towards the kitchen area.

"Coffee?" He asked me.

"Yeah, please" I stood awkwardly.

"Take a seat, I'll bring it in for you".

I walked over to the couch and nervously sat down. I'd never been to a boy's house before; in fact, I had never been inside a boy's room even in the care home.

CHAPTER 8
TRAVIS

I can't believe Cole pulled that stunt today, well I mean I knew he was a bit of a perv and liked to prey on girls like Tiff, but even I didn't think he would actually try to push himself on Tiff. Push is a bit of an understatement from what Chance said. Forced would be more like the word that should be used. Just thinking about it makes my blood boil. Frank text to say that he had fired Cole and that Cole had left with a black eye. I'm assuming my uncle punched him. Frank taught me everything I know, him being ex-army and all. With my parents being on the other side of the world it landed on my uncle to teach me how to defend myself and during my school years he taught me how to channel my anger in the form of boxing. I spend a lot of time with Frank in the gym lifting weights and boxing, it's sort of like our bonding time, I guess.

Tiff fell asleep not long after she finished the coffee I made her, she didn't talk much, just said thanks and thanks again. I guess she is still a bit shaken up. Having her here feels so right. I rub the stubble on my chin as I watch her sleep, yeah nothing creepy about that! She looks so small and fragile with her long black hair spread across the red couch pillows, her fist clutching the corner of the pillow in a vice-like grip. I'm guessing she has seen just as much shit as I have. My phone vibrates in my pocket, and I pull it out to see Clint is ringing me. I hope he has that info I asked for. Even Frank was shocked when I told him why I wanted Tiff's info.

I quietly head to my room to take the call so that Tiff won't overhear anything.

"Clint"

"Trav, I got some info for you on Tiff".

"Go on"

"Her dad committed suicide a month after her mum was buried, her mum is the woman you couldn't save, sorry Trav".

"I knew it, fuck" I ran my hand down my face. It all made sense now, my need to protect her. It's like fate had made us meet and wanted us to be together.

"Trav, that hotel she is staying at, you need to get her out and soon".

"Why? What's up?"

"Her bank accounts show she only has a couple hundred left, and that hotel manager is known for taking advantage of his female customers that can't afford to pay".

"What do you mean Clint?" I could feel my anger rising again.

"He makes them pay for the room with sexual favours for him and his mates".

"Tiff wouldn't do that" I shouted down the phone at him.

"Man, she has little to no money and nowhere else to go, what would you do if you were her? It's obvious she isn't going to ask for help or tell you what's going on".

Clint had a good point; I need to find a way to get Tiff to open up to me.

"Clint, do you think Amber could get close enough to Tiff to make her open up and spill the beans, without me having to tell her I know about her?"

"I don't know man, I really think you should just sit down and talk to her, tell her everything".

"If I do that she may just run. Chance told you what happened with Cole this morning?"

"No not yet. What happened?"

I relayed this morning's events to Clint and with every word my blood started to boil again.

"That fucking bastard, I'll rip his fucking cock off" Clint yelled at me.

"Frank fired him and gave him a black eye, but I'm yet to dish out my justice".

"You know he will be at Nancy's bar tonight, right?"

"Really? Maybe we can do practice and head out for drinks after" I smirked.

"I like you're thinking, but if Tiff is with us, we need to play it cool and not throw the first punch or insult".

"Clint, she is my girl. I think seeing her in my arms will be enough to set Cole off on one".

"Does she know she is your girl?"

"I'm not sure, I think she overheard me saying it to Chance earlier, but she hasn't said anything since so I may be mistaken".

"So, everyone knows she is your girl except for her?"

"Something like that"

"You really need to sit down with her and tell her everything".

"I know, but what if she runs from me?"

"That's a risk you have to take if you want her in your life".

"What if I talk to her after she has met Amber. Then she will have someone to confide in"

"That could work, I'll let Amber in on the plan then, but you need to talk to her soon man" Clint advised me before hanging up.

Now I had even more on my mind, she was the daughter of the woman I couldn't save, and her dad committed suicide not long after. Now she was jobless, no money to speak of and practically homeless. How could social services not be aware of her situation? Hopefully Amber will be the friend that Tiff needs right now, it sure as hell looks like she doesn't have another soul in her life right now yet alone a best friend to talk to about girly shit or whatever it is girls talk about. I know this isn't going to happen overnight and will probably take a while, and in the meantime, I'll do whatever I can to protect her. I fired off a quick text to Clint.

Hey, I think we should get Amber to be best friends with Tiff first before I tell her about her parents and me being there. I want her to have someone there for her when she gets mad at me. I will tell her though that she is my girl. Everything else can wait until she has a good firm friendship with Amber.

Clint replies within seconds.

Probably the best idea you've ever had. Amber is onboard with it and can't wait to meet her tonight.

At least he has spoken to Amber already and she is happy to go along with this plan. I just hope that Tiff doesn't hate me when it all comes out. I head back into the kitchen and put the coffee maker on again. I should wake Tiff up in a bit and have some lunch with her. Shit, I haven't done the shopping yet. Pulling my phone out my pocket I open up the delivery app and place an order for lunch for us. I hope she likes sweet chilli chicken subs. I took the 2 mugs of coffee I'd just made and walked into the living area placing the mugs on the coffee table. I knelt down on the floor in front of Tiff's face and gently brushed the back of my hand over her cheek.

"Tiff, time to wake up" I whispered to her and enjoyed watching the goosebumps rise on her skin as her breath hitched her eyes open slowly.

"Hey, good sleep?" I asked her as I backed away slightly.

"How long was I out for?"

"About two hours. I've ordered lunch, hope you like sweet chilli chicken subs".

"One of my favourites, although I haven't had it in ages" she smiled at me as she sat up tucking her feet underneath her.

"It shouldn't be long" I sat beside her on the couch and pulled her feet onto my lap as I gently massaged them.

"I need to go home after lunch to get changed if tonight is still on" She looked at me with those beautiful ocean blue eyes of hers and smiled. I could so easily get lost in her eyes.

"I'll drop you off after we have eaten, although you look ok for going out tonight to me".

"I really should go home and change. I'll get the bus so you can get back to work".

"No need, Frank gave me the rest of the day off".

"that's nice of him, but really, I can get the bus".

"Look I let you have your way last night about not dropping you of at home, but after this morning I will be dropping you back off at home and walking you to your door, so I know you are home safe and sound, then I will be picking you up from home to take you out tonight".

"You can't do that" she looked at me with scared and pleading eyes.

"I can and I will" I held her feet in my hands still massaging them and surprised she hadn't pulled them away yet.

"Travis I will catch the bus, and you will let me".

"Now I know your hiding something from me".

"I'm not hiding anything" her eyes flickered to the door as she pulled her feet away and went to stand up.

"Don't even think about it Tiff, you won't make it as far as the top step before I catch you and haul your arse back in here" I knew she was thinking about bolting.

"I don't want you taking me home" she crossed her arms over her ample chest as she glared at me. I stood up facing her.

"Tiff, I've seen all sorts of homes you know, you don't have to be embarrassed" I tried to reason with her in the hopes she would tell me, but nope the stubborn girl turned on her heels and ran barefoot towards the door. I laughed and ran after her grabbing her arm as she turned the doorknob. I turned her around and wrapped my arm around the top of her thighs. I hauled her up and over my shoulder before marching her back towards the spare room. I kicked open the door and threw her onto the bed. She sat up and started hitting me as I stood over her. Fair play her punches hurt and would leave bruises.

"Let me go, I said I'd catch a bus, you can't make me go with you".

"I'll let you go when you agree to me dropping you off at home or tell me what you're hiding" I grabbed at her fists and wrapped my hands around her wrists to stop her hitting me anymore.

"I can't" she whimpered trying to pull away from me.

"You can, you just don't want to. Why?" I asked her. I quickly fell on top of her pinning her to the bed as her knee was about to connect with my balls. Yeah, not happening.

She squirmed beneath me, her hands now pinned above her head, my hips pinning hers down. Fuck my cock was getting hard and I hoped she wouldn't feel it through our jeans.

"Stop squirming and talk to me" I said between clenched teeth.

"I can't," She sobbed as tears fell from her eyes. I released her wrists and wiped away her tears as I gazed into her eyes.

"You can Tiff, you can tell me anything and I won't judge you, not ever" she stared back into my eyes and her breathing hitched again, maybe she is having the same urges and feelings as I am right now.

"I don't have a home" she sniffed and turned away from me tears spilling onto the sheets beneath her. I pulled myself off her and then pulled her onto my lap stroking her hair as I cradled her to my chest.

"What do you mean you have no home? Where are you staying?" I asked even though I already knew.

"I left the care home as soon as I could and lied about staying with friends, I stay in a hotel, but that won't be for much longer as my money is running out now".

"What hotel?"

"Shady Oaks on Oak Street"

"Fuck, why? Tiff that neighbourhood is bad, like really bad".

"It's all I could afford after paying off my dad's debts and his funeral expenses. I have no one and nowhere" she sniffed again and buried her face into my shirt.

"After lunch we are going to fetch your stuff and you can stay here with me".

"I can't Travis"

"You can, you're my girl and my responsibility now".

"You meant it yesterday and earlier when you said it?"

"Meant what?" I asked her.

"That I'm your girl? You hardly know me".

"I don't need to know you to know that you make me feel happier than I've ever felt before. You're my girl and have been since you first said it's T.J sir" I chuckled, and she smiled a weak smile.

"So, are you, my girl?" I asked her, hoping she would say yes.

"I guess, but can we take it slow?"

"As slow as you want. But you are moving in today. You can have this room, it's the spare room."

"Do I have a choice?"

"Nope"

"Guess I'm moving in then" She smiled at me with a smile that made her eyes sparkle and my cock twitch. Shit this was going to be hard to go slow with my cock acting like a sex starved teenager.

CHAPTER 9

T.J AKA TIFF

Here I am sitting on Travis' couch eating the sweet chilli sub he ordered for lunch. Guess he isn't the douche bag I thought he was after all. He's been nothing but kind, sweet and generous with me today. He picked me up after Cole made a pass at me and then he let me sleep on his couch. Sleep, that's something that doesn't happen very often as even living at the hotel I have to have my wits about me, it's like living in the care home, always listening for the rattle of the door handle and someone trying to get into your room. Every night for the past 3 years I've had to sleep with one eye and ear open, the one night I fell into a deep sleep at the care home some knob head of a boy actually managed to get into my room and start feeling me up, imagine his surprise when I pulled a knife out against his throat and kneed him in his ball sack. Yeah, living in a care home is not like they show it to be on the kid's television show. Its hell on earth. You have no privacy and very little freedom, everyone knows your business and why you are there, and the boys seem to think that all the girls are an easy lay or begging for a fucking. Not to mention the staff screwing each other and smoking weed. Hey, they even share their drugs with the care kids on a good day. Like I said hell on earth.

Some might say that it's moving too fast with me and Travis moving in together when we've only known each other for a day but I'm not moving into his room, in a way I'll just be a lodger. He's agreed to go slow, so I know I'm not under any pressure to sleep with him, especially as it was his idea and suggestion for me to have the spare room. I'm his girl now and it kind of makes me feel safe and wanted, something I've not felt in 3 nearly 4 years. It will be 4 years next Thursday since mum was killed, I miss her so much, her smile and the way she would whisper secrets to me and the nights we sat on her bed when dad was working away, we had a movie and lots of chocolates and cakes after we ate pizza. Mum was my best friend as well as a parent and some junked up thug took her from me and is still walking the streets free as a bird as the police never caught him.

"Penny for them" Travis voice broke into my thoughts.

"Huh?"

"You were scowling, like you were deep in thought and angry. Not over Cole?"

"No not Cole, the bastard who took my mum from me".

"You want to talk about it?" Travis offered"

"Not really, well not today, maybe one day"

"Whenever you're ready" he bumped a shoulder against mine making me smile shyly at him. He's actually a really nice guy when he isn't being a moody bastard.

"Thanks, for everything"

"No thanks needed. When your finished eating I need to stop by the garage and then we need to go collect your stuff"

"Drop me off to pack and pick me up again when you've finished what you need to at the garage" I suggested.

"You sure you'll be, ok?"

"Yeah, won't take me too long to pack the few bits I have there" Honestly it wouldn't take me long at all considering I had very few personal belongings. Not my choice though, when the police took me to the care home, I didn't have time to grab any of my things, only the picture of me and my parents together on our last family holiday. Even when the house was sold to pay off the remaining mortgage I didn't get to go back in and claim any of our things, not that much was left after it had been burgled several times when people realised the place was empty.

Half an hour later Travis pulled up outside the seedy run-down hotel I'd called home for the past 9 months. He got out of his car and held me in his arms as we stood outside.

"What's your room number?"

"Six, why?"

"So, I can come up when I get back and help you carry your stuff out to the car. "

"That would be nice, but you don't have to".

"So, give me your number so I can ring when I get here then".

"About that, I sort of don't have a phone".

"I thought as much, how about we get you one tomorrow on the garage accounts for work purposes" He winked at me and wrapped his arms around my waist pulling me against him.

"I'd like that" I rested my head against his chest as my arms wrapped around him, breathing in his scent of oil, petrol and just him.

"I'll be back in less than an hour" he pulled away from me, kissing my forehead gently.

"Ok, I should be all packed up by then" I smiled at him as he jumped back into his car and headed off to the garage.

I turned and slowly walked towards the hotel front door for the last time ever I hoped.

Gary sat behind the counter he looked up as I walked in and gave me his usual smile showing his black decayed teeth.

"Your back early, something wrong?" He asked me.

"No, just coming to collect my stuff."

"Why's that then?"

"I'm shipping out today, moving on you could say" I didn't want to give him any details, the man honestly creeps me out.

"Really? How come?"

"I got an offer I couldn't refuse, you could say" Gary was now approaching me and didn't look to happy either.

"I thought you were staying on here for a while".

"Things change" I quickly stepped away from him and pushed the door separating the foyer from the rooms open.

"Do you need any help?" he asked as he stepped towards me following my steps. Why is he following me?

"Nope, I can manage on my own thank you" I tried to let the door swing closed but Gary was quick to stop it and step through following me down the corridor. I quickly opened the door to my room and turned to close my door, thankfully Gary hadn't caught up with just yet so that task was easy. With my door now closed and locked I pulled out the one and only suitcase I owned and started to put my clothes and the one picture I owned into it along with my college folders and books. All my belongings packed away into one small suitcase. Not a lot to show for nearly 18 years of life. I sit on the bed with the only family photo I have in my hands, tears springing to my eyes as I trace a thumb over my mother's face. My own mind is lost in thoughts and memories of happier times. I failed to hear the lock on my door click as Gary let himself into my room.

"You ungrateful bitch, I let you stay here for cheaper than any other person and you still pass up any opportunity I give you to be with me, and now you tell me you're leaving. You're not going anywhere without giving me what you owe me" he sneered at me as he launched himself across the room at me.

"I owe you nothing, I always paid up on time what I owed" I jumped back away from him and further onto the bed.

"You owe me bitch and I intend to collect" he grabbed hold of my ankle and pulled me towards him. Why the fuck do I end up in these situations? I'm not even that pretty, yet boys seem to think they can force me to be with them. Fuck my life. I kick out my legs and raise my fists ready to punch if given a chance. I don't get that chance though.

"What the fuck are you doing to my girl?" Travis yells as he yanks Gary away from me. Gary's back hit the wall opposite me with Travis hand clamped around his throat. The anger pouring off Travis was visible in the tension across his shoulders and the seething look drawn on his face.

"Who the fuck are you?" Gary asked as he struggled for breath and tried clawing at Travis's hand still wrapped around his throat.

"I'm her boyfriend and you dared touch what belongs to me, and without consent" Travis told him in a cool, calm yet scary voice. Wait! Did he say boyfriend? I know I agreed to be his girl, but I guess I didn't think what title that gave him to me. Boyfriend, yeah holy shit balls I guess he's right I have a boyfriend. A smoking hot, grease monkey boyfriend who is already saving my arse from perverts like Gary.

"That frigid bitch doesn't have a boyfriend, you're lying" Gary practically spat in Travis face. Travis grabbed Gary by the shoulders and threw him to the floor.

"I suggest you get your miserable rapist arse out of my sight before I really get angry" Travis rolled his shoulders, his muscles rippling in a tantalising way as he did so. His fists clenched at his side as he moved his head from side to side as if loosening up for a big fight.

"You haven't seen the last of me bitch" Gary sneered as he scrambled to his feet and left the room. Travis stepped over to me and ran his knuckle down over my cheek.

"You, ok?" He whispered in my ear.

"Yeah, let's get out of here" I grabbed my bag and Travis grabbed the suitcase and picture from the bed.

"Is this all of it?" He asked with a raised eyebrow.

"Yeah, this is all of my stuff".

"Come on then, let's get going".

I followed Travis down the hallway and out the foyer to his car which he had parked in the drop off zone right by the front doors. The drive back to Travis' apartment was silent, not awkward silent but still a slightly uncomfortable silence. Travis wasted no time in getting the suitcase and my bag out of the car and walking into the apartment, still not saying a word to me. Now it was getting unbearable. The anger was still rolling off him in waves, his shoulders hunched with tension.

"Travis..."

"Don't, don't you dare try to worm your way out of this" he turned, dropping the case and glared at me, his face contorted with rage. He stalked towards me making me take steps backwards away from him.

"Travis, I don't know what I've done".

"Really? You pay your way by sleeping around with the hotel staff, and then you try to act all innocent" My hand came up without a second thought and connected with his face, the sound of the slap ricocheting around the room.

"How dare you fucking insinuate that I'm a slut. I paid with what cash I had left over from my parent's life insurance. Want me to provide a bank statement to prove it?" I grabbed my suitcase and bag before running out of his apartment and struggling towards the stairs. I gave up with my suitcase and just threw it. I had enough clothes in my duffel bag to last me for now. I reached my hand out to grab the banister by the stairs only to have my elbow gripped firmly and my whole body spun around to face Travis.

"Tiff, I'm sorry" I could see the words were meant in his eyes. He genuinely was sorry, but it didn't stop me from opening my mouth and hurling abuse at him. I'd lived for three years with the stigma of being a slut because I was a care brat and apparently all care kids are sexual deviants.

"You're no better than the rest of society. Just because I was in care doesn't make me a trouble making, drug taking, rampant sex starved thief. Not all care kids are bad you know" I pulled my elbow out of Travis grip and started to turn back to the stairs. Tears stung my eyes threatening to spill over.

"Tiff, please I mean it, I'm sorry".

"This isn't going to work. I'll find somewhere else to stay and see you at work" my feet left the floor, and I was spun in the air before being thrown over Travis shoulder for the second time today. His arm firmly clamping my legs down against his hard body stopping me from kicking him, with only my arms free I punched him repeatedly with my fists while screaming at him to put me down. He stalked back into his apartment and headed straight towards the spare room. I heard the door click shut and then what I think to be a key turning in the lock.

Travis placed me gently on the bed and stood in front of me. I watched him slip a key into his back pocket.

"Now, you are going to listen to me and let me speak before butting in" he folded his arms across his chest and looked at me with a raised eyebrow daring me to argue with him.

"Just let me go" I stood up and tried to grab for his pocket only to be pushed back down onto the bed.

"Not happening, you will listen and talk to me, if after that you still want to leave then I'll let you go".

"Fine" I folded my arms and huffed.

"Good. I know not all care kids are bad, you're not bad. I'm truly sorry that I jumped to the wrong conclusion about the set up with the hotel manager, but I'd like you to explain what he meant when he said you owed him, and it really did look like that owe was a sexual favour from the doorway."

"He hinted more than a few times at me paying with sex if I ever got short of money, I'd never do that though. I'd rather sleep on a park bench than lower myself to that degree".

"So, you have never given him the impression that you would give him a sexual favour?"

"No never, if anything I've always brushed him off and ignored him" Travis stepped forward and dropped to his knees in front of me, his hand reaching up and gently stroking my cheeks.

"Was today the only time he had tried anything with you?" Travis asked me with worry evident in his voice. I could only nod my head to confirm that today was the first time that Gary had tried to do anything to me. The tears that threatened to spill earlier could no longer be held back as the enormity of what could have happened if Travis hadn't walked in dawned on me, and I sobbed into my hands. Travis stroked my hair and held my head to his chest and let me sob until I could cry no more and fell asleep leaning against him.

CHAPTER 10

TRAVIS

Tiff had every reason to be angry with me and slap me like she
did. I was totally out of order when I accused her of sexual favours to
pay her rent on the room, she was using at that god awful seedy hotel.
I just saw red when I walked in and saw that pervert grabbing at her
and hearing him say she owed him. It was obvious what he thought
she owed him by the way he said it and the way he was grabbing at
her. Fuck what if I hadn't turned up when I did? Or if she continued
staying there. It was obvious that sooner or later he was going to
rape her unless she complied and willingly slept with him. Tiff said
she would rather sleep on a park bench, but I know when the chips
are down and you're desperate enough especially on those cold dark
winter nights, that you will do near enough anything for a warm bed
and shelter from the cold. I know because I did a few nights sleeping
rough on the streets as part of a charity drive to raise awareness of
the severity of homelessness in our town. Just one night and I was
begging in my mind for a warm bed and shelter from the wind and
rain. She was also right about society judging care kids to be out of
control and trouble. Some were bad news but not all of them. Some
kids it was genuinely because they had no parents or relatives to take
them in during a crisis or death in the family, others it was because
they lived in a single parent family and the parent was too sick to care
for them others it was because their parents were abusive to them or
just couldn't care for them. Yes, there were the kids whose parents
were in prison or doped up on drugs all the time but that didn't make
the kid bad. Sometimes the kids went off the rails as that was their
coping mechanism, a way to deal with the crap life had dealt them.
Not all kids were a product of the despair that life threw at them,
some like Tiff were kind, caring, considerate and wanted to have a
normal life. I wanted to give Tiff that normal life, or at least a better
life than what she had currently been having these past few months

or years. I held Tiff as she sobbed in my arms. Everything today had been intense and scary for her, first Cole, then that man in the hotel trying to do unspeakable things to her. She yet again cried herself to sleep in my arms and I gently laid her back down on the bed and left her to sleep while I carried her suitcase and bag back into the apartment. She didn't really have much stuff. I spotted the family picture she had been holding on the floor by the door. I picked it up and noticed the glass was broken but the frame was homemade, seashells and glitter were stuck onto it, it obviously meant a lot to Tiff. I rummaged around in the cupboard I used for storing junk until I found the box holding all my family portraits in and looked through them for a frame the same size. Finally finding one I took it to the table along with Tiff's photo and carefully swapped the glass over. I quietly set the photo on the bedside table next to Tiff's bed where she was still sleeping. She looked so peaceful and relaxed like this, a vision of pure innocent beauty.

I let Tiff sleep for a bit before I woke her up so we could head out for my band practice.

I gently shook her shoulder as I whispered her name in her ear.

"Tiff, it's time to wake up".

She turned and looked up at me as her eyes fluttered open.

"What time is it?"

"It's just gone five, you slept for nearly two hours again" I chuckled.

"Sorry, I guess all those sleepless nights finally caught up with me" She absently told me as she sleepily rubbed at her eyes. She tensed as she realised what she had said.

"Sleepless nights? Want to tell me about them?" I asked her, thinking it would be nightmares from her parents dying especially her dad given she was the one that found him hanging.

"I never slept properly, always listening for someone trying to sneak into my room. I haven't slept solidly at night for nearly four years now."

"Since you got taken into care?" I asked her.

"Yeah, at first it was nightmare's keeping me awake but it soon became apparent that boys would try to sneak into the girl's rooms at night for a quick grope or more if the girl was up for it, I eventually started moving my drawers or desk in front of the door every night".

"Well, you don't have to worry about that anymore. You're safe here, even from me "I laughed.

"Thank you"

"I mean it Tiff, this room is yours, no strings attached, no rent needed, I just ask that you do your fair share of keeping the apartment clean, and maybe bake me a cake at your class" I winked at her making her giggle, and God did that giggle sound like the most amazing sound I'd ever heard from her in the two days I'd known her. Two Days is that all? It felt like I'd known her my whole life.

"I think I can manage that "

"Good, now get ready as we have practice to get to" I walked to the door and smiled at her.

"Practise? Oh, shit I forgot, what do I wear to a football or sports practice?"

"Just what you're already wearing" She still thought it was a sports thing I practised at, I really couldn't wait for her to see what practice I actually did.

An hour later I pulled up outside Clint's house. He lived in his parent's old house and rented it from them, they downsized a couple years back to a small bungalow just a couple miles away from here but closer to the town centre. Tiff looked at me puzzled.

"Come on, let's go in so you can meet the guy's" I opened my door and quickly got out and jogged round to Tiff's side, the car holding my hand out to her.

"Umm, I thought we were going to a sports club or something".

"I don't do sports Tiff, yeah, I use Franks gym and do weights and stuff but I'm not a sports person".

"So what practice is this exactly?" She asked me as we stepped in through the front door. "And why are you just walking into someone else's home?"

"This is Clint's place, we kind of always just walk into each other's places, sort of family really" I explained to her as we walked down the hallway into the living room.

"Trav baby, you came" Amber jumped up from her seat and walked over to me. "And who is this beauty?" She asked as she looked at Tiff. I knew that Amber already knew as Clint would've told her already.

"Amber this is Tiff, Tiff this is Amber a real good friend of mine".

"Hey" Tiff sounded so timid and shy, not the girl who shouted out in the garage just yesterday. Holy shit was she intimidated by Amber or jealous even.

"Hey, come on let's get some drinks while the boys set up" Amber wrapped an arm around Tiff's arm and pulled her towards the kitchen. Tiff turned to look at me and honestly, she looked like a scared rabbit caught in the headlights of a massive truck.

"Trav man, you made it in time for a change" Clint walked in behind me from the room we used for band practice, originally it had been the dining room when his parents lived here. Clint had thought it better suited our practice needs as it was larger than the garage or the living room.

"So that's the girl then?" Clint smirked at me.

"Yeah, that's my girl. When are the other's getting here?"

"Chance is on his way and Brad is just walking in the door now".

"Did I hear my name?" Brad walked into the living room with his usual cocky swagger and grin. Brad was from Latino American descent and had tanned skin with dark hair falling around his ears.

He was also a ladies' man, using his Latino side to woo girls into bed with him, the cocky man whore.

"Brad, how's things?" I asked him as I grabbed his hand in our fist shake and patted his back in our brotherly way.

"You mean after you ditched me to deal with the psycho bitch? Yeah, I'm just peachy".

"I heard about that; take it she bitched all night over getting a beating from Trav's girl then?" Clint asked as he too gave Brad the usual fist shake and pat on the back.

"Man, she is still bitching, and she said she will be at Nancy's tonight to see her man" Brad winked at me.

"Who is coming to the pub tonight?" Amber asked as she and Tiff walked back into the room with beers for us all.

"Claire is" Brad told her and watched her grimace.

"That bitch from the burger place?" Tiff asked as she handed me a cold beer.

"Yeah, you really pissed her off, you know" Brad chuckled.

"I'll get big Ben to stop her from getting in, He's on the doors tonight" Amber pulled her phone out.

"No let her come, I'm not scared of bitches like her" Tiff told her while flopping down onto the oversized couch.

"You sure?" Brad asked her "She has a temper on her and is extremely possessive over Trav here".

"I'm sure, and she can drop the possessive thing as Travis isn't her man "

"You heard the lady," Clint smirked at us as he opened his beer.

"Sorry I'm late, Cole collared me as I locked up earlier" Chance practically ran into the living room.

"What did he want?" I asked as different emotions flicked over Tiff's face. Anger, fear and confusion.

"He wanted to know where you had taken Tiff to so he could apologise. Told him to do one if he knew what was good for him."

"Now we are all here let's get this practice started shall we, sooner we start sooner we can hit the bar" Clint looked at us all.

"You ok Tiff?" Amber asked her as she followed us into the 'band' room.

"Yeah, just not sure how to feel about Cole wanting to apologise".

"He's known to be pushy and flirty with the girls but talking to him has to be your decision at the end of the day" Amber told her. If I had anything to do with it the fucker wouldn't get a chance to talk to her ever again, but Amber was right the decision has to be Tiff's.

I watched as Tiff looked around the room, her eyes bugging out of her head as her jaw dropped to the floor.

"Practise? As in band practice?" She asked me.

"Yeah, and we are pretty good as well" I smiled at her as I took my place behind the drums and Brad and Chance hooked up their guitars to the amps and speakers. Clint checked the mic over making sure it worked.

"Let's start with 'firefly' and then move on to' call girl'".

Firefly was my personal favourite song to play. Thinking about it, it sort, of sounds like Tiff, the fiery flight of a young girl escaping realism and looking for a brighter future. I started the beat and then Brad and Chance stepped in with their guitars before Clint started with the lyrics.

Midnight sky, blacks and blues
the moon hidden behind the clouds.
Sights and sounds of the busy crowds.
Drown her sobs and painful sounds.
Misunderstood, misused,
This girl was broken and bruised.
She looked up to the darken sky.
and shouted out why?
Then like a firefly her smile grew and lite up her eyes.

Her flight or fight gave a kick.
now she stood with determined force giving her hair a flick...
She walked with strength in her stride.
A smile on her face a mile wide
And like a firefly she drew a breath she did not hold
and her blue green eyes shone bright and bold.
With majestic grace she fluttered by
just like a firefly.

Clint sang on as I watched Tiff from behind my drums, her eyes glistening as she took in the words, I watched as she swallowed and pressed a hand to her heart when Clint sang the verse about starting again with determined strength and facing up to a future alone yet still being strong. Then just like that she stood up and ran out of the room. I threw my drumsticks down and went to chase after her, but Amber shook her hand and motioned that she would go instead. I knew she would be good with that as Clint would've filled her in on all the details and I Knew that Amber wouldn't spill that she knew anything about Tiff to her.

CHAPTER 11
TIFF

I never in a million years thought that Travis played drums yet alone was in a band, and a good band at that. Clint sang with a passion in his voice that was hard to achieve by other basement bands I'd heard. But the song lyrics he sang hit so close to home for me and hit a chord in my heart as memories of being lost and alone yet having to be strong and fight on when dad died hit me full force. I couldn't listen anymore and needed to get out of there fast. I heard the beat of the drums stop and hoped that Travis wouldn't follow me, I needed a moment to myself. Some things from my past I didn't want to share just yet. Mum being killed was hard enough to deal with then dad giving up on life and in turn giving up on me was awful but being in care was by far the most traumatic time for me. That's where I learnt the true meaning of the term 'flight or fight' and I quickly learnt that fighting was the better option as fleeing to your room or anywhere else only made things worse the next time round. It's not a time in my life I wish to revisit. Yeah, there were a few good times like ice skating a few times and the time we went frog hunting in the pond and brought back a toad. But the rest was miserable. The kids didn't do drugs as much as the staff did. In fact, one member of staff took me and a few of the boys to a pool hall and openly dealt drugs while smoking a joint. And that was a good day. My broken nose was courtesy of another girl in the home who just didn't like my face apparently. Anyway, that song Clint was singing triggered something in me and my flight or fight slipped into flight mode, and I legged it out of that room faster than a cat on a hot tin roof. I needed space and some alone time to collect myself again and lock those feelings away again.

"Tiff, wait up" Amber called out to me.

"Please just leave me alone".

"Tiff, what's wrong?" Amber asked me as she brushed my hair behind my ear when she caught up with me.

"I just need a minute; I'm fine go back in please" I practically begged her.

"Tiff, you are far from alright or fine, your tear-stained face says that just as much as you getting up and running out here".

"Just leave it Amber " I pushed her away from me and started to walk away from Clint's house. I had no idea where I was or where I was going but I couldn't be here right now.

"Tiff, let me walk with you at least or I'll have to call Travis to come get you".

"Fine, but don't fetch Travis and don't try to psychoanalyse me either".

"Wouldn't dream of it, but when you're ready I'm here for you".

We walked for ages in complete silence, I did notice that she texted someone a few times, probably Travis. Eventually Amber broke the silence between us.

"So, the guys are heading to the bar now, you want to join them?"

"Yeah, sure why not?" Remembering that a certain blonde bitch would be there was a ticket to help me get back into the right frame of mind, or at least the one I'd been living in these past few years. My flight or fight needed to get back to fight level instead of flight mode and that bitch could just well be the answer. I mean I get that Travis is a catch but let's be real here he's just a normal man, nothing special, no godly like features about him, he was just a normal man who just so happened to be in a band, own his own apartment and car, plus work in a garage all at just 20 something years old. Yeah, ok so he's not some hot shot CEO but he's my hotshot, hell that sounds good my hotshot! yeah, if I'm his girl then he's my hotshot and that blonde bitch best stay the fuck away from him.

"Oh, goody as I just asked them to pick us up, my feet are killing me and I still have a shift behind the bar to do" Amber smiled at me with a big goofy smile

"You work at the pub?"

"Work? I own and run the place, the boys help out sometimes and they bring in a good crowd when they perform".

"Guess you guys are real long-term friends then?"

"Been friends with the guys since we were all about 6 maybe 7 years old".

"Wow, that must be nice to have friends like that" I could feel my mood slipping again to unwanted territory.

"It has its advantages and disadvantages. Like Clint is an arsehole to any guy who looks at me wrong and then Travis will beat anyone up who tries anything with me, Brad and Chance are the goofballs always trying to prank each other and us but they can be just as protective in their own way".

"So more like family than friends?" I asked her. Sure, it sounded nice though whatever way she put it.

"Yeah, guess you could say that. How about you? Any friends or family?"

"Nope, just me myself and I" I waved my arms around indicating that it was just me.

"Well not anymore, you got me now so suck it up biatch cos you just got yourself a bestie" She looped her arm through mine and smiled at me.

"Guess I have" I laughed at her.

"Oh, here come the boy's now" She waved down a beat-up Ford pick-up truck.

"Chance, taking your truck today then?" Amber asked him as she swung the door open to face Clint and Brad already sat in the back seats with Chance driving.

"Travis is behind so Tiff can ride with him," Clint told her.

Sure, enough Travis pulled up behind and called me over.

"See you at the pub Tiff" They all said at the same time as Amber climbed into the truck. I slowly made my way over to Travis's car and climbed in.

"You, ok?" Travis asked me as he followed Chance in his pick-up.

"Yeah, I'm fine now, just needed a bit of space. "

"You sure?"

"Yeah, I'm sure. Now let's go get some drinks and annoy a bimbo or two" Travis literally roared with laughter at my comment.

"Yeah, let's do that firefly".

"Firefly?" I asked, feeling slightly confused by the nickname.

"Yeah firefly, like the girl in Clint's song. You're that girl".

"You think I'm that girl? That girl who was beaten and lonely who found strength and the will to carry on with a smile on her face?"

"Hell yeah, you Tiff are my Firefly, my flight or fight girl and I see that fight in you same as it's in me. I know you've seen and experienced some shit in your life, I don't know everything. I see it when you talk about the little things you have shared with me. But despite all the hardships and struggles you're still here fighting strong and carrying on, that's my Firefly".

Firefly, I'm his girl, his Firefly! I actually like the sound of that.

"Ok hotshot I'll give you that".

"Hotshot?" He raised an eyebrow at me.

"Yeah, your no super model or God gift man or a CEO but you're my hotshot, my hotshot drummer".

"Yeah, ok I'll give you that" He used my words back at me.

When we pulled up outside a pub called Nancy's Travis went back to his moody scowl look, the one that said he had seen shit and didn't want to deal with your bullshit as well, or it could just be his resting bitch face, either way this was the Travis I first saw in the garage.

"You ok Trav?" I asked.

"Yeah, why?"

"You've got that look on your face like you did at the garage. You know that 'don't fuck with me cos I'm a moody arsehole who will rip you a new one' look".

"You mean my usual look? Sorry it's just the way I am, but with you I feel lighter and free. Being with people that aren't friends or family tends to make me uneasy and moody, especially women. I've been burnt and had my trust smashed apart so many times it's hard to relax. If I upset you at the garage, I'm sorry, it's not you trust me, it's those twins especially Cole".

"Yeah, Cole would probably make me like that after this morning as well".

"You know he might be here tonight?" Travis looked at me as he held my hand while we walked into the pub.

"I can deal with him Travis, just like I can deal with Barbie doll".

"I'm right here with you if you need me".

"Usual Trav?" Amber shouted from behind the bar.

"Yeah, and a coke for Tiff"

"Coming up "Amber replied as she pulled down glasses, did a little spin and started making our drinks. The pub was busy, and the bar staff moved seamlessly around each other occasionally doing a little spin or twirl as they passed each other getting drinks or getting to the tills.

"Travis baby" That God damn awful voice of the bimbo shrieked across the pub as Claire walked over and grabbed Travis bi-cep and leaned against him. Travis grabbed her hand and pushed it away from him with a scowl on his face.

"Oh, lookie here it's the barbie bitch from last night" I smiled at her.

"Bitch, what are you doing here?" She glared daggers at me as she tried and failed to grab Travis' arm again.

"I came with hotshot here; you know my boyfriend? "I watched as Travis struggled against her octopus' arms, still trying to grab at him.

"Travis isn't your boyfriend bitch, he'd never date an ugly freak like you, and definitely not a schoolgirl. I mean how old are you? 12" She sneered at me with her hands now on her hips instead of grabbing at Travis.

"Claire" Travis warned but she ignored him.

"Look bitch, I don't know who you are or think you are, but you're not welcome here so go back to your little playhouse and your dolls and have a tea party with them" She flicked her hair at me as she turned away to face Travis. I don't know what hurt more the words she spoke, or the fact Travis sat there and let her say them, either way I'd be damned if she was going to get my man or get away with talking to me like that. I tapped her shoulder making her turn to face me.

"Are you still here?"

"Thing is barbie, Travis brought me here along with his friends who I've just spent most the evening with, so I'm guessing since you weren't there that means they wanted me around not you. After all they invited me to come here tonight with them, did you get an invite?" I reached my hand across the bar towards Travis who immediately grabbed it and rubbed his thumb over my knuckles.

"I don't need an invite to join Travis, he knows I'll show up because he's my man" She grabbed my hand and ripped it away from Travis and my other hand came up in a fist and caught the side of her face making her head whip to the side. I heard a few "ouch" comments from some college guys sitting on a table behind us.

"You show up like a bad smell, then linger just as long as one, do us all a favour barbie and vanish before we have to call pest control" Yeah, maybe I was a bit harsh after hitting her, but she was literally getting on my last nerve and Travis just sitting there saying and doing nothing was not helping my mood right now. Claire raised her fist to strike at me, but Travis grabbed it in time stopping her as Amber walked over from behind the bar and whistled loudly with her fingers between her teeth. Two doormen walked over and nodded at Amber.

"Ben, Clive take the trash out please" Amber asked them as she spun a finger over Claire's head.

"Sure, thing Amber " The biggest guy answered, he was easily 6 foot 4 tall with dark hair shaved so close to his skull it could have been bald if he wanted.

"Thanks Ben," Amber replied. Guess big dude is big Ben then making the shorter yet broader man with blonde spiky hair Clive. Claire stood facing me hands on her hips looking smug as if she thought it was me being thrown out, stupid bitch stood there with her fake tits near enough falling out of the top of that ridiculous small purple skin-tight PVC dress she was wearing, well if you can call it a dress that is considering it was so tight and small that her arse cheeks were practically spilling out as much as her fake tits were. Ben stood next to her, and I watched as that smug smile fell from her face as she realised that it was her being thrown out, then panic showed on her face as she started to shout when Ben grabbed her arm.

"Come on Claire, sorry Barbie" he told her.

"Wait no, this is bullshit she hit me it should be her getting kicked out not me" she squawked whilst struggling against the grip Ben had on her arm as he pulled her away from us.

"Did she? Sorry I only saw you going to hit her" Clive answered in a deadpan way as he winked at me making me chuckle.

"Travis tell them baby; tell them she assaulted me" She begged Travis as Ben carried on dragging her by the arm towards the door followed by Clive.

"Sorry didn't see anything Claire, you see anything Amber?" Travis yelled over to Claire and Amber.

"Only Claire trying to hit my new bestie" Amber smiled and winked at us both." Thank God the trash has been taken out, now do you two need a refill?" Amber stood looking at me with a bar towel slung over her shoulder.

"Yeah, same again Amb" Travis replied as he stood behind me, hands on the bar either side of my body, his chest pressed against my back as he lowered his head and kissed my neck.

"Fuck off Trav, you stood and watched that shit show and did nothing".

"Firefly, do you know how fucking hot you are when you get all fired up like that and take on bitches like Claire?"

"Nice try Trav, but you are supposed to be my hotshot and you did nothing".

"Because I knew you could handle her, and she needed to see that you don't need me standing up for you because you are stronger and more mature than her. If I thought it was getting out of control I would've stepped in and done something, but you handled it so well and fuck was it hot" Travis trailed kisses down my neck making me feel things between my thighs I'd never felt before, like what the actual fuck?

"Drink up Firefly we need to get home, work in the morning and it's getting late" Travis pushed away from me and downed his drink and nodded at mine for me to drink up. I quickly drank up and Travis grabbed my hand pulling me towards the door as he waved at the guys to let them know we were leaving.

CHAPTER 12

TRAVIS

When Tiff ran out back at Clint's I admit I was worried, But Amber went after her and texted me a few times letting me know they were fine, and that Tiff just needed some time to process her emotions that had been stirred up from the song. Amber was a care kid too so if anyone knew what Tiff went through in the care home then it would be Amber. Amber never told us guys much about her time in care she just said it wasn't all fun and games like that T.V programme shows it to be. Clint filling Amber in on the other stuff as well meant that Amber knew better than any of us how Tiff might be feeling. Getting the message back saying to pick them up on the way to the pub was such a relief to me, I was worried that maybe Tiff might have gone down a rabbit hole of dark depression and wanted to hide away so knowing she was willing to still come out with us to the pub was a weight removed from my shoulders. Admittedly I was still worried about going to the pub tonight knowing that Claire and Cole might turn up tonight, well Claire definitely would, she always turned up like a bad smell that wouldn't disappear, I just hoped that Tiff would have the strength to deal with Claire's crap today.

"Right guys, tonight was epic, and I think that new song is going to kill the crowd on Saturday night, good call Brad with those lyrics. Let's pack up and go find the girl's" Clint bossed us around as usual.

"Wait guy's, I need to tell you stuff about Tiff, so you know why she is the way she is, but she doesn't know that I know yet so keep it on the down low and don't ever let on you know" I knew I was taking a risk with telling them, but I also trusted my longest and best friends.

"Yeah, what was with her running out during Firefly?" Brad piped up.

"You lot better listen to Trav, it's not good, that girl has been through hell and back" Clint looked at both Chance and Brad as he set his mic to one side and started to switch off the amps and speakers. Packing away never took long as we kept most things set up and plugged in except for the guitars of course, they always got unplugged and packed away into their cases. The guys finished packing up and sat down as I filled them in on Tiff's past or what Clint and I knew about it anyway.

"Shit, that's a tough life, holy fuck no wonder she fled like she did" Brad had a small tear fall down his cheek as he quickly wiped it away, he was the softest most sentimental one of us and always showed his emotions.

"How are you holding up though Trav? I mean it's her mum you saw die after all" Chance asked as he clapped a hand on my shoulder.

"I'm doing ok, actually I think Tiff is my saviour and is going to help me deal with my shit just as much as I'm going to help her" I honestly believed it as well, just that I didn't know how or when I was going to tell her that I was the one who helped save her dad that fateful night.

"Guys, she doesn't know about Trav being there that night yet, so obviously be discreet about it" Clint told them as he stood up.

"Yeah sure, no problem, guess we have our own real-life Firefly now then" Chance commented as he too stood up. Firefly, Tiff is my own Firefly and that nickname sounded so damn good and right.

"Right enough moping let's go get those girl's and hit the bar" Brad stood up and raced towards the door "Last one there buys the first round" He shouted back over his shoulder.

"God damn it you little cheat" Chance shouted as we all ran towards the door to catch up with him.

It took us ten minutes to catch up with the girl's as they had probably been walking for over an hour now while we practised. Amber jumped in the truck with Clint and the boys while I called Tiff over to join me in my car, she didn't hesitate which I took to be a good sign.

"You, ok?" I asked her.

"Yeah, I'm fine. Now let's go get some drinks and annoy a bimbo or two" I couldn't help myself as I roared with laughter at her reply. Annoy a bimbo or two, yeah definitely at least one bimbo as I know for a fact that Claire will be there tonight just like every night.

"Yeah, let's do that Firefly" I used my new nickname for her.

"Firefly?"

"Yeah, Firefly, like the girl in Clint's song. You're that girl" I looked over to watch her face and reaction to make sure I hadn't upset her.

"You think I'm that girl? That girl who was beaten and lonely who found strength and the will to carry on with a smile on her face?" She asked me with an eyebrow raised.

I went on to explain to her why she was my Firefly and from her expression I knew that she was shocked but also happy. Yeah, she was my Firefly alright.

"Ok hotshot, I'll give you that" She winked at me.

"Hotshot?" I asked, raising an eyebrow at her waiting for her explanation of that nickname.

"Yeah, you're no super model or god gift man or a CEO but you're my hotshot, my hotshot drummer" She grinned at me with the biggest smile I'd seen on her yet. I admit I liked her nickname for me Hotshot, hell yeah, I could be on board with that, and she was right I wasn't a looker per say but that didn't stop women throwing themselves at me, guess I was a good-looking bloke for an average Joe. I mean let's face it most drop dead gorgeous looking men are as Tiff put it super models or actors or bigwig CEO billionaires or some schmuck from a romance model that doesn't actually exist in real life.

Pulling up outside Nancy's the pub I felt my mood shift slightly, I hated being around people especially leeches like Claire. I'd been hurt and burned too many times by fake friends and wanna be girlfriends and being around people put me on edge, something that Tiff noticed.

"You ok Trav?" she asked me.

"Yeah, why?"

"You've got that look on your face like you did at the garage. You know that 'don't fuck with me cos I'm a moody arsehole who will rip you a new one' look".

"You mean my usual look? Sorry it's just the way I am, but with you I feel lighter and free, being with people that aren't friends or family tends to make me uneasy and moody, especially women. I've been burnt and had my trust smashed apart so many times it's hard to relax. If I upset you at the garage, I'm sorry, it's not you trust me, it's those twins especially Cole" I explained to her as I grabbed her hand and walked into the pub heading straight to the bar. Amber served us almost straight away and then Claire happened. She pawed at me wrapping a hand around my arm and resting her hair on my shoulder, I tensed and watched as anger flicked over Tiff's face and then it happened.

"Oh, Lookie here, it's the Barbie from last night" Tiff smiled a fake smile at Claire.

"Bitch, what are you doing here?" Claire spat at her still trying to wrap herself around me as I kept trying to remove her arms from my body.

"I came with hotshot here; you know my boyfriend?" oh shit that last bit was sure to wind Claire up.

"Travis isn't your boyfriend bitch, he'd never date an ugly freak like you, and definitely not a schoolgirl. I mean how old are you? twelve?" Claire sneered at Tiff with her hands now on her hips instead of all over me thank God.

"Claire" I warned her, I really didn't want Tiff upset again today and Claire was going down that real bitchy path again, I knew if I didn't step in soon then fists would fly. Before I could say anymore or react Tiff spoke up and in my peripheral view, I spotted Amber and the guys watching the show with interest and worry. I knew they would step in and defend Tiff if needed.

"Look bitch, I don't know who you are or think you are, but you're not welcome here so go back to your little playhouse and your dolls and have a tea party with them" Claire flicked her hair at Tiff as she taunted her with harsh words that made my blood boil, the only child here was Claire. I saw a flicker of hurt flashover Tiff's face and went to stand up, but Amber tapped my arm and shook her head. Tiff needed to show Claire that she was not a child. I watched and Listened as the argument continued between the two girls and Tiff was on fire with her replies and comments, I noticed a table of college boys behind us watching with interest as well as my guys and Amber, I also noticed Amber had signalled Big Ben the doorman to come over, yep Claire was going to get thrown out yet again. Claire getting tossed out by Ben and Clive was a regular occurrence here. At some point Tiff had reached for my hand on the bar and I'd started stroking her knuckles with my thumb which Claire noticed and ripped Tiffs hand away from me and then Tiff clocked Claire in the face with her fist, and holy shit if it wasn't the hottest thing I'd seen. Just as Claire went to retaliate with her own hand, Amber grabbed at it and stopped her before whistling loudly to Ben and waving a finger over Claire's head in a signal to remove her from the pub. Claire stood in her usual smug stance as if she thought it was Tiff getting kicked out, her shrieking and shouting got attention from everyone as Ben grabbed her arm and started to pull her away from the bar towards the door with Clive following. In typical Claire style she started banging on about Tiff assaulting her and it should be Tiff getting kicked out, and as usual we all denied seeing anything. Like I said, seeing Tiff give Claire a run for her money and then punching her had been so hot and dick was rock hard as my balls ached. I knew Tiff wasn't ready to step into that level of our relationship just yet, but my dick needed sorting soon before I got blue balls. I stood up behind Tiff as Amber got us more drinks, my hands on the bar top either side of Tiff as I leaned over pressing my chest to her back and started kissing her neck. She was tense and pissed at me and she told me as well. She was pissed I didn't stand up for her and sort Claire out myself but I explained my reason why as I continued kissing her neck and I felt her body relax and the little tremble she gave, hell she was getting turned on and it made me even harder knowing that I had done that to her, we really needed to leave now before my balls exploded from the pressure building up inside them thank God for decent denim to hide the bulge in my pants. One cold shower and wank coming up. We said our goodbyes as I practically dragged her out of the pub to head home.

CHAPTER 13

TIFF

Today was just full of raw emotions and encounters. Admittedly setting Claire straight after the emotional turmoil I was going through after hearing that song was just what I needed. Travis explained why he didn't interfere with the whole Claire situation, and I admit I understand now why he didn't step in. He was right Claire needed to know that I could stand up for myself and that she wasn't his girlfriend. Her face when Big Ben dragged her out the pub was priceless. Amber and the guys all standing up for me when she said I hit her first, which was technically true, showed me that I had friends now. For the first time ever, I actually feel like I belong and have friends. Travis dragged me out of the pub and started heading towards the car when Cole stepped out from the shadows and headed towards us. I was hoping he would just walk past us but how wrong could I be?

"T.J can we talk please?" Cole asked me and Travis wrapped an arm around my waist pulling me closer to him in a protective way.

"What's there to say? Are you sorry? That you didn't mean to scare me. That you would never hurt me. Save your breath I've heard it all before one too many times in my life for it to mean a damn thing to me" Truth is so many people have said sorry only to hurt me or let me down again that I have major trust issues with the meaning of that word now.

"It's true, I'm sorry, and yeah, I would never hurt you".

"Really? You want to tell your face that as it looks like it doesn't agree with that statement" Coles eyes showed no sign of regret or remorse, just pure hatred and anger directed at me.

"Look I'm not sorry that I like you ok, I can't apologise for that, but I get it you're not interested in me but that won't stop me from trying" Cole looked at me again his hands in his pockets and eyes boring into mine.

"I suggest you back off and leave my girl well alone Cole" Travis growled at Cole as his fists clenched and his arm pulled me even closer to his side.

"Your girl? Really Trav? How long will this one last? An hour, maybe a week if you're lucky before she runs away screaming. Oh, how's Claire taken the news given how she seems to be telling everyone she is yours?"

"Actually, Claire knows who Travis belongs to, I made sure of that just before she got kicked out the pub" I informed Cole who looked shocked at the information.

"Really? That explains her mood then, you need to be careful of Claire, she is a vindictive person and holds on to a grudge as much as a dog holds onto a big juicy bone".

"Noted, now if you don't mind, we were just heading home".

"You're going home with him?" Cole asked with anger lacing his voice.

"Yeah, problem with that?" Travis asked him.

"Really T.J? I never pegged you as a cheap easy slut, especially after the run around you gave me this morning, hell maybe I should have pushed harder, maybe being forced and given it rough is your thing after all you are sleeping with Travis" Cole sneered at me. His words cut deep and took me back to days long gone when I was bullied and pushed around at school and the care home. That one word setting my mind in a downward spiral 'slut'.

"Cole, I suggest you watch your mouth; Tiff is renting my spare room not sleeping with me, yeah sure we are dating if you want to label it, but we certainly aren't fucking or sleeping together not that it is any of your business anyway" I needed to do something and fast before these two ended up fighting, I'm certain that Amber wouldn't approve of a bloodbath in her pub car park.

"Cole you dipshit, you say you're sorry and then you insult me. Are you really sorry or just saying it to try and impress me?"

"Look, I'm sorry, I stepped out of line and for that I apologise, I'll back off, but I really need the job at the garage. Trav you've met my dad you know what he's like" Cole pleaded, and I did feel sort of sorry for him, but his actions and words hurt me more than he knows.

"Wait, so you're apologising just so you can keep your job?" I couldn't believe my own ears at Cole's words.

"No not at all, I'm saying sorry because I am sorry" Cole looked at me and this time I did see regret in his eyes.

"Look I'll talk to Frank in the morning".

"Tiff what are you doing?" Travis spun me around to face him and stared at me with worry in his eyes.

"Everyone deserves a second chance; we all mess up sometimes".

"You're too soft hearted" Travis kissed my forehead before turning to look at Cole.

"Be at the garage 8;30 sharp and don't screw this second chance up".

"Thanks, Trav, I won't let you down, I promise".

"Don't let Tiff down either, stay away if you can't be civil and just a work colleague" Travis warned Cole.

"I won't"

"Good, now get out of here" I snapped, wanting to get away from the situation as my mind was still whizzing with past memories and mixed emotions that had built up throughout the day. Cole walked off towards the pub and Travis led me back to the car with his arm still wrapped around my waist.

"Come on let's get you home and I'll run you a nice bath" Travis told me as I got into the car.

True to his word when we got back to the apartment Travis ran me a bath while I sat quietly trying to collect my thoughts and emotions together before they spilled out, although holding them back was getting harder and harder by the second as my mind was racing over the words from that song, the words Cole said about me, the encounters I had today, shit I had been attacked three times in less than 24 hours.

"Hey, baths ready. You, ok?" Travis was standing in front of me, I'd been so caught up in my own mind I didn't hear him come over to me.

"Yeah, I'm fine. I'll just go have my bath then, thanks for running it for me".

"Anything for you firefly. I'm just going to grab a shower, so I'll see you in a bit" He kissed me gently before leaving me so that we could both go clean up.

I climbed into the bath and immersed myself in the water before emerging again and resting my head on the back of the bath.

"Ok google play my soundtrack" I shouted at my phone that was sitting on the side of the sink. Monsters in my head by Welshly arms started to play. The song resonated with me on a deep level given that the words were like they were written for me and my mind. I drew my legs up and hugged my knees as I sat forward in the bath, my long wet black hair clinging to my back as the tears started to fall. The song changed to Down in a hole by Alice in chains and the crying turned into uncontrollable sobs that wracked my body. Every word echoing in my head from the song and from words spoken to me today and in the past. I looked at my thighs and the urge to repeat my secret was so strong that it was probably a good job that my wash bag was still in my room. I put my head onto my knees that I was still hugging and sobbed for ages as one song blurred into another.

"Tiff, are you ok in there?" Travis gently knocked on the door. I stood up and stepped out of the bath grabbing a towel and turning the music on my phone off.

"Tiff?" Travis's worried voice sounded through the door. I wrapped the towel around me and checked that it was big enough to cover my thighs before opening the door to a worried looking Travis.

"I'm fine"

"Really?"

"I said I'm fine" I snapped at him.

"You want to tell your face that as it looks like it doesn't agree with that statement" damn he used my words to Cole earlier against me.

"I'm fine, it's been a long day and I'm tired" A half lie, I was tired but far from fine at this present moment. I pushed past him and walked into my room locking the door behind me. I changed into some pyjamas and sat on the bed staring at the wall opposite, my mind still working overtime. Would everyone see me as a cheap easy slut? Was I a slut living with someone I'd only just met? Maybe I should look for a place to live tomorrow. Yeah, that's what I'll do. I'll look for a place to stay tomorrow.

"Tiff, I got you a hot chocolate" Travis knocked on my door. I walked over and opened the door stepping aside for him so that he could walk in. He set the two mugs down on top of the drawer's and turned around to look at me. Without saying a word, he pulled me into his arms and against his chest as he held me. After a few minutes he gently and slowly walked me back to the bed and pulled me down to lie next to him with his arms still wrapped around me.

"You know you can talk to me about anything, anytime you want" He whispered to me.

"I know, maybe one day".

"Whenever you're ready" He kissed my head and then tugged at me to sit up before passing me my drink.

"I'll look for somewhere to stay in the morning".

"What? No way. Is this because of what Cole said earlier?"

"Partly"

"Ignore him, what does it matter what people think? People will always have an opinion on others. It's life, and life is too short to worry about what others think or say about you".

"Life is too short" I sigh remembering my parents and how short their lives were.

"It is, now stop worrying and say you'll stay here".

"For now,"

"Good, it would be a waste of time moving out to only move back in again when our relationship gets more serious" Travis grinned at me, and my heart fluttered.

Travis took my empty mug from me and then settled us down on the bed again with my head on his chest, my fingers stroking against his smooth skin as we lay there in silence Travis arms wrapped around me and twirling my hair in his fingers. Being in his arms gave me a feeling of safety and love I'd not felt in years, and I drifted off to sleep cuddling up against him.

CHAPTER 14

TRAVIS

I had planned on taking a shower and jerking off to get rid of the massive hard on I had after watching Tiff tear strips of Claire, but then Cole happened. Fucking Cole ruined both our moods tonight. I knew Tiff had already had an emotional and testing day today, but Cole just had to tip that iceberg and sink the titanic that was Tiff and her chirpy mood. I could've killed him for calling her a slut, and it didn't go unnoticed how she flinched and suddenly became tense in my arms at his words. Obviously, there was stuff in her past that caused her issues, the more time I spent with her the more I realised that her smiles and sass were a front, like a defence mechanism, I wanted to know what had happened to her besides her parents and being in a care home, but I wasn't going to pressure her into talking, I'd wait until she came to me and talked. Earlier after I'd had my shower, I happened to walk past the bathroom door and heard Tiff's music playing, the song was full of emotions in the words, despair and longing along with feeling lost and depressed I listened to the words and felt the raw emotions that Tiff must be feeling after the horrendous day she had had today, and then I swear I heard a sob, I stopped and listened carefully and sure enough I heard her sobbing her heart out, my chest felt restricted and it became hard to breath knowing my girl was suffering in there on her own. Knocking on the door I asked if she was ok, it felt like ages before she eventually opened the door wrapped in only a towel, her ocean blue eyes dull and no longer sparkling, they now just looked red and swollen from crying.

"I'm fine" was all she said as she looked at me standing in the doorway.

"You want to tell your face that as it looks like it doesn't agree with that statement" yeah, I know a cheap shot using her own words from earlier. But I thought it might get a smile.

"I'm fine, it's been a long day and I'm tired" Was all she said as she pushed past me and walked into her room locking the door behind her. I could've gotten the spare key and let myself in but that would be invading her personal space and I got the feeling she needed a few minutes to change. Walking into the kitchen I spotted the hot chocolate that Amber left her for when she and Clint come over, she loves the stuff. Maybe Tiff would like some, all girls like chocolate, right? I made us both a mug each and knocked on her door. I was surprised and relieved when she opened the door and stepped aside to let me in. I placed both mugs on top of the drawers and turned to face her, on instinct I reached out and pulled into my chest and held her tight my arms wrapped around her. We stayed like that for a bit before I slowly backed us up to the bed and pulled her down with me so that she was lying next to me, my arms still wrapped around her.

"You know you can talk to me about anything, anytime you want" I whispered in her ear. I wanted her to know I was there for her no matter what. I'd dated and fucked countless women, but Tiff made me want to stop fucking around and just settle down, with her. She was mine and I'd be damn sure to make sure that every other fucker out there knew it.

"I know, maybe one day" She quietly answered me.

"Whenever you're ready" I kissed the top of her head and pulled us both up to sit and handed her the mug of chocolate I'd made for her.

"I'll look somewhere to stay in the morning" she told me with no emotions to her face or voice, it was like someone had sucked the life out of her.

"What? No way. Is this because of what Cole said earlier? I knew that the bastard had gotten into her head.

"Partly"

"Ignore him, what does it matter what people think? People will always have an opinion on others. It's life, and life is too short to worry about what others think or say about you" I spoke softly but inside I was raging with anger so deep it burnt into my heart. How dare Cole cause Tiff to feel like this.

"Life is too short" She sighed, and I knew she was thinking about her parents.

"It is, now stop worrying and say you'll stay here".

"For now," Those two words had my heart suddenly feel so much lighter and free.

"Good, it would be a waste of time moving out to only move back in again when our relationship gets more serious" I gave her a grin and watched as her lips twitched with a smile. I took her empty mug from her and placed both mugs back on top of the drawers before tugging her against me as we both lay down on her bed. Her head resting on my chest and one hand gently stroking across my chest next to her face. My arms wrapped around her, my fingers twirling her long black hair around them. We lay in silence and eventually Tiffs breathing even out. I knew she had fallen asleep as her hand also stopped its soft stroking. I gently manoeuvred myself out from under her and pulled the blanket over her before heading into the living room to grab my phone. I needed to talk to Mac, the guy I hired a year ago to find Joyce's killer. Tiff needed answers to her mum's death just as much as I did, and we both also needed closure on the matter to help us rebuild and become stronger together. Mac had gotten several leads, but they had all fallen through whenever we got close. Grabbing my phone, I called Mac.

"Trav, what's happening?" His gravelly voice sounded through the speaker pressed against my ear.

"Mac, have you got any new leads?"

"Actually kid, I was going to ring you tomorrow and arrange a meet up. I've found some more information on Joyce and her husband".

"On the Governs? What info?"

"I'll tell you when we meet up. How's things going for you anyway?"

"I got a girlfriend" I scratched the back of my head as I stood awkwardly by the couch. Did I really just say I had a girlfriend?

"Whoa, there kid, a girlfriend? As in your going on dates and doing normal shit?" Trust Mac to come right out with it.

"Yeah, but Mac she's Joyce's daughter. I didn't know they had a kid, and it wasn't planned. She kind of just stormed into my life at the garage and I knew then that she was mine, even before I knew who she was".

"Shit, when are you going to tell her?"

"When the time is right, she doesn't know about me being there yet".

"Time is never right for this kind of stuff Trav, don't leave it too late to tell her".

"I won't Mac, so we're meeting up. Tomorrow lunchtime?"

"Yeah, same café as before?"

"Same place same time" I answered.

"See you tomorrow kid, and look after that girl, her life could depend on it" Mac hung up. Strange way to end a call. Why would Tiff's life depend on me looking after her? Not that I wouldn't look after her after all she is my girl now. More interesting though is the fact that Mac said he had information on Tiff's parents, what information could he have on them? Feeling alert and not sleepy I switched on the T.V and sat down to watch some shitty late-night show. I wasn't really watching though if I'm honest as my mind was taken over with thought about Tiff and what Mac might have learnt about her parents. A couple of hours later I heard whimpering coming from Tiff's room and so I walked quietly over and pushed the door open. She was thrashing her head from side to side and whimpering. As I got closer, I could see the sweat on her face and the pain in her scrunched-up face. She was having a nightmare. I sat down on the bed and stroked her arm soothingly.

"Tiff, wake up you're having a bad dream".

"Stop, no stop .... I said no ...stop please" She mumbled.

"Tiff, wake up baby" Baby? I'd never said that before. Tiff's words scared me though. What was she dreaming about? Her past? What happened to her? I gently shook her again and as I did so she screamed and her eyes flew open, her breath coming out in short pants as her eyes landed on my face. I scooped her up and pulled her onto my lap stroking her head as I cradled her against me.

"Ssshhhh it's just a dream, I'm here now so you're safe and sound" I whispered as her body shook with fear and sobs. I sat with her on my lap until she stopped crying before we both lay down on her bed facing each other.

"You want to talk about it?" I asked her.

"Not really"

"You get some sleep; I'll be in my room if you need me".

"Trav, can you stay here with me tonight? Please" Well hell, how was I supposed to refuse her?

"If you want me to".

"Please Trav"

I pulled the blanket back over us both in answer to her question and pulled her against me. This would be a first for me sleeping with a girl as in actually sleeping.

We both fell asleep, Tiff in my arms and me holding her close chasing away those monsters tormenting her mind as she slept.

CHAPTER 15

TIFF

Waking up I found myself still wrapped in Travis' arms, my back against his bare sculpted chest. Memories from yesterday and my nightmare last night started filtering into my mind, making my heart race and fear grip me tight. Memories of the kids bullying me in the care home and the fights I got into circling my mind like a swarm of angry bees. Travis' grip tightened around me as he pulled me against his chest.

"Morning firefly" Travis kissed the nape of my neck sending shivers down my spine. "Did you sleep ok?" he asked me.

"Better with you next to me. I'm sorry if I woke you up last night, I've not had nightmares in a while, in fact I haven't slept that good in just as long".

Travis pulled me around, so I was lying on my back as he leaned over me staring into my eyes like he was trying to find my soul.

"Why haven't you slept properly for so long?" his concern tugged at my heart as I answered him, eyes looking around the room, looking anywhere but at him.

"Fear, living in a care home it's kind of hard to sleep knowing someone might come into your room at night, then the hotel was also because of fear and wanting to know that no one could get to me while I slept".

"Well, I'm the only one here and I'll only come into your room if you ask me. You're safe here and safe with me" He climbed over me hovering just above me resting on his elbows which were placed either side of my head, his fingers toying with my hair. He leaned his head down and his lips pressed against mine coaxing me to part mine in a passionate yet soft kiss. My hands came up and gripped his neck, my fingers twisting themselves in his hair as I lost myself to his kiss as his tongue slipped inside my mouth capturing mine. The kiss was so sexy and passionate it sent heat down my spine and straight to my most intimate area making me moan against his lips. Travis lowered himself so that his bare chest was pressed against me, my nipples aching and poking into his bare muscled chest, the sensations I was feeling were more than I'd ever felt even when I touched myself. His hips pressed against my stomach and the obvious sign of his desire was digging into my stomach and turning me on so much. Yeah, these feelings were new to me, but I wasn't a prude. I'd touched and fingered myself on occasion, but full sex and stuff was something I had never experienced so knew little about. Shit I'd never even watched TV for so long I had no idea really how things really worked. I needed a girlfriend to talk to about this stuff, then it hit me I have got a girlfriend, Amber. I could get Travis to ring her later and arrange some girly time maybe.

Travis moved so that his solid cock was pressed against my pussy through our pyjamas, I gasped at the incredible feeling as he rubbed it against me, he kept moving and rubbing against me, his lips fighting with mine and our tongues intertwined. I felt the oncoming of an orgasm as my back arched, my fingers pulling at his hair as he trailed kisses over my neck and then I was undone as I let go and came with his pyjama clad cock pressed against me. Travis gave a long moan and grunt as he stilled and looked into my eyes with a smile on his face. The dampness I felt between my thighs now evidence that I wasn't the only one to let go and come.

"Fuck, Tiff that was awesome" Travis gave me a quick kiss as he moved to lie beside me on the bed and pulled me against him so that my head was resting on his chest.

"The best orgasm I've ever had" I admitted as I blushed.

"Really? So, you had boyfriends before then?" Travis rolled onto his side and propped himself up on his elbow as he looked at me.

"No, but you don't need a boyfriend to experience orgasms Trav, pretty sure you have used your own hand before" I laughed as him.

"So, you're not one of those prudish girls then? Wonder what else you get up to or wouldn't mind doing in the bedroom. Wait, are you a virgin?"

"Does it matter?" I wanted to know if it made a difference to him whether I was or wasn't a virgin. I know some men like Travis would run a mile thinking that the girl would get all clingy and shit if they took her virginity. But me, I didn't really care about all the forever lovey dovey shit. Being in care I'd seen too many kids come from broken homes and families in which the parents had either cheated on each other or just fallen out of love so yeah, that shit didn't bother me. But that said it didn't mean I would be a slut and sleep around contrary to what the kids at school and the boys in the care home thought about care home girls.

"Nope, I'm just curious. If you are I want to make sure that if your first time is with me then its special"

"I don't need special Trav, if I give you my virginity then it will be heat of the moment and no planning involved, I don't want that anticipation shit I just want things to happen naturally".

"You sure? Most girls want romance and shit their first time".

"In case you hadn't noticed I'm not like most girls" I grinned at him then slapped his chest as I sat up.

"Yeah, your one of a kind and fucking gorgeous with it" Travis sat up and swung his legs over the side of the bed.

" I'm going to make breakfast and some tea; do you want anything?"

"Toast and tea please"

"Sure thing" Travis kissed me on the head before heading out the room to go make breakfast. He stopped at the door and looked me up and down before smiling at me.

"I'll just clean up and then make breakfast, it will be ready in a few minutes".

"I'll get cleaned up as well before I get dressed and then I'll be right out" I answered him. He closed the door behind him leaving me on my own to get dressed. I quickly cleaned up and pulled on my work trousers and a black t-shirt over the top of my plain black bra. The girls needed support given that I'm big busted for my slim frame. I hated wearing them but us women have to suffer through this and periods because we are the stronger sex despite what men say.

I sat with Travis at the breakfast bar eating my toast.

"Are you ok with seeing Cole at work today?" Travis asked me.

"Yeah, you will be there to keep an eye on him, so I feel ok about it".

"Good, I got a track day on Saturday if you want to come and be my lucky mascot" Travis winked at me.

"Track day, hell yeah. Can I drive?"

"You got a licence?"

"Do I look like I have a licence?"

"Then no, sorry but no licence no track unless you are the passenger".

"Boo, spoil sport" I crossed my arms and gave a fake pout making Travis smirk.

"Clint and the guys will be there as well".

"Will Amber be there?" I asked secretly hoping he would say yes.

"Yeah, she never misses track day".

"Good, I was going to ask you to ring her to arrange some girly time".

"Why are you blushing?" Shit, he saw me getting embarrassed about why I wanted to talk to Amber.

"I'm not blushing, I just never had a friend before that I felt like spending time with and chatting to"

"Ohh, that kind of girly time, I'm sure I can make us guys disappear for a bit to give you girls some space. Actually, why don't

I ring her and see if she is free to go to town with you after lunch today?"

"I don't have the money to go to town just yet, not until I get my apprenticeship wage that is".

"You need to get yourself a phone so take my card and get one, plus some new jeans and tops maybe, before you argue you can pay it back by doing the cooking tonight and baking cakes and shit for a picnic lunch on Saturday. Deal?"

"Deal, even though I still feel bad, but I know that if I argue you will just get Amber to buy it anyway" I didn't know that for sure, but I had a gut feeling I was right.

"You know me so well" Travis pulled out his wallet and handed me his credit card. "Don't buy the cheap shit either, buy quality that will last" He smiled at me as I took the card and popped it into my back pocket.

"Will do Sir" I teased but his eyes darkened with a heat and lustful look that had me gasp and clench my thighs together as heat pooled in my lower stomach. So he likes being called Sir, something to note for another day maybe.

"Come on, we best get to work before Cole turns up, won't do to tell him not to be late and then we arrive late".

"Good point" I hopped down from the bar stool and followed Travis out to his car.

Cole was sitting in the staff room waiting for us when we arrived at the garage.

"Cole" Travis looked at him.

"Trav, T.J" Cole nodded at us.

"T, my girl there you are, can you give me a hand with this brake bleed please" Mitch strolled in and called out to me.

"Mitch, fuck off" Travis glared at him.

"I'll be out in five Mitch" I shouted over my shoulder. Frank walked past Mitch and sat down opposite Cole at the table.

"Right then boys, T.J we need to sort this shit out and see if it will work with you all working together. Trav, I know that T.J is your girl now but don't be a possessive dick about it, especially in my garage"

"Not a problem uncle" That was the first time I had heard Travis call Frank that.

"Good. Right now about yesterday morning, Cole you were bang out of order and I won't tolerate that kind of behaviour from one of my employees, T.J has been kind enough to offer you a second chance and despite both mine and Travis better judgement we are willing to agree, but if you screw up like that again then not only will you be thrown out of here but I will ensure you get reported to the police as a sexual predator. Understood?" Damn Frank was a scary arse dude when he wanted to be.

"Understood" Cole replied and nodded at both me and Travis.

"Good, now all of you get to work and pretend yesterday never happened, I don't want any awkwardness here, Understood?"

"Understood" We all replied in unison.

"T.J bleed those brakes with Mitch and you two get on with sorting out those other cars parked in your bays. Frank stood up and went back to his office.

The morning flew by and before I knew it Travis was calling out to me and Mitch.

"You two finished with that Golf yet? Travis asked as he stood behind me wrapping an arm over my shoulders.

"Yeah, just wrapping it up now," Mitch answered him.

"Ok if I steal Tiff away?" Travis asked him.

"Yeah, sure thing dude"

"Thanks" Travis took my hand and led me to his car.

"I'll drop you off at home to get cleaned up and changed, Amber will be picking you up at 2 to go to town, she's really excited" I hadn't realised he had already rung Amber.

"Why is she excited?"

"She normally only hangs with us guys, being a busy pub owner takes up a lot of her time, luckily for you she had some time off today".

"Ohh, I'll make sure to make the most of it then".

"You do that" Travis smiled his panty dropping smile at me. Travis dropped me off at the apartment and drove off saying he had some business to attend to. I hopped in the shower to wash off the dirt and grime from working on that old Golf earlier. That car had turned out to be a right bitch to bleed the brakes on, but we got it sorted in the end between Mitch and myself.

Before I knew it Amber was knocking on the front door to pick me up. We drove to town in her purple Suzuki Jeep singing along to the radio as Goddess by Jaira Burns played. We parked up in the multi storey and Amber turned in her seat to look at me.

"So, what did you want to talk about?"

"Wow you psychic or something?" I laughed.

"Most girls have time like this because they want to talk about something that's bothering them, so spill. What did Travis do?"

"Travis didn't do anything, it's me. God this is embarrassing. I'm a virgin"

"Whoa, wasn't' expecting that".

"Meaning? Look just cos I was in care doesn't make me some bed hopping slut you know" I snapped back at Amber defending myself against her opinion of me being a care brat.

"Whoa that's not what I meant; shit girl I was a care kid too you know" Amber held her hands up in surrender to my outburst.

"Sorry, guess years of being labelled a slut just because I was in care make me get angry quickly".

"I get you; I really do. Why do people judge us care kids so badly? You know I was a virgin until I turned 19 and slept with Clint one drunken night, God was that a night to remember".

"So, you got stuck in care as well?"

"Yeah, and not just from the boys but from kids at school as well, I got a scar on my back from a boy who stuck a knife in me when I turned him down in front of a room full of other care kids."

"I just got bullied and beaten up a lot, but it sticks with you, the torment and stuff. How do you deal with it?"

"Tiff, you gotta let go of that stuff and look towards the future, you can't let that time and those kids rule your life and define your future. But if you ever need to talk about it then I'm always here for you. So, I'm gathering you didn't want to talk about that seeing as you asked for girly time".

"So basically, I know about orgasms and shit, I'm not a prude and have you know ....." I blushed as opening up to someone about masturbation was slightly embarrassing even if it didn't feel like it earlier with Travis.

"Ohh, right yeah, that's a good thing most girls like us don't even touch themselves, you know being in care it's a bit risky, I mean what if someone burst into your room and caught you".

"Exactly, but I left care and started living in a hotel, I locked my door and did most of that stuff in the bathroom with the door locked as well."

"Do you own a vibrator?"

"No, no way that's going a little too far, isn't it?" I blushed at the thought.

"Nope, girl we need to get you one asap, come on let's go shop" Amber dragged me out the car and towards the shops, guess we are buying my first vibrator then.

We shopped for hours and when we finished, I had a full rundown on what to expect from sexual intercourse, my first vibrator, sexy underwear and new clothes as well as a mobile phone which Amber helped me set up and I sent my first text to Travis.

Tiff: - *Hey hotshot I'm heading home now x*

Travis: - Hey firefly, I've just got in now, missed you today. X

Amber dropped me off and went back to work, I carried my shopping bags up the stairs and Travis opened the front door to greet me.

"Looks like you had a good time shopping" He grinned at me and tried to take the bags from me.

"Sure did, and Amber was amazing with helping me out" I quickly pulled the bags behind me out of his reach, the embarrassment if he saw the bag containing all my sexy stuff and the vibrator, the label on the bag would be sure to give away what I brought.

"Good, go put those bags away and we'll head out to get some food shopping as I believe you're cooking tonight" Travis eyed the bags and smirked before winking at me as I all but ran towards my room.

"Give me a few minutes and I'll be right with you."

I dropped the bags in my room and headed back to Travis to head out for more shopping.

CHAPTER 16

TRAVIS

After dropping Tiff off back at the apartment I drove back towards the garage and the café to meet Mac. I was intrigued and anxious to find out what information he had for me today. I walked into the small cafe and spotted Mac sitting in the far corner away from prying eyes and ears.

"Mac, you ordered?"

"Not yet I was waiting for you".

The waitress strolled over with her notepad and pen giving me a wink as she popped her gum in her mouth, something I detest.

"What can I get you two fine gentlemen today?" She asked the phrase she probably got told repeatedly to say to all male customers just to be polite.

"Coffee and a club sandwich please love" Mac ordered.

"Bacon cheeseburger and salad with a glass of ice water please" I told her as I focused on the folder Mac was holding under his arm on the table.

"I'll get that for you both right away" There waitress strolled away, and Mac shoved the folder at me.

"Mr Govern was not as clean as we first thought, he was having an affair with a woman called Marie Simpson".

I opened the folder and stared at the pictures in front of me. The woman in the pictures looked young but her eyes were hollow and empty lacking any emotion, almost like she was on drugs. I looked back up at Mac and raised an eyebrow at him.

"Yeah, she is in rehab right now, seems that after he killed himself, she lost her way a bit and started on drugs and drink, she also had a miscarriage from the stress of his death, the child was his".

"Why do you have pictures of my sister?" The waitress screamed at us.

"Your sister?" I asked as Mac stood up and went to stand behind her. This girl could be the lead we need into finding out who killed Tiff's mum.

"Yeah, that's my sister, but why do you have pictures of her? What are you some sort of pervert or stalker?"

"No nothing like that, but you better sit down if you want to know why?"

"I'll just tell Betty I'm taking a break" she walked off and spoke to the elderly lady who owned the small café, before walking back over and sitting down opposite me and Mac who now sat next to me.

"Your sister was seeing this man" Mac slid a photo of Tiff's dad in front of her.

"Yeah, that's Daniel. He died four, maybe five years ago, killed himself and made my sister lose her baby. That's what set her on a downward spiral, losing him then their baby like she did, still doesn't answer why you have her photo".

"Did she know he was married?"

"Yeah, she knew but his wife was murdered in a mugging gone wrong or something, but he loved his daughter and kept saying he needed to protect her, so he never made their relationship official, she was always his dirty little secret. The day he died she had told him about the baby, and he wanted her to get rid of it, she refused and told him to take responsibility or end the relationship and she would bring the baby up on her own, she lost the baby and any chance of being a mother ever again a few days later".

"Did either of you meet his daughter? And what was he protecting her against?" my mind was spinning and all sorts of bad things happening to her were running across my mind. I swore to myself that no matter what I would protect her at any cost.

"Look, you still haven't answered me as to why you have her photo".

"I am looking into the mugging and who killed his wife, if there was maybe a motive as a witness said some interesting things that suggest it was more of a warning than a murder, but things got out of hand" Mac explained as I watched this girl's face for any sign, she may know more than she is letting on.

"You think something dodgy was going on with Daniel? I never liked the bloke to be honest, I mean he was hiding an affair from his wife and kid so yeah, I never trusted him and tried so many times to talk my sister into walking away, but you know what they say, love is blind and all that crap" She popped her gum again making me clench my teeth in annoyance.

"Do you know any friends or acquaintances he may have had? Places he used to go to?" Mac asked.

"He used to go to this little back street bar, here I'll give you the address, but don't tell anyone where you got it from, it's dangerous" she quickly scribbled down an address and handed it to me.

"Be warned this place is not for people like us, it's dangerous and probably illegal, I only know about it after following Daniel a few times and watching from a side" she stood up and left us as Betty brought our food over. On the tray under our plates was a note with the waitress's name and number on it.

"I'll case this place out and get info on it before we make our next move. Travis, stay away from it and don't do anything daft" Mac warned me as he bit into his sandwich. This guy knows me too well, and if he thinks a warning will stop me, he is deluded. I know this place and the area it's in, it's bad, like really bad. so bad even the police try to stay away from it.

"You can't do it alone Mac, this area hell this place is really bad, you need me to help you, or you will get killed".

"Travis my boy, I know you are wanting answers and you think I'm old and past my years but trust me this sort of place will swallow you up and spit you out, I've done this stuff for years and have a few guys I can get in to check this place over without giving away the fact someone is looking onto them".

"Fine, I'll stay away but use the back up and stay safe old man" I laughed trying to lighten the mood a bit.

"You have my word" Mac stood up and shook my hand "I'll call if I get any more information.

"See you soon Mac " I shook his hand and stood up to leave as well. I needed to let off some steam before getting home to my girl. The punch bags at the gym were calling me and I knew that would be the perfect way to release some of my pent-up anger and frustration. I spent a few hours at the gym getting all the frustration and anger out before I headed home again. Tiff had texted me a few times making me smile. I stood by the front door of my apartment waiting for Amber to drop Tiff off. I didn't have to wait long before I heard the girls giggling and Tiff told Amber she would see her later. I spotted the pink and black bags she was carrying and offered to take them to her room, but she quickly hid them and ran to her room effectively hiding them from me. I knew the shop that those bags came from and the thought of Tiff showing me what was inside those bags had my cock twitching. I even spotted the small plain black carrier bag she had and knew that it contained sex toys, how? Because only one shop in town does those small black bags and I'd know seeing as I shop there a lot. The thought of Tiff using a sex toy had my cock go from twitching to rock hard in a millisecond. Damn now is not the time to get a hard on. I willed my cock to go down by thinking of oil changes on French cars, thankfully it did the trick, and I was back to decent just as Tiff came back out of her room ready to go food shopping.

I knew I'd have to tell her that it was me who saved her dad during the mugging that killed her mum, but how? I didn't want to lose her. I also knew I'd have to tell her about Mac investigating it and the fact her dad was cheating on her mum and owed people money.

Shit how would she take that news? Maybe I should take her with me next time I meet up with Mac and explain it all then. That sounded a more logical idea to me, at least then she had someone else there to verify that it's all true and not some made up shit, plus it would also show that I'm not some sick stalker pervert type guy who deliberately went after her just to get my kicks. I wanted her as soon as I heard that voice on day one in the garage, and that was before I saw her or knew about her parents.

We got our shopping and Tiff made a delicious spaghetti carbonara with garlic bread, it was the best meal I had ever tasted.

"Fuck that meal was amazing, who taught you to cook?" I asked her.

"Books mostly but doing a baking course at college has helped a bit. Most of it is just common sense though. Talking of the baking course, I need to get going or I'll be late" Tiff placed the dirty dishes by the sink and wiped her hands.

"You got a lesson tonight?"

"Yeah, I need to go if the bus is running late, I will be late, so I get the earlier one to make sure I'm on time. It's not compulsory I go, it's more of a hobby really but I hate missing a single lesson".

"I'll drop you off and pick you up".

"It's ok really, the bus will be fine".

"Tiff, I said I'd drop you off and that's what I'm doing no argument. Besides I can call in on Frank for a drink while I wait for you"

"Only if you're sure".

"I'm certain"

"Fine" She relented and went to fetch her bag. I really need to get her a new one as that one she has now is old and tatty, an old canvas satchel type bag with leather straps and buckles. The straps looked like they might snap any second and the canvas had holes in it and old patches that had obviously been sewn on over holes in order to hold the bag together. I'll have to search the internet for a similar one as given the state of the one she is currently using I'd say it is sentimental to her in some way. Maybe it was once used by one of her parents.

"Ready?" I asked her as I grabbed my keys from the side.

"Yep"

"Let's go then, can't wait to see what you make tonight" I smiled at her.

"I get to bring it home, so you not only see it but get to taste it too".

"I'd love to taste it, and other things" I wink at her as she blushes and slaps my chest.

"Maybe" She smiles at me. Maybe? Jesus this girl is driving me and my cock insane tonight.

I dropped Tiff off at college and went over to Franks to fill him in on the information that Mac had gathered, and the waitress had provided us with.

"Shit Trav, that's a lot to take in. You think that her dad owed money?"

"Almost certain of it, given the type of bar he went to and the mugging. What's more is that I now don't think he killed himself".

"What are you saying? You think he was killed?"

"Yeah, I think he owed far too much and couldn't pay it, so they staged his death to look like a suicide".

"Careful Trav, you don't want to get yourself in too deep with this. What if these people don't like you snooping and come after you?"

"I need answers Frank, if it wasn't for Tiff, I might walk away but now, now I need to know for her sake".

"Just be careful Trav".

"Always old man" I laugh at Frank as we drink our coffees on his patio.

"So, you and Tiff huh" He winks at me.

"Yeah, she is a great girl and I actually think she may be the one, you know?"

"Never thought I'd see the day that my nephew settled down "

"Never thought I'd find a girl as perfect as Tiff is. Yeah, I mean she has a bad history, but she is perfect to me".

"Well, you best look after her then boy and not fuck it up" Frank gave me his 'I'm serious 'look and I smiled as I shook my head at him.

"I promise"

"Good. You decided what car you're taking to the tracks this weekend?"

"Yeah, I'm taking the Lexus this time, might chuck some spare wheels in the truck too in case we do burnouts and doughnuts".

"Good plan, Mitch going with you?"

"Think the twins are meeting us there. Amber and the guys are coming, and I asked Tiff as well".

"Sounds like a reunion" Frank chuckled.

"Nah. Just some friends meeting up and having a good time".

"Well, you best take the spare helmets as well then".

"Thanks Frank, I best get off and pick Tiff up".

"You do that boy. I'll see you in the morning, don't forget Tiff has college tomorrow".

"Noted".

I left Frank's and drove to the college with a smile on my face. Frank always had a way to make me feel better.

CHAPTER 17

TIFF AKA T.J

Baking class today went by quicker than I thought it would. Before I knew it, I was standing outside waiting for Travis to pick me up, while holding a fresh baked apple and cinnamon cake in my hands. I lost myself in my thoughts as the past few days whirled around in my head. First day at work then Cole and Claire, Travis wanting me as his girlfriend, Amber being a care brat like me, the band and finally having not just a home but actual friends. So much happening in such a short time. Maybe this was all just some warped dream and I'll wake up any second and still be stuck in that awful seedy hotel. Or maybe I'm actually living some form of fucked up Matrix style dream life and nothing is real. I'm so lost in my thoughts that I don't hear anyone walk up behind me.

"Hey, you, ok?" A tall thin man asks me as he taps my shoulder. His grey hair looked scruffy and unkempt along with his beard. He reminded me of a homeless person but something in his eyes and the way he looked at me set me on edge.

"Yeah, I'm fine, just waiting for my boyfriend to get the car" I lied, maybe if he thought that Travis was close, he would leave me alone.

"Pretty lass like you shouldn't be on her own out here at night. Lots of weird people out here" his eyes roaming my body as his tongue swept over his bottom lip.

"He won't be a second" I stepped back a bit away from the guy, my heart beating like crazy.

"Well, I'll just wait with you. Wouldn't want anything nasty to happen to you" He stepped in closer to me making my skin crawl and an unsettling feeling ran over me. I'd run into guys like this before and dealt with them swiftly so I knew if it came to it I could handle him. And as I was thinking that thought he made his move and grabbed my arm pulling me towards him, he spun me around so fast

I dropped the cake I was holding as my back collided with his chest and both arms wrapped around me holding me firm.

"He said you were pretty, but I thought he was joking, thinking I might have some fun before returning you to your rightful place" He sneered in my ear. What was that supposed to mean? My rightful place? Is this guy crazy? I threw my head back hitting him in his Adam's apple before using his sudden slight release of my arms to my advantage and thrust both elbows back into his ribs and raised a foot up behind me to connect with his crown jewels. Success, he released me as he doubled over in pain screaming at me. I didn't wait around as I ran straight towards the main road hoping that Travis would pull up any second. Seemed luck was on my side as I skidded to halt before toppling in front of Travis car as the brakes screeched to a halt the car only just missing me as my hands landed on the bonnet. My heart beating out of my chest as panic and relief set in simultaneously. Travis practically leapt from his car as he ran round to me grabbing me in his arms.

"Tiff? What're you doing out here? I thought I was picking you up from the front door." He stepped back with both hands on my arms as he looked me over before hugging me close. His voice laced with worry as he spoke "

Tiff? shit you're shaking. Did something happen?"

"Just take me home, please" I almost begged him but managed to keep my voice steady despite how much I was shaking.

"Yeah, sure. Come on let's get you home" His arms wrapped around me as he guided me to the passenger door and helped me get settled and buckled in safely before he got in the driver's side and drove back home. The drive home was silent, he didn't try to ask what had happened, but I could see him looking over at me with concern every now and then. My head was replaying the whole incident. Return me to my rightful place? And he was told I was pretty by someone? Was someone out to get me? Who? And more importantly why? I was so lost in my thoughts again trying to work out what was said and what it meant that I must have blindly walked up the stairs into our home as next thing I know Travis is handing me a cup of hot chocolate and pulling my trainers off my feet. I've also got a blanket draped over my shoulders as I'm sitting on the couch, my cheeks feel wet, a sure sign I had been silently crying without even realising it.

"Tiff? Can you tell me what happened?" Travis knelt on the floor in front of me, his hands on my knees as he looked up at me.

"I was waiting for you, He .... he... he started talking and then grabbed me, he said he was returning me to my rightful place but not before having some fun...... Trav said he was told I was pretty.... I'm scared" I finally broke down and sobbed big heavy ugly body wracking sobs as Travis took my mug, placed it on the table and pulled me onto his lap as he sat next to me, he pulled me in against his chest and kissed my head.

"Tiff, I think we need to talk but I need to make a few phone calls first and you need to meet someone, is that ok?" He told me, I just nodded my head. When I finished my ugly crying Travis set me down on the couch and went to make his phone calls, I must have dozed off as the next thing I heard was Travis talking to two other people in hushed voices, keeping my eyes closed I tried to listen in. One voice was Frank the other I didn't recognise but it was another male.

"You sure now is the time to tell her?" The male voice said.

"I think Travis is right, this incident tonight maybe connected somehow" Frank spoke.

"Am I sure? Fuck no, I'm scared she will leave and want nothing to do with me when she hears the truth, or worse blame me for her mum's death" Now that got my attention.

"Why would you be blamed for my mum's death?" I jumped up and stared at the three men in front of me. Travis started to walk towards me as I stepped away, fear gripping me and making my chest feel tight.

"Was it you? Did you kill her?" Travis wouldn't, right? It couldn't be him? Could it?

"No, it wasn't me, but I saw it" He sighed as he looked at me with sorrow in his eyes.

"What?" It took me a few seconds to figure it out "You... you were the one that saved my dad?"

"Yeah, but I didn't know it was your dad until after I met you, I had no idea you had to believe me" Travis stepped closer, but I held my hand up for him to stop as I backed up a bit more.

"Hear the boy and us out" The other man spoke.

"T.J please hear us out on this, none of us knew until the following day when we pieced it altogether" Frank stepped forward.

"You all knew? Who else knows?"

"The band and Amber" Travis answered me as he looked at me, tears shimmering in his eyes. "I told them about your care home issue, as well. I only told them as I wanted to protect you".

"Protect me? Protect me from what? I don't need protecting I can handle things myself just like I've been doing for the past four fucking years".

"Tiff, please... things aren't safe right now, things are happening, and we think it's all connected. Mac, ring that waitress and get her to meet us at Ambers pub please, some things need to be heard from her" Travis looked between me and the other guy, well at least I had a name now for him. Mac walked off with his phone in his hand as both Frank and Travis stepped towards me almost like they were herding me in.

"T.J sweety, we only want to look after you and protect you, but you need to know the facts, all of them" Frank placed a hand on my shoulder that I instantly shrugged off as I scowled at him.

"Why should I listen to you? You all kept this from me "I glared at Travis "Is this why you want to be my boyfriend? Guilty conscience? Survivors' guilt or just wanting to be a hero for the poor broken girl" Travis stepped back a look of anger flashed in his eyes before the look of pain and hurt replaced it.

"Your past has nothing to do with my feelings for you Tiff, I want to be with you because you're amazing, sweet, kind, caring and yet strong and sassy with it. I love that about you, and you make me feel happier and more alive than I have felt in years. I wanted to be your boyfriend before I found out and still want to be yours now. Please tiff you have to believe me" His voice had a sound of desperation in it.

"She's meeting us there in fifteen minutes" Mac told us as he came back into the room.

"Tiff, come with me and meet someone who can help us explain what we know so far and why we think you need protecting. But that's not why I want to be with you, I swear" Travis held his hand out for me, but I brushed it away and walked towards the door slipping my feet into my shoes.

"Well, what are we waiting for? I want answers "I glared at all three of them. Travis grabbed his keys before Frank stopped him.

"I'll drive I think you and T.J will need a few stiff drinks for this conversation".

"Frank has a point kiddo" Mac added.

Travis sighed and put his keys in his pocket before looking at me.

"Come on then, guess we are going in Frank's truck. You're following us, Mac?"

"Yeah, I'll see you there kiddo".

I followed Travis and the others out to the cars and watched as Mac got into his beat-up Volvo. Who is he? And what has he got to do with what is happening? And who the hell are we meeting with? All this is starting to give me a headache.

We pulled up outside Nancy's bar and Travis tried to hold my hand again, I again pushed it away. I was too mad and confused to even entertain being anything with Travis. Although even the thought of him not being with me or in my life sent pangs of hurt and pain to my heart. Was it too early to love him? Because I'm sure this feeling I have for Travis is love.

"Flick" Mac greeted a woman with blue hair cut into a bob.

"Stalker" she replied as she looked over to Travis "Second stalker" She shot at him. I eyed Travis suspiciously.

"Tiff this is Flick she can answer some questions you may have when you hear everything".

"You Daniels kid, right? You have his eyes" She looked at me with pity in her eyes. How did she know my dad?

"Shall we" Frank opened the door and led us through the bar to the back room.

"This room is private so we can talk openly in here and Tiff can hear about everything we know" Travis told us all. Amber walked in and took drink orders before disappearing again.

"Spill" I snapped at them all.

"I saw the mugging, I tried to save your mum I really did but her wounds were just too severe for me to stop the bleeding. I'm sorry I couldn't save her. I never got a good look at the guy who did it, he was wearing a hoodie and a mask. Something he said though made me think it wasn't just a standard mugging. He said, 'Your debt is still outstanding, this changes nothing' The police didn't take any note of that though and just put it down to a mugging gone wrong and are still looking for the mugger but nothing so far. Clint is working on the files and cameras trying to help me as much as he can, yeah, he works for the police" Travis told me.

"Wait so, the mugger gave my dad a message about a debt? Why aren't the police investigating that? What debt? My dad never owed anyone except the bank for the mortgage".

"Guess daddy dearest wasn't honest with you or your mum" Flick said as she popped her gum and Travis clenched his teeth. Guess I found something that annoys him.

"What is that supposed to mean?" I glared at her "And how do you know my dad?"

"Have you ever seen this woman?" Mac shows me a picture of a young woman who looks similar to Flick except she looks broken and lost, no emotions on her face at all.

"No" I look at Mac and Flick, she has tears in her eyes as she looks at the photo.

"She was my sister Marie".

"Was? Where is she now?" I ask.

"In rehab, thanks to your waste of space dad" she snapped at me.

"My dad wasn't a waste of space".

"Really, he was having an affair with Marie and got her pregnant, he wouldn't leave your mum or you. Not even after your mum died, did he do the right thing".

"You're a liar" I stood up and clenched my fists, Travis grabbed my arm and tried to pull my back down I shook his hand away and glared at him.

"How could you? You set this up, didn't you? I thought you liked me, but you just want to hurt me" I shouted at him. Travis stood up and pulled me into him, wrapping his arms tightly around me.

"I'd never do anything to hurt you, I just want you to know all the facts".

"I've done my research Tiffany, I'm a private investigator and it's my job to get the facts and make sure they are the truth" Mac spoke up as Amber came in and placed drinks and a bottle of whisky on the table before leaving us again.

"I hired Mac, well we did, me and Frank. The mugging and what the guy said haunted me and were messing with my head so we hired Mac to try and solve what the police can't solve".

"So, Mac is doing what the police can't or won't do?" I asked as I pushed Travis away and sat back down.

"Yeah, you could say that" Mac chuckled. "Anyway, your dad was indeed having an affair with Marie, and she later took an overdose, she is now in rehab".

"What does her being in rehab have to do with my dad?"

"He got her pregnant and told her to get an abortion, she refused and then a few days later he killed himself, she lost the baby due to stress and later started taking drugs, she is now in rehab "Flick said with tears rolling down her cheeks.

"My dad did that?" I asked still not wanting to believe what I was hearing.

"That's only the beginning, we think he owes a debt to some big-time gangsters who run several backstreet gambling rooms, if he did then you may be in danger" Mac looked at me with a serious look on his face.

"The guy from tonight said I would be in my rightful place.... what does that have to do with all this?"

"What guy?" Both Mac and Frank said together, guess Trav hadn't told them yet then. I sat back and told them about the guy outside college earlier tonight and watched as Mac and Frank looked at each other.

"What did he look like?" Flick asked.

"Tall, skinny scruffy homeless looking with a beard and grey hair. Why?"

"We need to report this to the police" Frank spoke up while Travis pulled his phone out and text someone on it.

"I'll do that now" Mac said as he walked out the room.

"That sounds like Gus" Flick said.

"Gus?" Travis asked her.

"Yeah, he is always snooping and asking questions about my sister, even asking if I knew where Daniel's kid was, he's been bugging me for years now. Told him over and over again that I didn't know where the bastard's kid was, but he never believed me".

"My dad was not a bastard."

"Whatever helps you sleep at night, truth is my sister nearly died because of him" She snapped back at me.

"Ladies please. "Clint said as he walked into the room "Trav what you got for me?"

"Tiff was attacked outside the college tonight, any chance you can pull up the cameras?" Travis asked him.

"Already done, and the police are out searching for the guy already, but Trav, Tiff this guy is connected to some very nasty yet powerful people, you are swimming with sharks if you get in any deeper".

"Clint, they came after Tiff and from what Flick here says they have been after Tiff for years" Travis filled Clint in.

"Shit Tiff, what the fuck was your dad involved in?"

"Nothing that I know of but seems he kept me in the dark about a lot of stuff" I admitted looking at Flick.

"He probably only did that to protect you, I shouldn't be taking it out on you. What your dad did to my sister wasn't just on him, my sister took the drugs and still kept seeing him even knowing he was married, it's as much on her as it is him" Flick sort of apologised to me.

"Well, Mac and I will liaise with the police and hopefully get more answers soon. Trav take Tiff home and maybe stay there until we know more" Clint set his laptop down and opened it up.

"Come on Tiff, let's get you and Trav back home" Frank stood up and pulled his keys out his pocket. Travis looked at me as he stood up and held out his hand, this time I took it and watched as Travis visibly relaxed.

We followed Frank into the main bar and out to his truck, the ride home was silent but this time it was a comfortable silence as I forgave Travis with just a look.

CHAPTER 18

TRAVIS

Well, that was a shit storm of a meeting and Tiff finding out about her dad's affair. Flick was a total bitch to Tiff and it's not even Tiff's fault that her dad did wrong by Marie. Why do the children have to suffer the parent's misdoings? A question I have often asked myself. Tiff was tense the whole ride back home and didn't say a word to me, she did give me a look which I assume means I'm forgiven. I hope so at least because I really don't want to lose this girl, I think my heart would just shatter if I did. Tiff threw her shoes off and then threw her jacket onto the couch before heading to her room.

"Tiff, are we ok?" I asked her with my hand scratching the back of my neck. I'd never felt so out of depth than I did right now. Tiff stopped and turned to face me.

"Trav, you didn't tell me the truth even when you found out. Were you ever going to tell me? You deliberately kept me in the dark, were you hoping I'd never find out?"

"I was going to tell you honestly, I just wanted to have more to give you and maybe catch the bastard who killed your mum" I took a step towards her "Please Tiff, I can't lose you, I wanted to tell you I really did, I just didn't know how, and I wanted to give you what you needed to catch the killer" I watched as tears ran down her cheeks and her shoulders slumped. I stepped up to her, wrapping my arms around her and pulling her closer to me.

"You should have told me Trav".

"I know that now, and I am sorry."

"Stay with me tonight, please" She looked up at me with watery eyes and tear-stained cheeks, how could I possibly say no?

"Come on let's get you into bed".

Waking up in the morning with Tiff draped over me was the best feeling in the world. We spent some time last night lying in bed talking everything through and she understood why I didn't tell her, and all was forgiven. We even promised to tell each other everything from now on no matter how bad it was. She eventually drifted off to sleep wrapped up in my arms, her head on my chest and that is how she was still when I opened my eyes this morning. She looked adorable with her little lips slightly parted as she breathed softly. Her thick lashes resting against her pale freckled cheeks. This girl was just adorable, and she was mine. Frank sent a text earlier telling us to stay home and not come into work until we knew what the hell this Gus bloke wanted with Tiff. The police still haven't found him yet, but they have enough evidence on the CCTV cameras from his attempted assault on Tiff that they can charge him with assault and attempted kidnap when they find him. I however have little faith in the police force to actually do just that which is why Clint, and his cousin Chance are following up any leads. I'm so lost in my thoughts while stroking Tiff's arm that I don't realise she has shifted slightly, and my hand is now stroking over her breast until I feel a hard nipple suddenly under my finger and Tiff gasps as her eyes open. I stop what I'm doing and look down at her.

"Don't stop" She almost pleads with me, so I slowly bend down and capture her lips with mine as I continue with my slow strokes and gently twirling my finger over her hard nipple as it tries to poke out through her t-shirt. She moans into my mouth as she pulls herself closer to me, her pyjama clad pussy rubbing against my hip. She pulls back and lifts her t-shirt over her head throwing it onto the floor exposing her naked pert breasts to me with both nipples pink and hard poking out at me. She is fucking perfect. I lean over her after shedding my t-shirt and slowly push her back down onto the bed as I hover over her gently kissing and nibbling her lips. Somehow during the kissing and nibbling we both end up naked her body rubbing against mine, my cock hard as rock pressing against her stomach as she rubs herself against me trying to find some friction,

I reach my hand down and gently part her folds as I slip a finger over her clit and gently massage it making her buck and gasp with the pleasure I am eliciting from her body. I slip a finger inside her and circle her clit with my thumb as I kiss over her breasts and suck each nipple in turn. I kiss feather light kisses over her breasts and down over her stomach, by now she is a writhing moaning mess and I intend to make her moan a lot more. Slowly I tease my kisses further down as I spread her legs wider before blowing a soft breath over her clit and then swiping my tongue over it, she bucks and gasps at the feeling as I continue circling my tongue over her sensitive bud slipping it into her pussy every other swirl and as her body starts to tremble with the tell-tale signs of her impending orgasm I slip two fingers into her pulsating wet pussy and motion them into a curl with a come here signal as I hit her G-spot and another swipe of my tongue followed by a suck on her clit has her lift her hips from the bed as she screams out my name with the force of the orgasm ripping through her body. I keep moving my fingers inside her as I suck her juices up while she comes down from the orgasm. Her body sinks back into the mattress as I kiss back up over her stomach towards her breasts my cock now pressed against her pussy practically begging to be let in, but I won't until she gives me all clear. Shit I've got no condoms in here, guess it won't be today then. Just as that thought enters my head Tiff wraps her legs around my waist pulling me closer as she whispers.

"I want you".

"Tiff as much as I want to go further, I don't have a condom in here".

"I'm on the pill, so as long as your clean".

Shit that was all the permission I needed as my cock found her entrance and I slowly pushed inside her tight wet pussy. She tenses as I reach that barrier and with a soft kiss and thrust, I push my way in and relax against her kissing her lips softly. We made love soft and slow as I moved on top of her, letting her feel how much she meant to me, and she meant the world to me. Is it too early to say I loved her? fuck it if it is because I can't deny that I have feelings for Tiff that I have never felt for anyone else, so this must be love, right? I placed my hand against Tiff's pussy as I made love to her my fingers grazing her clit as my other hand teased her nipples, she came again her tight walls pulsating and squeezing my cock in a vice like grip as she milked my cock as I came hard pouring all my seed into her. Filling her to the brim. We both lay on the bed catching our breaths while cuddling into each other.

"You, ok?" I asked her after a few moments.

"I'm good. You?"

"Fucking fantastic" I grinned at her as she smiled back at me.

"I'll admit not how I wanted your first time to go, but you did say you wanted spontaneous spur of the moment and not pre planned".

"That was perfect Trav" She leaned up and kissed me before her stomach rumbled making us both chuckle.

"Best feed the beast" I laughed at her as I swung my legs over the side of the bed and stood up to retrieve my sweatpants.

"I'll just grab a quick shower and strip the bed" Tiff waved her hands at the blood-stained sheets with a look of embarrassment on her face.

"Hey, that's normal for the first time. How about you go get cleaned up and I'll sort the sheets out before making us some breakfast, or I could order take out. Breakfast muffins maybe?"

"Sounds perfect, can you order a caramel latte as well please".

"Anything you wish for Firefly" I kissed her again before she went into the bathroom, and I got to work stripping the sheets and ordering our breakfast. After putting the washing on and grabbing clean sheets I walked back from the linen cupboard by my room towards Tiff's room and heard her singing. It was a song I'd never heard before, but her voice and the lyrics were sad yet strong and full of raw emotion and feelings. I quickly whipped my phone from the table and pressed record as I listened to her soft voice.

You thought you broke me thought you shattered my last resolve took away a piece of my heart

fractured my soul but I'm not that girl anymore not broken or scared not used or abused I'm so much stronger than you I'm not broken I'm not shattered or lost I'm free from the chains of my past you can't take from me what's already taken can't break what was already broken you left me feeling alone

feeling abandoned unloved and lost but I'm not that girl anymore not broken or scared not used or abused I'm so much stronger than you my future is peaceful and new I'm not abandoned

not feeling alone I'm free from the chains of my past you stood by idly and watched me grow I grew to be stronger than you know those names that you called me those punches you threw the heartache you caused me the chains that clawed me to my sorrow well they are all gone for now because I'm not that girl anymore not broken or scared not used or abused I'm much stronger than you I've moved on with my life I'm living and breathing

not trembling and weeping not scared of my past

I'm not that girl anymore I'm stronger than ever before stronger than you will ever believe my future is brighter now that I'm stronger I'm not that girl from before not that girl anymore not broken or scared not used or abused I'm free from the chains of my past I'm not that girl anymore.

Shit my phone rings and Tiff looks straight at me standing in her doorway. I quickly answered it hoping she didn't see me recording her singing. I need to send that to Clint and ask if he has heard that song before because I sure as hell hadn't.

"Hey" I answered my phone while watching Tiff brush her hair.

"The police have Gus in custody" Clints voice came over the phone.

"Hang on I'll put you on speaker".

"Hey Clint" Tiff called over to the phone as I walked over to her side.

"Hey Tiff, right Gus is in police custody being questioned as we speak, I've got the detective to loop me in and give me any information he might gather but so far, he isn't talking, just giving the usual 'no comment' crap".

"Can we pressure him in any way?" I asked.

"Actually, he's requested to speak to Tiff before anyone else but that was before we showed him the video evidence from last night".

"Put the deal to him that if I talk to him, he tells us everything. I'm ready to listen" Tiff shot out before I had a chance to shoot the idea down.

"Tiff, you can't be serious. He tried to kidnap you and God knows what else he might have done" I said as I pulled her down onto my lap as I sat on the bed.

"I'm sure. He's in police custody he can't do anything to me and if this is what's needed to find out what the hell happened to my mum and why they want me then I'll do it" she said with so much conviction my chest swelled with pride.

"If you're sure Tiff, I'll put the offer to him via the detective and get back to you as soon as we have an answer. In the meantime, stay home and sit tight. We don't know what's going on just yet but from what we've heard you are wanted by some dangerous people Tiff" Clint almost sounded scared for Tiff as his voice was laced with worry.

"I'll be keeping her safe Clint don't worry".

"I know your idea of safe Trav" I could almost hear the smirk on his face.

"Too late man" I laughed knowing that Clint would get what I was saying.

"Too much" Clint shot back at me as he laughed with me "I'll get Amber to drop by later and we can do a song lyric run through at yours tonight".

"Cool, look forward to it" with that I hung up the phone and turned Tiff round on my lap, so she was straddling me.

"Was there some sort of inside joke going on with you and Clint?" Tiff asked me as she wrapped her arms around my neck.

"Maybe. What was that about though? You saying you'll talk to Gus? I'm not happy about that, he could be dangerous".

"Trav he's locked up in a police station and will probably have cuffs on when or if I talk to him, plus there will be officers in the room as well".

"I know that, but I still worry".

"You're so sweet, now when is breakfast getting here?" her stomach rumbled loudly again and as if on cue, the doorbell rang.

"Right about now" I laughed as I stood up placing Tiff on her feet as I went to answer the door. I sent Clint the recording of Tiff singing while I'm answering the door and taking our breakfast from the kid delivering it. I swear these delivery drivers are getting younger, what did he cycle here? An hour later Clint shoots me a text.

Hey, I have not heard that song before and can't find it online either. She has an incredible yet haunting voice, we need to use it in some of our stuff, it could be dynamite for us.

I chuckle and shoot him back a message.

Tell me about it, I couldn't stop watching her as she sang. She doesn't know I recorded her or that I sent it to you, be a nice surprise later when I play it to all the guys.

It had me wondering if it was an original song or an unreleased song that Tiff had stumbled across.

"Hey Tiff, that song you were singing earlier, where'd you hear it from?"

"You heard me?" She looks over from the kitchen area to the couch I'm sitting on, her cheeks flushed red with embarrassment.

"I did, and it was phenomenal" Her blush grew redder with my words.

"It's just something I sort of made up and sing when I'm feeling good about stuff".

"Talking about feelings, come here a minute I want to talk to you about something that's been bugging me" I wanted to talk to her about the scars on her thighs.

She walked over and sat crossed legged on the couch and looked up at me.

"You want to know about the scars, don't you? I saw you look at them earlier and the other day. I don't do that anymore though I haven't in a long time. I wanted to the other day, but I didn't".

"Why did you start?"

"Started when I went to the care home, guess my teenage head couldn't deal with the shit show that was life back then. I had no control over any aspect of my life. My parents were dead, and I had no choice but to go into care. They changed my school as well, so I lost all my friends and my parents. Everyone I knew was gone and my life was no longer my own. Cutting myself made me feel in control of something, like I control how deep and long each cut is. I control how much blood I want and how many lines I score on my body. I stopped when one day I lost my control and wanted to end it all, all the hurt, anger and pain I felt. I just wanted it to stop but was too much of a coward to slit my wrists so I cut deeper than ever before into my thighs over and over again, blood poured out from each cut but with each cut I felt free, so I carried on and then the night staff came to check and found me crying my thighs covered in blood, at first, she thought I'd been raped until she saw the blade in my hand. She sat with me and just held me while I cried. She helped clean the wounds and promised she wouldn't tell anyone as long as I promised to talk to her if I ever felt like doing it again. She talked to me most nights after that until I left the home. That night was the last time I cut myself, I keep my promises and keeping that promise in turn gives me something else to control".

"Tiff, you really are my little firefly, so strong and like you said in that song, you aren't that girl anymore" I kissed her cheeks kissing away the tears that slipped out of her eyes. We sat watching films on the couch for a few hours when the doorbell went. I stood up and answered it to two police officers and Clint.

"Clint, what's going on?"

"Gus wants to talk to Tiff, so we've come to escort you both to the station, he only said she was in danger unless he talked to her" Clint looked past me to Tiff

"What danger?" Tiff asked as she walked over to us while I let them all into the apartment.

"He didn't say but we are treating it as a serious threat".

"OK. Best get going then, the sooner I talk to Gus the sooner we get this mess sorted out".

This girl was so strong amidst all the trauma she had suffered and the shit she was going through right now. How much more could she endure before her walls crumpled and left her a mess that is beyond.

CHAPTER 19

TIFF

Clint drove me and Travis to the police station in his truck with a police car following. Whatever was going on concerning me and my father it seemed pretty big and looked like I was in danger. In just a few weeks my life has gone from a lost orphan escaping the system to being an orphan running into trouble at every turn. And on top of that I suddenly seem to be every man's wet dream as I've been sexually propositioned several times in just one week. I admit I'm nervous and scared about this talk with Gus, but I know that in order to find out why I'm suddenly being hunted I need to talk to him to get answers. The mere thought of being in a room with him is enough to make my skin crawl and bile rise in my throat.

"This mic will feed back to the tapes everything that is said in the room" Clint tells me as he securely sticks tape over the wires of the mic set onto my skin and hides it from view with my top.

"Remember he's handcuffed so he can't do anything to you and an officer will be in the room at all times. Also, the mirror is a two way and we will be behind it watching everything"

"Still don't know why I can't go in with her" Travis grumbled as he stood behind me running his hands up and down my arms in a soothing manner.

"Because he said he will only talk if Tiff goes in on her own, it was hard enough getting him to agree to the officer in the room" Clint replied as he stepped away from me now seemingly happy with the mic placement.

"You sure you want to do this Tiff?"

"Trav, I have to. if I don't then I will never get answers and I could be running for years from a threat I know nothing about"

"Ready?" Clint motioned to the door.

"Not really, but let's get this show on the road shall we".

"Clint, is this Miss McGovern?" A tall stocky man with a shaved head wearing a suit asked as he walked into the room.

"Wesley, yeah this is Tiff".

"Nice to meet you Tiff, I'm Wesley, the lead detective in the case. We believe that Gus in there may have information on a big drug dealer and supplier in the town as well as other sickening things. Get what you can out of him and hopefully it will help us pull the rest from him later on. Remember he's a criminal and criminals lie... a lot, so don't believe everything he says. He may try to antagonise you, so try to stay calm. If it gets too much just tap your thigh and we will pull you out of the room"

I nod my head at him, my tongue suddenly feeling swollen in my now dry mouth.

"Right, if we are all, ready let's get some answers" Wesley showed me out the room and we followed him down the corridor to another door.

"He's in here, we will be next door watching you at all times" Wesley knocked on the door and another officer inside the room opened it letting me step inside.

"Little Tiff. You've grown up a lot since I last saw you properly" Gus said.

"You saw me last night remember".

"Yeah, but it was dark and street lighting doesn't do you any justice. You have your mothers' eyes" Now that got my attention, how did he know my mother?

"You knew her?"

"Not exactly, I'm sorry it was me who killed her, but I didn't mean to" the shock of his words had me stumble backwards before the shock was replaced with pure anger. This man killed my mother.

"Why? Why did you kill her?" I asked while trying my best to rein in my temper and overwhelming need to cry.

"It was an accident, I was meant to just put the frighteners on your dad, he owed a lot of money and was refusing to pay his debt. Said he wouldn't sell his own flesh and blood no matter what. He tried to fight me, and your mum got in the way, and I accidently stabbed her".

"What do you mean sell his own flesh and blood?"

"He couldn't pay back his debt in money so he either gave up your home or you. The boss wanted you. Your dad refused and tried to hide you by sending you to your aunties except as you later found out you have no living relatives".

"I remember going to Sharron's for a few weeks. Is that why dad suddenly decided I needed a break?"

"Yeah, he needed you to disappear in the hopes of the boss not finding you. Your dad he said you had died and for a while the boss believed him until one of his runners saw you at school and reported back, that was when I was asked to do the mugging".

"Why me?"

"I don't know, honestly if I was to hazard a guess it's because he wants you as his wife. He's obsessed with getting you at any cost as long as you are unharmed. You aren't safe, neither are your friends. You can't run this time he has eyes everywhere" I watched as Gus looked over my shoulder at the officer standing by the door.

"Well, he can't have me. I'm with Travis and I'm never going to be with a man who is wanted by the police for nefarious crimes".

"You think that will stop him? What the boss wants he gets regardless of what others say or do. He wants you and he will get you" as he spoke, I heard the door lock click and saw the officer step closer to me in the corner of my eye.

"Really? You're going to try getting me in a police station? Good luck with that" I scoffed at him as the officer lunged at me, I side stepped turning to face him as he crashed into the table.

"Bitch" The officer slash brute shouted at me.

"I told you that you aren't safe anywhere, I tried to warn you" Gus shouted at me as the officer grabbed him and hit him on the head with his baton. With Gus now lying on the floor the brute lunged at me again waving his baton over his head. I reached up grabbing the baton as I twisted my body away from him and flipped him over my shoulder twisting his wrist in the process. He dropped the baton as he screamed out in pain, his wrist probably broken.

"At least now I know why dad insisted on self-defence lessons".

I could hear banging on the door and shouting in the hallway. Surely this brute knew that I was being watched and was rigged with a mic. Or maybe he was a dumb as he looked. The brute flipped over onto his front and jumped up, knocking me onto my arse.

"You bitch" he slapped my face so hard my head whipped to the side and made my head spin as dizziness set in. I scrambled around the floor with my hands blindly feeling for the baton, my only hope of subduing this brute. Finding it I quickly whipped round and slammed the baton into his side as he fell on top of me, and the door crashed open with a bang.

"Tiff, baby you, ok?" I felt Travis hands on my shoulders as someone lifted the brute from me. My vision was waving in and out of focus. When did I bang my head?

"Paramedics are on their way now, keep her talking and awake. Shit put pressure on that wound stem the blood flow" I heard someone shout. Blood? What wound? Who are they talking about?

"Tiff, stay with me baby" Travis' voice sounded far away even though I could feel his body holding me, my head now resting against his chest as he pulled me to a sitting position with my back against his front and his legs either side of me.

"Travis, he killed her" I mumbled.

"I know baby I know. You did good. Now stay awake keep talking to me" Travis desperate voice whispered in my ear.

"Tiffany McGovern aged seventeen no known allergies, this is her next of kin Travis Jones, stab wound to left side and head injury from hitting the floor hard, bruising and swelling on right cheek from a powerful blow to the face caused by this man's hand" I think I heard Wesley say. What stab wound? My name, when was I stabbed?"

"Hurry up" Was the last thing I heard from Travis before darkness consumed me.

When I next opened my eyes, I was in a white room, my head was throbbing, and I had a lot of pain in my side. I ran my hand down my side and felt the bandage under the standard hospital gown. I groaned as memories assaulted my mind.

"Tiff, you're awake, thank god" Travis hand suddenly gripped mine and his thumb brushed up and down my knuckles.

"I'll go get the doctor" I think Clint said as I blinked, taking in the room I was in and spotting Amber, Chance and Brad stood by a window all looking at me. As I swept my gaze to the door, I saw Wesley and then Clint walking back in followed by a doctor.

"You're awake, that's a good thing. We had to operate on you because the stab wound was very deep and had punctured your kidney, all's good though and we managed to repair the damage. You have a concussion and a large lump on your head but no damage so that will start to feel better in a day or two."

"Stab?" I barely managed to ask.

"The officer stabbed you with a hidden flick knife he had in his sleeve" Wesley answered as the grip on my hand from Travis got tighter.

"What happened?" I asked as Amber handed me a glass of water.

"Gus did try to warn you about the officer with his subtle looks behind you that we noticed, but he locked the door from inside before we got there. Gus is dead, the blow to his head caused a massive bleed on his brain and unfortunately it killed him" Wesley filled me in. I reached a hand up to my head as the throbbing got worse.

"I think that's enough for today. You have five minutes then you all clear out so that my patient can rest" The doctor ordered.

"I'll be back tomorrow kid. You did well today. I have some trusted men stationed outside your door" Wesley patted my arm before leaving the room.

"You scared the shit out of us," Chance said as he swept a hand through his hair.

"Yeah, Travis here even cried, like big fat ugly sobs and tears" Brad joked as he grinned at me.

"Shut up Brad, I never cry" Travis replied as he punched Brad in the arm.

"You so did cry Trav" Amber laughed as she sat on the edge of the bed next to me.

"Girl, you sure know how to get all the attention," Amber nervously laughed.

"What can I say, I guess I'm just super special".

"You're wanted Tiff, that's what you are, and not in a good way" Travis replied as he leant over and kissed my head.

"What do we do?" I asked as I looked at my friends.

"We look after you and keep you safe, you're our family now and we look after each other" Brad said as he sat on a chair at the side of the bed.

"What he said" Chance stood behind him with his arms crossed over his chest.

"Exactly, your family now and we protect family" Clint stood next to Amber.

"You have a plan, don't you?" I looked between each of them and smiled when my eyes landed on Travis.

"Sure do. You have to get better enough to leave the hospital first though" he winked at me.

"What about work? And giving a statement about what happened? I'm sure the police will want that even if it was all on camera" I asked with a slight panic in my voice.

"Not a problem I'll sort that out with Wesley and the team, should have it all sorted by the beginning of next week. Clint spoke before anyone could speak.

"Ok, so I guess we are going away then".

"We all are, Brad here managed to get some cheap holiday chalet by the coast for a couple of weeks. Fancy a holiday with us?" Chance almost shouted.

"So, we took a chance and booked it, we leave on Monday, all of us" Clint said.

"You ok with that Tiff?" Travis asked me with clear concern in his voice.

"Hell yeah, I've always wanted to go abroad".

"This is going to be epic" Chance fist pumped the air making us all laugh.

"Right, we should go and let you rest up" Amber stood up and gestured to the boys to leave, they all stood up except Travis.

"You too Trav, she needs her rest" Amber scolded him.

"I'm staying, I'll rest on the plane".

"Trav, Amber is right you need to rest too. Tiff is safe and there are guards on the door. She will be fine." Clint looked at Travis.

"What, like she was safe in that room with that officer? Sorry man but I can't trust anyone with her safety right now apart from us, so I'm staying".

"Fine, but I'll take over from you in a few hours, we will work out a rota so one of us is here with Tiff" Clint suggested.

"I said I'm not leaving; you can sit with me but I'm staying here until Tiff is allowed home".

"Trav, you need rest as well" Brad tried.

"I'll rest when I'm dead" Travis glared at each of his friends.

"Fine have it your way "Clint shook his head and they all walked out the room leaving just me and Travis.

"I should never have agreed to you going into that room".

"I needed to Trav; you know that. And we couldn't have known the officer was corrupt and going to attack me".

"He killed her Tiff, Gus killed your mum, it was him I saw that night" Travis looked at me with watery eyes.

"I know Trav, but it's not your fault, none of it is".

"Seeing you lying there bleeding was like being back in that alleyway, I thought I was going to lose you" A small tear slipped out of his eye and rolled down his cheek.

"I'm safe Trav, you saved me" I held my hand against his cheek and wiped away the tear with my thumb.

"For now, how can I keep you safe from whoever this boss is? I can't lose you".

"We will find a way and we will also find a way of dealing with this boss once and for all" I say with determination. "We can get as much information as the police already have and I can work my street smarts on some of the kids I know that deal drugs and I'm sure eventually we can find out who this boss is and get him off my back somehow".

"I don't like the idea of you mixing with those people Tiff".

"Trav, we have this thing called the internet and social media, I can make contact without even seeing them, I was a care brat remember and kids like us are trusted by low life scum who deal in drugs and shit, even Amber could help me on that side of things as well".

"I'd feel better about it with Amber helping you and you promise no meeting up with anyone".

"Deal. But this will all have to wait until we get back from holiday though".

"If things heat up here then we may not be returning for a while you know?"

"Who cares? Stay or come home it doesn't matter to me as long as I'm with you and the guys".

"Always firefly, always" Travis pulls me into a hug making me groan with pain before he quickly releases me.

"You should get some rest; I'll pop over to the canteen and get us some drinks".

"And chocolate?" I ask as I snuggle down into the pillows and close my eyes.

"And chocolate" Travis kissed my head tenderly.

CHAPTER 20

TRAVIS

Watching Tiff in that interview room with that scumbag was bad enough, then hearing how he was sent to scare her dad but ended up killing Tiff's mum by supposed accident was almost unbearable.

"Did he just give a warning look and nod at the officer?" Clint asked. This got my attention back on that scumbag talking to Tiff.

"I thought that as well, he just hinted that Tiff isn't safe anywhere as well" Wesley replied. Now I was watching the officer while listening to the conversation Tiff was having.

"Shit he just flicked the inner lock, call back up now" Wesley shouted as Clint ran for the door. I stood frozen to the spot watching my girl get attacked by the officer, she fought back hard but I saw the glint of silver and then watched as he hit her hard in the face making her head whip to the side and hit the floor hard. My eyes flickered to her body and then I saw it, the blood seeping out from her top. My girl was injured and needed me. I ran out towards where Clint Wesley and a few other officers were trying to break the door down.

"Clint, he has a knife, she's been stabbed" I yelled at him.

"Fuck, get armed response up here and a fucking taser NOW" Wesley shouted out his orders while they all started charging at the door before someone came running up with a big battering ram or 'door opener' as Clint called it. It took two hits before the door swung open and I saw Tiff with the attacker lying on her, Clint yanked him off as two more officers cuffed him, I ran to Tiff pulling her up against my chest, legs either side of her.

"Tiff baby, you, ok?" she looked so pale and weak as her eyes kept rolling in her head which she could barely hold up.

"Paramedics are on their way, keeping her talking and awake. Shit put pressure on that wound stem the blood flow" Wesley yelled at me. I quickly pressed my hand down on her side against where the blood was pouring, my hand instantly turning red. Clint threw some gauze at me from a medical box and stood over us running his hands through his hair cursing at the shit show we just witnessed.

"Travis, he killed her" Tiff spoke in barely a whisper as her head rolled to the side again.

"I know baby, I know. You did good, now stay awake keep talking to me" I whispered in her ear, the sound of desperation dripping from each word. I couldn't lose her.

"Tiffany McGovern aged seventeen no known allergies; this is her next of kin Travis Jones. Stab wound to left side and head injury from hitting the floor hard, bruising and swelling on right cheek from a powerful blow to the face caused by this man's hand" Wesley gave the paramedics the run down as they set their bags on the floor next to me.

"Hurry up" I yelled at them as I watched Tiff's eyes roll to the back of her head and she fell limp in my arms. Shit no this can't be happening.

"She's gone into shock, Travis, was it? You need to lie her down and move back so we can treat her".

I moved back and watched them work on her setting up a drip and sticking bandages on her side. They tried to bring her round, but she wasn't responding to them talking to her.

"We need to get her to hospital now" One of the paramedics spoke to Wesley.

"Yeah, I have a team outside so it's all blues and twos to the hospital with police escort as well, this girl needs protection so my officers will be stationed outside every and any room or cubicle she gets placed in" Wesley replied.

"Let's go... on two lift her onto the trolley".

I zoned out again as I watched them lift her onto the trolley then panic before starting CPR on her. It felt like hours before they stopped and started running for the door. I couldn't tell you what happened as my mind went into panic mode and shut down.

"Trav, you ok man? You, going in the ambulance with her" Clint shook my shoulders pulling me back into the here and now.

"Yeah, yeah sure" I said numbly.

"Trav, she will be alright, that girl is a fighter" he slapped my shoulder as we ran after the paramedics and my girl.

As soon as we got to the hospital, they rushed Tiff through to the emergency room while I was pulled to the side to give the receptionist as much information about her as I could. Then it was just a waiting game. Police stood in every corner, some with guns, some without. Wesley sat next to me while Clint had gone outside to ring the guys and Frank. He said he wanted to fill them in as they had all grown fond of Tiff over the few short days, they had known her.

Only half an hour later Brad, Chance and Amber were giving me hugs and asking after Tiff, I had nothing to give them other than she was being treated, and just as I said that a doctor appeared.

"Travis Jones?" He asked, looking between us all.

"That's me"

"Right, ok. Tiffany has suffered a deep stab wound and has some internal bleeding, so we are taking her down to theatre in a second to sort that out. She is still unconscious but there is no brain damage so it's just a case of waiting for her to come round. We should be out of surgery within two hours and will be up on the ward. The nurse here will show you to Tiffany's room and I'll meet you there after".

"Thank you" I felt numb, my girl needs surgery as she has internal bleeding. What if she bleeds out? What if they can't stop it? What if she dies?

"Trav, get out of your head now, I know what you're thinking and I'm telling you now that girl is a stubborn one and she will fight and be back in your arms in no time" Amber slung her arm over my shoulder pulling me into one of her famous hugs.

"I can't lose her Amb, I think I love her" I admitted.

"Woah there did the big bad Trav just say the L word?" Brad laughed.

"Yes, he did" Chance agreed.

"Well boys suck it up because I know damn straight that Tiff has a place in all our hearts already" Amber laughed back at them, and she was right, Tiff had a special place in all our hearts whether she liked it or not.

"If you'd like to follow me, I'll take you up to Tiffany's room and help get the armed guards situated with as little disturbance to the other patients. She has her own private room on the ward, I will allow you all to stay until she comes round but after that you will have to leave as she will need her rest" A nurse who appeared from nowhere spoke up making us all jump. Wesley signalled to two of the officers holding guns and they immediately stepped into line behind us as we followed the nurse to Tiff's room. The lift was crammed with all of us in it, but it was only three floors before walking down the longest corridor I've ever walked down. Finally, we entered a ward and followed the nurse to a private room which also seemed to be on its own private corridor on the ward.

While we sat and waited Clint filled the guys in on everything that had happened, and they all agreed that it was their job to help keep her safe. Then Brad had a rare brainwave idea.

"Guys, why don't we get away for a couple weeks, give time for Wesley to set up surveillance and security while looking into any information they have gathered, and it gives Tiff time to heal without worry".

"That's not a bad idea" Wesley spoke up agreeing with Brad.

"Can you organise something Brad, seeing as this was your idea" Clint asked with amusement on his face, Brad was known for his quick and cheap getaways on the spur of the moment.

"You know it bro" Brad pulled his phone from his pocket and started scrolling for cheap places to stay.

Before long we had a holiday chalet on the coast booked and a plan in action to keep Tiff safe for a few weeks while she recovered. Eventually we heard some commotion, and a guard poked his head round the door to Tiff's room.

"She's on her way up now should be here in thirty seconds, ahh here she is now" he told us as we watched porters flanked by police wheel her bed into the room and the nursing staff started setting up the monitors and drips as we stood to one side watching. She looked so small and frail lying in the bed with drips sticking in her arms, one for blood and the other for fluid, I think. Blood bag though? That made me worried.

"Ahh, Travis? Surgery went well, we managed to fix the tear in her kidney and stop the bleeding, however she did lose a lot of blood and required a transfusion" The doctor pointed at the blood bag. "She did come too just before surgery, so all is good on the head injury front, it's just waiting for the anaesthetic to wear off now. She has come round since surgery but was still out of sorts so might not remember that bit. I'll leave you all to wait with her until she wakes up and then I'll be back to talk to Tiff herself".

"Thanks" I mumbled as the doctor left the room followed by the nurses. I sat on the chair at Tiff's bedside pulling it closer so I could touch her and hold her hand. The others dotted themselves around the room as we talked quietly between ourselves.

"Trav that recording you sent me of Tiff, did you ask her about it?" Clint asked me.

"Yeah, she said it's something she made up and sings every now and then when she feels good".

"So, original, sweet. We need to get her to sing it again and put music to it. Chance if I send you the recording you think you and Brad could get some music written up?"

"What? I'm lost man" Brad looked confused.

"Tiff was singing this morning and I recorded it then sent it to Clint and now he wants to make it a proper song" I answered with a quick summary of what Clint was asking them to do.

"Let's hear it then" Amber said as Clint pulled his phone out and pressed play on the recording. The room fell silent except for Tiff's haunting yet beautiful voice coming from the phone filling the room.

"That was... just.... wow" Brad was speechless for once.

"Shit, that girl can sing and wow what a song" Chance had tears in his eyes.

"That poor girl" Amber sniffed.

"Yeah, we can definitely get music for that written up, she sings on key, and I can match up her vocals to the notes needed on both acoustic and bass, Trav reckon you can drum out a beat for it?" Chance asked me.

"You give me the notes and yeah, I'll give it a go, think I might already have the beat down in my head".

"I think this song could be epic" Amber jumped up excitedly while wiping away tears from her eyes.

A few hours later Tiff finally woke up making me the happiest man in the room. We all surrounded her and filled her in on our plan to escape for a couple weeks. Her face at the mention of getting away was priceless, filled with so much happiness. It made me wonder when or if she had been away on holiday. Something I'd have to ask her later. The doctor came in and explained everything to Tiff and then a nurse came and kicked everyone out. I obviously refused to leave, even the guys tried to get me to go but I wanted to stay and keep Tiff safe. They eventually gave in to me after promising to do shifts with me watching Tiff. I watched Tiff snuggle down and her eyes close as she drifted back to sleep. I knew then that I would die for this girl, I would do everything I could to protect her. She was my world and owned my heart and soul. I was screwed but in a good way.

CHAPTER 21

TIFF

Being in hospital is so boring, I want to get out of here like yesterday, but the doctor said I still need monitoring. Travis hasn't left the hospital at all and is starting to get on my nerves with his hovering. He looks worn out as well and needs a wash and some sleep. Frank is popping in today though and I'm hoping he can help persuade Travis to go home for a wash and sleep for a few hours. The guards at the door have changed over so many times now but still remain a constant reminder of the danger I am currently in and all thanks to the man who was supposed to love and protect me from birth, my father. The man I looked up to and idolised, seems he was a villain and not my hero after all. Travis and the guys missed out on their track day as they wanted to spend the day with me instead, which was nice but now I feel guilty that they missed out on something that they love because of me and my drama. I miss the days when all I had to worry about was making sure no one could get into my room at night. Maybe I should ditch the guys and the job along with college and run away from here, as far away as possible and let them live normal lives without my problems worrying them.

"Tiff, you, ok?" Travis asked me as he walked into my room with mugs of coffee.

"Yeah, just thinking about stuff".

"Want to talk about it?"

"Not really, you'd probably call me crazy and go all caveman on me if I told you".

"If you're thinking what I think you are thinking then you can get that thought out of your little head now young lady" Frank's voice boomed through the door as he stepped in behind Travis.

"Hello to you too Frank" I scoffed at him.

"How you doing?" he asked me as he patted my shoulder before sitting down on the chair next to the bed leaving Travis to perch on the edge of my bed.

"Bored and stressed" I answered honestly.

"Bored I can take care of as I just picked up some assignments from the college for you, stressed I can help if it's to do with this ugly mug here" Frank pointed at Travis.

"Hey, insulted here" Travis pouted making me chuckle then wince with pain.

"Yeah, Trav is sort of stressing me out. He needs sleep and a wash but won't leave the hospital".

"I'm not leaving you Tiff".

"Travis, get your arse back home, wash up and rest, you look and smell like shit" Trust Frank to put it bluntly.

"Woe two insults in less than a minute, ow I am feeling really insulted".

"It's true though, as much as I love having you here, you are starting to smell a bit ripe and it's making me feel a bit sick if I'm honest".

"You as well? Great now I know how you really feel...... you love having me here is all I need to hear baby" Travis leaned over and kissed my cheek.

"Yeah, I love having you here when you don't stink".

"You heard her son, now go get cleaned up and rest, I'll stay with her until you get back. Maybe we can go over some of these assignments together?"

"Thanks Frank, that would be great".

"Fine, fine, I'll go but only for a couple hours, anything happens you call me, and I'll come straight back".

"Deal, now go I got work to do" I laughed as he stood up and hugged me.

"Look after her old man" Travis smirked.

"Be off with you kid" Frank shot back as they both laughed before Travis left my room and hopefully the building.

"Thanks Frank, he was starting to get on my nerves".

"He can't help it; he loves you more than he lets on. That's the thing about us Jones men, we love quickly and fiercely and protect what is ours will all our heart".

"Wait, back up love?"

"Yeah, that boy is head over fucking heels in love with you. Any fool can see that".

"But he's only known me just over a week."

"Love is love and has no time frame. His heart is all revved and primed ready to run alongside yours".

"Love though? Really? Seems everyone who has claimed to love me before has turned out to never have given a rat's arse about me".

"Tiffany, how does he make you feel?"

"I don't understand what you're asking?"

"Your heart misses a beat or go crazy, your stomach does flips and feel full of butterflies, you grin like the Cheshire bloody cat when he texts you".

"My heart feels like it steps up a gear and revs at the thought of him wanting me to be his" I grin knowing full well I look like that bloody cat Frank referenced.

"That grin and your words tell me you are just as head over heels with Travis as he is with you. True love and soulmates do exist, and I believe that is you two. You were destined and fated to meet and be together".

"You believe in all that fated and soulmate stuff?" I asked as Frank started placing textbooks on my hospital table.

"Don't you?"

"I never thought about it until now, but I guess it makes sense when you put it like you did".

"So, you agree then that you love Travis?"

"Yeah, yeah, I do"

Frank smiled at me and opened the first book for us to work with.

Before we knew it three hours had passed, and I had completed most of the assignments. My stomach rumbled, making Frank laugh.

"Shall I see what's on the menu for you today or shall we see if we can sneak down to the canteen?" Frank aske with a mischievous grin on his face.

"Let's escape" I chuckled as Frank stepped out the door in search of a wheelchair.

"Your chariot awaits" Frank wheeled in a wheelchair and had one of the guards already stood next to him.

"We can escape but Uncle Fester here has to come with us" I laughed at Frank's nickname for my guard of the day. Although he did look like Uncle Fester with his bald head and hunched shoulders.

"I've heard worse" Fester grunted.

"I can see that" Frank replied as I carefully climbed from the bed and flopped into the wheelchair.

"Quick run before Travis gets back and stops me".

Fester took the handles and leaned forward before charging towards the corridor with Frank and the other guard running behind, we must have looked at a right funny sight. Sitting in the hospital canteen was relaxing and felt normal for a change. Yeah, I was sitting in a wheelchair in my pyjamas, but beggars can't be choosers these days.

"Want another drink?" Fester asked me.

"Yeah, please and some cake too if they have any" I smiled at him before my face turned to panic as my phone started ringing and Travis name appeared on the screen.

"Give it here" Frank took my phone and answered it

"Yeah....... no, she is fine son....... we are in the canteen......... ok we will make our way back up now...... she is fine, and we have the guards with us so stop blowing my ear off" Frank hung up and waved Fester back over from the queue.

"Travis is back, and the doctor is waiting for Tiffany here, so we best get back to her room".

"Right, let's see how fast we can get back then?" Fester laughed as the other guard who didn't speak once stood up and laughed as well.

We ran back to my room and as we entered it, we saw that Travis was pacing up and down by the window almost nervously while a big bag sat on the bed.

"Ahh, there you are!" The doctor made us all jump as he spoke from behind us. Travis whirled around to face me, and I watched as the panic and worry left his face and relief replaced it.

"Thank god you're back, I was worried about you" Travis walked over to me and helped me from the wheelchair and lifted me up bridal style before carrying me back to my bed and placing me back into it pulling the covers over my lap before sitting down next to me.

"Right, now you are back. I can let you know that as you are healing well and all your tests and vitals are good, we can release you from the hospital with strict instructions to not go running any marathons any time soon. The nurse will be in to give you all the after-care information you need and the pain medication to take with you" The doctor told me, and Travis squeezed my hand with joy.

"Thank you doctor" I smiled.

"You're welcome, but please don't come back in for a good long while and stay safe" The doctor smiled back at me as he left.

"I'll ring Wesley as he will want to arrange all safeguarding measures to get you to a safe house" Fester said as he pulled his phone from his pocket.

"I'll let Clint know as well" The other guard told us as he left the room and made his phone call. Something about him didn't seem right. He not once tried to interact with us when we made our 'escape' earlier, he didn't even introduce himself really either.

"Travis, that guard who just left, is he new?"

"Yeah, I think so... I've not seen him up here before. Why?"

"It might be nothing, but something just feels off about him".

"I'll ask Wesley when he gets here" Frank interrupted us as he spoke up "I thought he was a bit off too when we went down to the canteen".

"It's not just me then".

"Not at all Tiffany. Travis you better ring Amber and let her know that our Tiffany is coming home".

"Already texted her, Doctor told me when I came in and you weren't here. I brought you clothes but didn't know what you would prefer to wear so brought a lot of choices" Travis cheeks flushed a pinkish colour making both me and Frank chuckle.

"Well, I can't get dressed, with you lot in my room now, can I?"

"You can use your bathroom; I'm not leaving this room unless you are with me" Travis folded his arms across his chest.

"Fine"

Travis lifted me from the bed and carried me into the bathroom before setting me on my feet and Frank passing the bag to me. They both left and I locked the door behind me deciding to take a quick shower before getting dressed. At long last I am finally leaving this hospital, and on top of that the guys have arranged a sort of holiday for us all to go on to help me recover and avoid my dramas. Let's hope their plan works that way and I can be just a normal girl for a short while. Normal? I don't even think I know what normal is these days, I mean the past four years have been anything but normal for most girls my age. But damn it if I won't try to enjoy doing normal things and having fun like I should be at my age.

CHAPTER 22

TRAVIS

I had only meant to go home for a quick wash and grab some clean clothes for Tiff but when I fell onto my couch exhaustion caught up with me and I must've fallen asleep. Next thing I know three hours had passed. I quickly showered and shoved some clothes into a bag for Tiff not knowing whether she would want jeans or leggings or even sweats given where her stitches were situated. Grabbing my keys and the bag I raced to my car and floored it to the hospital only to find her room empty and no guards at the door, panic set in, where is she? Has something happened to her? Why hasn't anyone rung me? A quick look at her bedside and I noticed her phone was gone, I pulled my phone out and rang her hoping she would answer it and be safe, it rang a few times before Frank answered it in his gruff voice. As I was talking to him the doctor came in looking for Tiff and I let Frank know, before hanging up and turning my attention to the doctor.

"Travis, nice to see that you finally took my advice and got some rest".

"Yeah, I sort of got bullied into it. Is everything alright with Tiff?"

"Yes, yes everything is perfect you could say. Is she around?"

"Canteen apparently but they are on their way back up now".

"Good, I'll be back when they arrive".

"Is everything ok?" I sounded worried now, my mind going a million miles a minute.

"Oh yes, I just wanted to let her know that we are releasing her today into your care".

"Today? Can she come home? "

"Yes today, she is healing well and moving around better than expected so I see no reason why she can't go home today, she has been here for what 5 days now".

"Feels like longer but yeah five days now."

"I'll let you settle her back down when she gets back and then I'll pop by to let her know".

"Thanks doc"

I pace the room waiting for what felt like hours but was just mere minutes before Tiff was wheeled back into the room by one of her guards with Frank and the other guard behind her. Relief flooded me at seeing her smiling and safe. Not seconds after putting her back into bed then the doctor showed back up and told her the good news. Both guards went off to make calls regarding safety precautions for moving Tiff to a secure location or safe house as they called it. I already knew we were staying at Clint's house until we leave for our little holiday on Friday. Two weeks of sand and sea with my girl and the guys, no work, no drama just us being us and enjoying life. I'd already texted Amber to let her know we would be over today while I was pacing the room waiting for Tiff to come back up. Now I was sitting here with Frank waiting for Tiff to get changed in the bathroom. She had suggested that one of the guards was making her feel like something was off about him, Frank also suggested the same so I will question Wesley and Clint when they get here which should be any minute now. And as if on cue the bathroom door opens at the same time Wesley knocks on the doorframe with Clint at his side.

"Hey guys" Tiff waved them in

"Hey, how are you doing?" Clint asks as he moves over to her side hugging her.

"Better now I can go home".

"About that" Wesley frowned at us all "Tiffany, you can't actually go back to Travis home as we think whoever is after you may now know that you are staying there".

"So where am I meant to go?"

"Mine" Clint smiled.

"Yours? What about Travis, will he be safe staying home?"

"Baby, I'm going with you" I pulled her down into my lap wrapping my arms around her.

"But won't that look like we are onto them if neither of us is home?"

"We have some men at the apartment now moving around and turning things on and off to make it appear like he is home" Wesley informed her.

"Amber is moving in as well, she said you will need some girl time and not just us men" Clint rolled his eyes as he repeated what Amber had told him the night before when we came up with this part of the plan in keeping Tiff safe.

"So, for the next three days I'm staying at Clints with Clint, Travis and Amber?"

"Yep, then on Friday we are travelling together in the minibus to the holiday chalet and enjoying two solid weeks of nothing but fun and relaxation" I kissed her neck gently as she started to relax a bit at the plan we had set into motion.

"Travis, I need you to go back to work for the next few days to make everything appear normal on that front and on Thursday make a big show about needing time away" Wesley commented.

"It's my birthday and my mum's death anniversary on Thursday" Tiff sighed as she tried to hide her face.

"Yeah, the day I saw her mum get killed" I added.

"Perfect excuses for you to need time away, Cole and Mitch need to believe the reasons too, Cole especially. I wouldn't put it past them to inadvertently let slip what's going on which is why so far, they are in the dark and think that Tiff is off work to concentrate on her studies while Travis is dealing with band stuff" Frank filled us in on what the other guys thought about us suddenly disappearing.

Wesley got a call and answered his phone while looking at us and smiling.

"Soon as the nurse has been we will be down, keep three by the door and the car running, we shouldn't be too much longer" he told whoever was on the end of the line.

"Car and security are all on standby" he told us as he hung up his phone.

"Good, I cannot wait to get out of here" Tiff laughed.

"I can't wait to get you back to bed" I whispered in her ear, making her shiver in my arms. I should maybe ask the doc if she will be ok for the kind of activity my cock and I have in mind. With that thought I quickly and gently stand up and place Tiff back down in my seat.

"I'm just popping to ask the doc some questions about Tiff's aftercare" Not a complete lie.

"Ask when the nurse will be in to sign her out as well while you're out there" Frank shouted after me. It didn't take long to find the doc.

"Doc, can I have a quick word?"

"Certainly, what can I help you with?"

"Well, erm... I know Tiff is doing well with her recovery and that but well... erm... will she be ok to have sex?" I have never felt embarrassed about sex before so why now?

"I see no reason why not, as long as she feels comfortable with it then go for it. You only live once so enjoy it" The doc winked at me as he patted my shoulder before walking off again.

I'd see how Tiff is tonight and maybe settle some of the tension running through us both with a long shower or bath followed by me showing Tiff just how much I fucking love her. My cock definitely liked that idea as it twitched in my boxers, thank fuck I wore jeans today. I walked back into Tiff's room to see the nurse standing there with a bag full of medicines and a handful of paper and leaflets.

"Ahh, Travis, as I was just saying this, here are all the notes from the operation and her stay here so if Tiffany should have any issues in the next few days she can present these to a doctor and they will be able to know what is the best course of action to take. There are also some leaflets and information regarding aftercare and exercises to do to help aid a faster recovery. In this bag we have all the pain medication and spare bandages. A district nurse will come by Friday morning before your holiday to change the dressing for the last time as she will show you how to do it yourself. Now scram, get out of here before the doctor changes his mind" The nurse laughs at us.

Wesley grabbed Tiff's bags while Frank grabbed the paperwork. I helped Tiff out of her chair, and we all walked out the hospital flanked by four guards. A big black car with dark tinted windows was waiting for us at the entrance with another two guards standing next to it.

"I'll drive your car back to the apartment and get Amber to pick me up from there to make it look like your home today" Clint held his hand out for my keys.

"Make it look like it's broken down when you get there so it doesn't look odd when you drop Travis of at work tomorrow morning" Wesley added.

"Will do, pile of shit probably will break down anyway".

"Hey, that's my car you're talking about, that baby is as reliable as I am" I stood tall and proud as Tiff slapped my chest.

"Yeah, yeah" Clint smirked as he walked off towards the carpark with Frank following him.

"Right let's get you safe and settled" Wesley ushered us into the car as he got into the front passenger side and one guard took the driver's side.

"Wesley, I was meant to ask earlier but one of the guards on the door upstairs, was he new?" I asked.

"Des? Yeah, he took over at the last minute from Lewis who usually watches in the day. Lewis fell ill last night. Was there a problem?"

"He just seemed off; I can't put my finger on it put something wouldn't settle in my gut about him" Tiff added.

"I'll take him off rotation then and keep an eye on him, hopefully Lewis will be back tomorrow".

"Will there be guards hanging around when we are away?" Tiff asked.

"No, we think we can pull them away once you are halfway down the motorway, so they will follow and then at the service station you will all drive off and they will watch to make sure no one is following before they head back here to wait for your return."

"We will be fine Tiff" I pulled her close to me as we drove back to Clints. I knew that we would have the house pretty much to ourselves once we got there as both Clint and Amber had work and the guards are stationed in the house over the road from Clint's which was up for sale and empty coincidently, this made it even easier to make Clint's house the safe house for the time being.

But as usual nothing goes smoothly and as we pulled up to Clint's I spotted the red convertible beetle that belongs to the super bitch.

"Travis baby, I've been so worried" Claire screeched as she ran over to me as I got out of the car.

"Fuck off Claire" I yelled at her as I held my hand out to help Tiff from the car. She winced a bit as she climbed out and I quickly picked her up bridal style.

"What are you doing with that whore?" Claire screamed as she tried to barge past Wesley.

"Whore? Bitch, are you really that dumb? The only whore here is you" Tiff shot back.

"Madam, if you could kindly step back, please or I will have to arrest you for causing a public nuisance" Wesley said in a calm and bored tone.

"Arrest me? You can't do that, you're not even a police officer. What are you some hired security?" Claire sneered.

"I am chief inspector Wesley Vine, and you madam are in our way".

"Travis, what's going on? Why are you carrying that bitch? What happened to you? "

"FUCK OFF" I again yelled at her as I carried Tiff into the house and set her down on the couch. I could still hear Claire outside demanding answers before she screamed and shouted "You can't do this to me, do you know who I am? I'm his girlfriend" then Wesley shouting.

"Your fucking delusional if you think Travis would want to be seen with you, that boy only has eyes for one girl and that girl was the one he was carrying over the threshold" now that gave me a warm feeling in my heart and a rather stupid idea. Was it really a stupid idea when I was already Tiff's next of kin on the hospital records? I was pulled out of my thoughts by Wesley walking back into the room.

"Fuck, that girl is crazy, had to arrest her as she wouldn't stop trying to get in the house".

"She's a crazy one alright" Tiff replied as she cocked an eyebrow at me.

"She is always telling people I'm hers, but I've never even spared her a second glance, she isn't my type for a start" I wink at Tiff.

"You have a team in the house over the road and an alarm button in each room on the wall by the windows should you need it. I'll leave you in peace now and hopefully all will be fine".

"Thanks Wes" Tiff called after him as he waved his hand behind him at us.

"It's just you and me now baby" I pulled Tiff up and hugged her before smashing my lips against hers in an all-consuming kiss. After a few minutes Tiff pulled back trying to catch her breath, cheeks flushed pink.

"We best stop before we end up doing something we probably shouldn't do given my injury".

"That's what I went to ask the doctor about" I smirked at her.

"Did you now? And what did the doctor say?"

"He said all good and it might help with recovery, but not to go too overboard" I grinned at her as she blinked and the pink on her cheeks turned to red with embarrassment at the thought, I had asked a doctor about sex with her.

"Did he now? I'm not sure if I can manage it" I could tell by the look on her face and her body language that she was lying and was as much in need of this as I was.

"How about a shower or bath to help you relax a bit?" I suggested, fuck I wanted to see her naked body again.

"I already had a shower, but I could do with a lie down" she bit down on her bottom lip, and that was all the encouragement I needed as I picked her up and carried her laughing into what would be our room. I let her body slide against mine as I slowly lowered her to the ground again, her bright blue eyes meeting mine sparkling with love and lust.

"Baby I'm going to take my time worshipping every inch of your gorgeous body".

"Is that a promise?"

"Damn straight it is' ' My hands slipped under the hem of her t-shirt before gripping it and sliding it up and over her head. I stepped back and admired her gorgeous round breasts as they sat in her pale blue lacy bra, nipples taut and pressing against the thin lace.

"Fucking perfect" I whisper as I smooth my hands over her arms and down her shoulders to the clasp of her bra before unclipping it pulling it down her arms and dropping it on the floor, her breasts now bare to me I pinch her nipple between my thumb and forefinger and gently tug on it making a small moan slip from her mouth, as I wrap my mouth over the other nipple and swirl my tongue over it nipping and licking, her hands reach out and her fingers slide into my hair pulling it lose from the band making it tumble down and brush against her breasts.

"Fuck" Tiff moans as I pull back and look down at her. Her skin on her chest and neck now a flushed pink, her eyes sparkling with need.

"What do you want, Tiff?"

"You, I want you, I need you".

With those words I pull her leggings down, taking her knickers with them, so she stands completely bare in front of me. The self-adhesive dressing is the only thing covering any part of her skin. I gently push her back towards the bed kissing her as I go. Her knees buckle as she hits the bed and I stop kissing and look at her with my eyebrows cocked.

"Thought you needed to lie down" I teased her.

"I do" she climbs on the bed and lies down trying to pull the cover over herself. I grip it and pull it away, the smile on her face full of mischief.

"You won't be needing that" I say as I throw all the covers onto the floor.

"But I'm cold"

"You won't be for much longer" I kiss down her body taking extra care around her wound before blowing hot air over her pussy making her squirm. My tongue glides between her pussy lips as my fingers part them, opening her up to me. I press my thumb to the edge of her opening as my tongue flicks over her clit teasing her and stroking her. A little nip with my teeth on her clit has her panting and bucking her hips I know I'm being a bastard taking her to the edge and not letting her fall off it and shatter into orgasm, but I want it to be the best orgasm she has ever had. I continue slowly teasing my tongue over her clit pushing my thumb in and out of her pussy teasing her.

"Travis please" At her begging I relent and then I slip two fingers inside her and press against her soft spongy G-spot rubbing my fingers over it as she shatters and spasms around me, filling my mouth with her juices while crushing my fingers in a vice like grip as she spirals and falls from the edge, I've been keeping her on.

Removing my fingers, I kiss up her body and grab my shirt as I rip it over my head and use it to wipe my face. Tiff lies there panting with post orgasm bliss etched on her face.

"You ok baby?" I ask her worried that she may be in pain.

"I'm fucking fantastic" she grins before pulling me down to kiss me, my cock straining even more against my boxers and jeans.

"Think you could manage my cock?" I ask her cheekily.

"Won't know until we try" with that I remove the rest of my clothes my cock springing free and aching to be buried deep inside her.

"If it gets too much just say and I'll stop" Tiff nods her head at me letting me know she agrees. I slowly lower myself over her and nudge the tip into her and slowly inch by inch push inside her savouring every second of this moment. Once I'm fully in I start to move in and out pressing myself against her so that her clit rubs against me as I make sweet love to her. Her legs wrap around my hips as I start to pick up pace, Tiff meets me thrust for thrust as we get faster then she clamps down on my cock as she comes again screaming my name, my hand slips between us as my fingers find her clit and I tease her rubbing her clit with my fingers while I thrust into her again and again, I feel her building up for a third orgasm and my own cock is aching to come with her a few more thrusts and she squeezes me tighter than before making my cock start to pulse as we both come at the same time looking into each other's eyes. Fuck if I didn't love her before I sure as hell do now. I slip from her and head to the bathroom to get a cloth. When I come back into the room Tiff is fast asleep curled into a ball. I gently cleaned her up, careful not to wake her.

Sleep will help her heal faster. I decide to get dressed and go make us both some food while she sleeps. Clint and Amber will be home soon as well so I suppose I should be a good house guest and cook for them as well.

CHAPTER 23

TIFF

I woke up feeling stiff and pain making me groan as I tried to roll out of the bed I'm lying on. I could hear muffled voices coming from the other room as I stood up and grimaced with the pain shooting up my side. I somehow managed to get my t-shirt and sweats back on before holding a hand to my side and slowly making my way out towards the voices, stopping at the door to grip the frame as the pain intensified at my movements.

"Shit, Tiff are you ok?" Travis was at my side in seconds.

"Pain" Was the only word I managed to mutter as I gritted my teeth before my legs gave way. Travis quickly scooped me up into his arms.

"Where to?"

"Couch, I want to be with you guys" Travis carried me over to the couch gently setting me down on his lap as he sat down, his arms wrapped around me as he kissed my head.

"Where are her pain meds?" Clint asked as Amber came back in with a glass of water handing it to me.

"On the counter by the kettle" Travis answered Clint as he stroked my back trying to soothe away the pain. Clint was back with the tablets in his hand in record time.

"Sorry baby, I should've woken you up when they were due to be taken".

"It's ok, I needed the sleep".

"Clint ordered pizza, should be here soon and the others are coming over as well, they want to plan out some trips while we are away" Amber sat down on the coffee table in front of us.

"Sounds like a good plan, not sure how much I'll be able to do though if this is anything to go by though".

"Don't worry we will work around it and still have a load of fun" Clint smiled at me.

"Hello, hello" Brad shouted from the hallway as he walked in with Chance right behind him.

"Hey, how are you feeling T?" Chance asked as he ruffled my hair.

"Better thanks"

"Lie's. She is in a lot of pain because I forgot to wake her up for her meds" Travis grunted.

"Sleep is the best cure" Chance shot back as he flopped in the armchair.

"True fact, she had them now, right? So don't sweat it bro. All's good and sleep helps the body heal faster" Brad added as he sat on the other armchair.

"Told you" I smacked Travis chest playfully.

"Yeah, yeah. Guys seeing as you are all here, we need to talk about that piece of music. I've got the beat down in my head and I think it will go with the music notes you sent over" Travis looked at each of the guys with a conspiratorial look.

"We already recorded our part and have mixed in the singing just needs your beat now" Brad added.

"Cool, I can do that now if you guys watch Tiff" Travis asked.

"Sure thing, Clint you go as well and maybe we can get it finished tonight" Brad replied.

"Actually, why don't all you guys go and record it together while we have some girly time?" Amber stood up hands on hips.

"Good call let's go guys" Brad stood up followed by Chance as they all ran into the music room and closed the door behind them.

"What's going on?" I asked Amber.

"They got a new song idea and need to record it before they forget it, it's always the same. If they don't record it, then it's forgotten, and they argue over who should've written it down. They have it mostly done now so shouldn't take them too long".

"Sounds intense, but why can't we sit in and watch?"

"When they record something for the first time, they like to do it privately until they perfect it, I'm sure we will hear it soon enough though".

"Good, I can't wait to hear it".

"Now enough about all of them, what about Travis and you?" She winked at me.

"Well, I'm not a nun anymore" I laughed as amber squealed.

"O.M.G you did the deed? When?"

"The morning before everything went to shit".

"Oh, not good about the after, but shit girl... morning sex? Fuck that is hot".

"Really?"

"Yes, most men are busy getting ready for the day to want morning sex so girl you hit the mother fucking jack pot with that being you're first time".

"He was very attentive and gentle, it was amazing" I felt my cheeks turn red with a blush.

"Guess you have to wait now until you are all healed up before a repeat performance though".

"Actually" I blushed even harder.

"No freaking way, what in the hospital?"

"No, God no not there, but Travis did ask the doctor about when was ok, before we left".

"Oh, well at least he got the all clear before he indulged, so sweet. Never knew Trav could be a sweet man" Amber laughed.

"He's not always grumpy" I laughed remembering when I first met Travis.

"He used to be fun before the stabbing he witnessed but something snapped in him that day and he became grumpy and angry at the world, but you my girl have brought him back to us, the old fun travis and I can't thank you enough. Shit, I think we all owe you, we thought we would lose him to his own self destruction".

"Things really got that bad?"

"Yep, he changed overnight back then and this past couple week it's like those past few years never happened. Witnessing your mum die left a big dent in his heart as he couldn't save her and didn't get a look at her killer. He felt like he had failed her and her family because the killer was never found".

"It wasn't his fault though".

"We kept telling him that, but he never listened, until you that is. He has a purpose now and something to live for and he's happy, probably happier than he has ever been. When his parents left, he was a bit upset but he chose to stay and he was happy with his decision, but I guess he always thought his parents would change their minds and stay behind with him. Truth is they never loved him enough to stay for him, Frank has always been there for him and always will be. Frank has been there for all of us growing up".

"He is a super guy, the shock on his face though when I turned up at the garage" I giggled at the memory.

"Yeah, he was expecting a dude not a sassy girl with attitude" Amber laughed with me before the doorbell rang.

"I'll just get that" She stood up and walked to the door.

"Is she here? I need to see her" Mitch's voice sounded down the hallway.

"Boy's please, she needs rest, and how did you know?"

"Claire told us," Cole replied. Fuck the last thing I want, or need is these two.

"Sorry Tiff, I couldn't stop them" Amber stood behind them as they barrelled into the living room.

"Thank God, we've been so worried about you. What did Travis do to you?" Cole asked with his fists clenched at his side.

"Nothing, Travis has been looking after me, he'd never hurt me".

"Bullshit" Cole shouted making me flinch.

"Travis hasn't hurt me Cole, now if you're going to call me a liar then you can leave" I shifted ready to stand up and winced at the sudden movement.

"You're hurt? What happened T.J?" Mitch sat down next to me and put his hand on my shoulder.

"I was stabbed, Travis saved me and got me help, that's all you need to know" I snapped at the twins.

"Travis was there? Why am I not surprised? Seems trouble always follows him" Cole spat.

"Cole, shut the fuck up, if T.J says he saved her and didn't hurt her then I believe it" Mitch shouted at his brother.

"Travis was fucking with her, if he cared about her, she would never have got hurt in the first place".

"Cole, I'm warning you. I know you hate Travis right now because he got T.J and not you but stop with this rant now before I smack you one" Mitch glared at his brother.

"Fuck you" Cole snapped before turning on his heel and walking out the house.

"He's angry because you chose Travis and not him, give him time and he will come round and be happy for you both. I better go after him. I needed to know you were safe after Claire shouted her mouth off that Travis was carrying you into the house. She made out you looked beaten up and broken and Travis looked like he hated you, she also said something about police and security?"

"Well, you can see for yourself that I'm fine, I'm staying here as I can't manage all those steps up to the apartment right now and Travis was angry with Claire not me. Police, well, obviously I was stabbed you know".

"True, I'll go and let you rest, call if you need anything though" Mitch ruffled my hair and walked with Amber back to the door. When Amber came back in, she was carrying a pile of pizza boxes.

"Grubs up" she smiled at me.

"I'll just go grab the boys" She walked towards the music room knocking on its door really hard before Clint poked his head out.

"Yeah?"

"Pizza's here, and the twins just left".

"Shit, ok good job Travis was in here then".

"You could say that Cole is very bitter and angry, even accused travis of hurting Tiff".

"What? How fucking dare, he" Travis roared as he pushed past Clint looking around the room before his eyes landed on me.

"I set him straight Trav don't worry" Amber told him as she walked past and opened a pizza box on the coffee table.

"Hey hotshot, you wanna sit down and feed me?" I grinned at him knowing he needed some distraction from the anger building up inside him right now.

"Firefly, you know I will feed you, but I'm more worried about the twins right now".

"Trav, we told them you didn't hurt me. Mitch believes me and says Cole is just angry because you got me and not him. He's just jealous and venting his anger. Claire didn't help though as she made out, I looked beaten up and you looked angry with me" I looked up at Travis as I spoke, needing him to see that I was fine.

"That bitch is always trouble, she only sniffs around the twins because they work with me, and she thinks it will get in with me. She is so fucking dumb" Travis shoulders relaxed a bit as he pulled me up and then sat down with me on his lap, Clint handed him a plate full of pizza for us both.

"How's that song coming on?" Amber asked as she handed Clint his plate of pizza while Brad and Chance laughed at each other stuffing pizza slices into their mouths.

"Done, Travis' beat was perfect, so it only took us a couple of run throughs before we got it recorded with the vocals, want to hear it?" Clint asked.

"Hell yeah" Both Amber and I replied. Clint stood up and pressed a few buttons on the sound system he had by the music room door and the room filled with the sound of the drums and guitars playing before a voice, no not just a voice but my voice sounded in the room. Me singing my song with their music played, filled the room. I looked at the guys with my mouth hanging open as they all grinned at me. The music was beautiful and perfect along with my voice and the lyrics, but how and when did they get my voice?

"I recorded you singing the other day, I was so mesmerised by your voice that I knew I had to share it with the guys. They agreed that we had to put it to music, especially since you told me it was your own song and not a copy" Travis told me, answering my thoughts.

"Tiff, we were wondering if you'd like to be a part of the band and maybe sing some songs with us?" Clint asked as Amber clapped her hands excitedly.

"I don't know, I've never sung in front of anyone before".

"Just give it a try, yeah? Your voice is amazing" Travis kissed my head.

"I'll try" I agreed, making them all cheer.

We spent the next few hours talking about what songs we could add my vocals to and what activities we could do while away. The beach and sunbathing, surfing for the guys, clubbing as long as we could get a VIP area as I would obviously need to sit down a lot and not dance or stand all night. Amber suggested the zoo which was agreed on along with the fairground noting that some rides may not be suitable for me in the first week but maybe the second week. I suggested the sea life centre which was put on the list for Brad to pre order tickets for. We had a sort of itinerary for the first week at least consisting of mainly hitting the beach during the day and clubs a few nights in the week if Brad could secure us V.I.P areas. Only two more days and then we could be away from here and be just normal young adults without any drama.

"Mind if we stop here Thursday night seeing as we leave Friday morning" Brad asked Clint.

"I was going to suggest that anyway, plus it's our new girl's birthday Thursday and we need to celebrate it" Clint replied giving Amber a knowing look, they had something planned for sure. I yawned and Travis chuckled before standing up with me in his arms as I was still on his lap.

"I'm going to take this one to bed, she needs her rest to heal as you all said earlier".

"Night you two" Chance chuckled at us.

"Don't do anything I wouldn't do" Brad waggled his finger at us.

"Meds?" Amber asked.

"I'll grab them" Clint stood up and walked towards the kitchen while Travis carried me into the bedroom placing me on the bed. Clint was behind Travis holding the tablets and a bottle of water before clapping his shoulder and leaving, closing the door behind him.

"Here, take your meds like a good girl" Travis whispered in my ear, making a shiver run down my spine. I took the pills from him, swallowing them with the water before looking up at him.

"What wouldn't Brad do?" I asked in a sultry voice.

"There is not much that boy wouldn't do, but you are still healing and not ready to find out, yet" He grinned at me as he tugged my sweatpants from my legs making me giggle.

"I think I'd like to know what you boys get up to, especially you".

"Tiff don't push it, you'll see what I like and enjoy in time, first you need to heal" Travis flopped on the bed next to me now only wearing his boxers while I lay in just my knickers and a t-shirt.

"Sounds ominous, can you not even give me a hint?"

"Let's watch a film shall we say fifty shades?" Travis asked with his head cocked to one side. Was that a hint or just his preference of film right now?

"Sure, Jamie Dornan is so hot in that film" I lied as I had never actually watched it, I had read the books but watching a film was something I never had time for.

"You think he's hot, do you?"

"So hot, like the hottest man I know" I teased Travis as he leaned over me pinning my arms to my sides on the bed as he hovered over me.

"So, I'm not hot then?" He kissed and nibbled at my neck.

"You're hot in your own league" I moaned as I spoke my pussy pulsating with need as Travis ground his erection against me.

"Is that right? So, I'm hot but in my own league, is that league higher than Mr fifty shades?" He sucked my nipple through the t-shirt making my back arch and a moan slip from my mouth.

"It's top of the leagues for you" I moaned again. Travis pulled both my hands above my head and pinned them down with one hand, his other hand trailed down to my knickers and he tugged on them, ripping them from my body before he pushed his boxers down and rubbed his cock against me again.

"Top league huh, that sounds like the perfect spot for me" his fingers on his free hand teasing my clit while his cock pressed just at the entrance to my desperate pussy.

"Trav, please" I whined, thrusting my hips against him trying to get his huge erection inside me.

"Please, what?" Travis whispered in my ear.

"Fuck me"

"I don't fuck you baby, I make love to you, sweet, sweet love. I make your body tremble as I pull every orgasm from your body that I can, and I intend on making you beg, scream and plead for each and every one of them in the future, but not yet, right now you get to come when you want. But when you're healed, be ready because baby I promise that you will be a trembling messy pile of shaking limbs when I finally let the beast lose on you." He whispered in my ear making my pulse race and my mind go a mile a second with desire at what he was saying. Damn it if I didn't want whatever he wanted to do or give to me.

"Travis please" I begged again.

He grinned against my mouth as he kissed me, slipping his tongue in and tasting every inch of my mouth fighting with my tongue as he slowly pushed his cock into me and started to in his words 'make love' to me. Every thrust sent me closer to orgasm as his fingers still caressed my clit with his other hand pinning my hands down to the mattress. I felt my body tense as my legs started the tell-tale sign of impending orgasm with their trembling.

"Let it go baby, come with me" Travis raspily groaned.

And with those few words my body let go as a powerful orgasm ripped through my body, my legs shaking, back arching as my pussy pulsated in orgasmic bliss around Travis thick shaft as he came undone with me, filling me with his seed. He slumped next to me, releasing my hands from his grip as we both caught our breaths.

"That was too fucking quick for me" Travis puffed out.

"Oh" I felt and sounded hurt, self-conscious, was it quick because he wanted it over with? Did I repulse him?

"Baby, stop with that negative thinking. It was quick because you felt to damn good, fuck you are amazing so stop doubting yourself" He pecked me on my lips before standing up and heading into the bathroom. Was I really that good that I made him come so fast? That was what he said? Wasn't it? If that's true, then hell I am a sex goddess. Travis came back with a warm wet cloth and cleaned me up gently before pulling the covers up over me and throwing the cloth into the pile of washing on the floor.

"I'll sort that out in the morning, right now I want to cuddle up with my girl and watch a film and sleep".

"I like the sound of that" I yawned as I snuggled up against Travis resting my head on his bare chest. He pressed play on the film after spending a few minutes finding it on whatever viewing platform he was using. We watched the first film, but I must have drifted off to sleep before the second began. Before I knew it, it was morning and the sun was streaming in through the windows, guess we forgot to close the curtains last night then.

CHAPTER 24

TRAVIS

It was finally Tiff's birthday. The guys and I spent most of yesterday planning a party for her, obviously we had to involve Wesley as we needed to make sure that Tiff was still protected during her party. It was agreed that five officers would be placed around the house to watch over her. They would blend in by saying they knew us from college or school. Tiff slept most of yesterday meaning that we got most of it sorted and the party would be a complete surprise for her, as long as I could keep her in the bedroom today that is. I had a feeling that wouldn't be a problem though. Today didn't feel as hard to cope with as the past few years had. Yes, it was the anniversary of me seeing Tiff's mum die, but something had changed in me and today didn't seem so bleak anymore. I knew I'd have to take Tiff to the alley and lay flowers down like I had done ever since that fateful day, maybe even take Tiff to the cemetery to place flowers down at her mum's grave. Some fresh air might do her some good. Tiff started to stir in my arms and her eyes fluttered open.

"Morning firefly"

"Morning hotshot"

"Cuppa?" I asked her as she stretched her arms above her head.

"Yes please"

I stood up and made my way towards the door before turning back to face her as she stood up from her side of the bed.

"Happy birthday beautiful"

"Thank you, sexy. Can we go see my mum later please?" She looked at me with sadness in her eyes.

"After breakfast we will go, now, go shower while I cook us something to eat".

"Yes sir" she winked at me as she threw her t-shirt at me running naked into the En suite. The little tease.

I set about cooking a full English breakfast for the four of us.

"Morning bro" Clint walked in flipping the switch on the kettle and getting the mugs out of the cupboard.

"Morning shithead" I smiled at him.

"Holy shit, did I hear Travis call you shit head?" Amber asked with a chuckle as she sat at the dining table.

"Yes, you did, holy shit babe, I think we have our Travis back" Clint grinned so wide I actually thought his cheeks would split open.

"Fuck you, arsehole" I shoved him playfully while I placed the bacon on a plate before grabbing the eggs.

"Good to see your back Trav, we all missed you" Amber smiled at me.

"Yeah, I kind of miss being me as well, guess I lost myself for a while" I admitted to the two people in my life who always had my back no matter what happened.

"Something smells good," Tiff said as she sat next to Amber at the table. She seemed to be in less pain today and had more colour to her cheeks.

"Yeah, Travis having a shower does make a difference" Clint smirked and ducked as I threw a tea towel at him.

"Fucker, I always smell good, don't I?" I winked at Tiff.

"Well...... you did smell a bit ripe back at the hospital" she giggled. I rounded the counter and stalked towards her before grabbing her and lifting her from her seat squealing as I spun her around.

"I like being all dirty with you firefly" I whispered in her ear as she slapped me playfully on the chest as I set her back down on her seat and went back to cooking breakfast.

"Eat up guys before it's cold" I slid four plates onto the table after dishing out the eggs and beans.

"Trav, I have missed your cooking skills so much, please say you will cook again soon" Amber practically drooled over her plate.

"Hey, I cook" Clint grumbled making us all laugh.

"Hmmm, yeah you cook if it's microwaved or takeaway" Amber laughed at him.

"It's still cooking" Clint argued.

"Nothing tastes as good as home cooked food" Amber looked at us all and we all nodded in agreement.

"So, what have you got planned today Trav?" Clint asked me.

"Taking Tiff up to see her mum and then grab some lunch at the diner. Are you guys all busy today?" I winked at them hoping Tiff didn't see me.

"Yeah, I got to talk to the new caterer at the bar as we are thinking of trying some pub grub next week and Clint has to make a run to collect some banners for a fun night I have planned for when we get back from our holiday" nice cover Amber.

After we had all finished eating, I loaded up the dirty dishes into the dishwasher while tiff went to dry and brush her hair. She looked so cute sitting at the table with her hair wrapped in a towel on top of her head.

"Catch you later Trav" Amber shouted from the hallway as she and Clint made their way out the door.

"Wait up, text Mitch and invite him and Cole over tonight will you" I asked them.

"Are you sure about that Trav?" Clint asked me, the confusion clear on his face.

"Yeah, let them see that Tiff is safe and happy with me, it might make Cole back off a bit and anything that makes Tiff happy is good for me" I answered with a shrug.

"Damn, where has this Trav been hiding all these years" Amber chuckled.

"it was a bloody long game of hide and seek that's for sure" Clint laughed as he pulled Amber back towards the door

"Later's" I yelled after them.

"They, gone already?" Tiff asked as she stepped up next to me while I wiped the countertop down.

"Yeah, but we will see them later. You ready to go?"

"Ready as I'll ever be. Do we have security with us today?"

"Wes said that someone will follow us from a safe distance, but we won't know they are there and to act normal".

"Sounds good"

"Let's go then" I grabbed my keys from the side and dragged Tiff out to the truck I was borrowing from Clint as my car was staying at the garage for the time being to make it look like it had broken down to cover why Clint was picking me up or I was using his truck and staying at his most nights. We stopped at a flower shop on the way towards the theatre that was not far from where Tiff's mum had died.

"Travis, I have your flowers ready. Who is this beauty?"

"Mavis, this is my girlfriend, Tiffany. Can you give me two more bunches really quick please for her mum?"

"Of course, just give me five minutes. Pop next door to the café I'm sure Doris would love to see you again" Mavis answered. She was in her late forties and short with a bubbly attitude. The first time I met her I broke down; it was a few days after the stabbing, and I wanted to show my respects so popped in here to get flowers to place against the wall. Mavis had pulled me into her back room and made me sit down while she pottered around making me tea and pulling a bouquet of flowers together for me. Doris is her sister and runs the café next door, both are very jolly people and always smiling. I try to pop in and say hi every few weeks as these women helped me a lot during the first few months. They are sort of a mother figure to me now.

"Doris here today, is she?"

"Everyday boy and you know it" Mavis clipped my ear as she shooed me away.

"Go say hi and I'll bring these flowers round once I'm done. When I get there, we can have a slice of cake and you can tell me all about this beautiful young lady you've kept hidden from us" She smiled warmly at me.

"Can you do another smaller one for my dad please?" Tiff asked Mavis a hint of sadness in her voice. Shit why had I not realised that maybe she wanted to stop by her dad's grave as well.

"Of course, dear, now you go with Travis and meet Doris, I'll be round in a few" Mavis smiled at Tiff and pushed us to the door. I took Tiff's hand and led her into the café next door, the bell ringing above the door as we walked in. Small round chairs with tables sat dotted around the room. The café had a very shabby chic feel to it with its mismatched furniture and dressers along the walls.

"Travis? Is it really you?" Doris walked towards us, a hand over her heart while the other was over her eyes like she was trying to see better. Typical Doris is always over acting.

"Hey Doris, how are you doing?"

"Better for seeing you boy. And who do we have here?" she looked down at my hand entwined with Tiff's.

"This is Tiff my girlfriend" I said proudly.

"Hello dear, I'm Doris and I run this fine establishment. I hope Travis has been treating you well" Doris did an exaggerated bow before showing us to a table for four.

"He has, thank you," Tiff shyly answered. Guess she isn't used to dealing with people like Doris and Mavis.

"That's good to hear. Tea, coffee, chocolate? What am I saying a girl like you is definitely a chocolate with cream and marshmallows girl. Am I right?"

"That is perfect," Tiff replied. What is it with girls and chocolate?

We spent a couple hours with Mavis and Doris in the café and as time went on Tiff started to relax more and laughed along with them when they made me the butt of their jokes. I didn't mind though I loved seeing Tiff smile and laugh so carefree without her usual scowl or sass.

"Well, it's been nice seeing you both again, but we have places to be" I stood up helping Tiff from her chair.

"Don't leave it so long next time Trav, and bring this young lady again, she is good for you" Mavis hugged me before Doris pulled her away.

"Give the boy some air Mavis, but yes boy don't leave it so long and look after Tiffany she is a gem".

"I will do Doris, I promise" I hugged her back before taking Tiff's hand and picking up the flowers in the other with Tiff grabbing a couple bouquets as well.

It took us another five minutes to reach the alley way that Tiff's mum had been stabbed in. I helped Tiff down from the car, tears already swimming in her eyes.

"Where were you standing when it happened?" She asked me. I swallowed the lump in my throat and pointed to the alley on the other side of the street.

"There, I was taking a shortcut back from a club. I tried to save her Tiff, I really tried but it was too late there was nothing I could do for her" Tears slipped past my eyelids as I closed them tight, willing myself not to break down here.

"Trav, it wasn't your fault, if anyone is to blame it's my dad" her hand caressed my cheeks as she wiped the tears away.

"We will sort it all out, I promise you. I will protect you Tiff" I bent my head down and kissed the top of her head pulling her in close to hold her tightly. Once I'd gathered myself together again, I pulled back and handed Tiff her flowers to place down. We both stepped up to the wall and laid our flowers against it. Taking a step back I whispered "I'm sorry" as I had done every year since she died.

I heard Tiff whisper, "I love you" Before she pushed her body into my side wrapping her arms around me.

"Let's go see your mum, shall we?" I hugged her close as I spun us around and headed back to the truck. We drove in silence to the cemetery. I parked up in the car park and took a deep breath, I hadn't been here since the funeral and even then, I stood back behind a tree leaving before anyone could see me, especially Tiff's dad. I remembered now seeing a teenage girl standing next to the man I did save that night; she was clinging onto his arm as she cried. Her black coat was too big for her, hanging from her skinny frame with the hood pulled up covering her face from view.

"Trav, you, ok?" Tiff shook my arm bringing me back from my memories.

"Yeah, just lost in thought. You wore a big black coat with the hood up" I looked at her as she looked back at me, tears once again swimming in her eyes as she nodded her head.

"Yeah, I wanted to hide away, I hated everyone back then and that sort of started me down the sassy pathway."

"I hated everyone too after that, I felt like everyone knew and blamed me" I answered her honestly.

"You were never to blame Trav".

"I know that now. Let's go put these flowers down and then find your dad, shall we?"

"Dad is with mum" Tiff replied as she opened her door. Well, that makes things a bit easier.

We walked down the winding path past the small forest part of the cemetery before Tiff headed off across the grass past several gravestones stopping at the angel statue.

"Hey mum, it's my birthday again. I'm 18 now all grown up and shit. Sorry, I shouldn't swear. I got my A levels just like I said I would and now I work in a garage fixing cars just like gramps and you did. I miss you so much mum" Tears poured down Tiff's face as she fell to her knees, I quickly wrapped my arms around her waist to stop her falling too hard as she shook with sobs pulling at my own heart as tears slipped down my cheeks.

"Mum, this is travis.... he tried to save you, but it was too late. I met him at work, and we hit it off. He didn't know you were my mum then though. I hope you like him" More sobs sent Tiff's body shaking again.

"I promise to always look after your daughter and protect her with my life Mrs McGovern" I said, making Tiff giggle through her sobs.

"Dad, I know what you did, I will find out everything. I don't hate you and I'm not angry. I'm just disappointed in you. You were supposed to look after me and protect me but instead you gambled me away literally. I know you tried to hide me away and that didn't work but you failed at protecting, at doing your job as a father. I miss you too dad" More sobs shaking her body as she buried her head in my chest, her hands fisting my jacket. I held her close, stroking her back as she cried into my chest. We sat there silently for a while as Tiff let all her emotions out before sitting back and wiping her face with her sleeve.

"I love and miss you both. I'm safe and loved now by my new family. They love and care for me just how I know you'd want me to be loved and cared for. Clint, Brad and Chance are like big brothers and Amber, mum you'd love her with her pink hair and excited eyes, she is like the sister I always moaned at wanting. Travis is my boyfriend and I know these guys love me and care for me more than anything so please don't worry about me. I love you guys to the moon and back times a million" Tiff sniffled and smiled as she stood up.

"Later's alligators" She laughed as she waved at the angel headstone. I stood up next to her.

"I promise we will look after your daughter" I grabbed Tiff's hand and walked with her back to the truck. That was extremely emotional, and I could tell it had taken it out of Tiff, she looked tired and drained. She can sleep this afternoon after lunch while we set up for the party.

Pulling up outside the diner I was relieved to not see Claire's car parked outside. At least we could eat in peace. I held Tiff's hand again as we walked into the burger joint slash diner. And Brad practically bounced on us.

"Hey birthday girl, what are you having? It's on me today"

"Brad dude, back off, give the girl some space" I pushed Brad back a bit while Tiff laughed.

"I'll have chocolate milkshake, pig belly buster bacon double cheese melt burger with dirty fries please" Tiff told him as my eyes went as wide as Brad's at her order. The pig belly buster bacon double cheese melt burger was huge, two burgers wrapped in bacon with cheddar cheese, Monterey jack cheese and a creamy cheese sauce layered throughout with onions, pickles and salad was the biggest burger the place sold.

"Are you hungry?" I asked her.

"Starving, all this exercise you have me doing in the bedroom builds up an appetite you know" She winked at me while Brad chuckled, and I laughed a full-on belly laugh.

"Coming right up, birthday girl, same for you Trav?"

"Yeah, why not"

We took a seat at one of the booths sitting opposite each other.

"Thanks for today Trav"

"Anytime Firefly"

We ate our meal in peace and then Brad brought over more milkshakes with chocolate cake.

"Can't have a birthday without cake, right?" Brad placed the cake and shakes on the table.

"I love cake," Tiff grinned. I loved her and seeing her so happy. But as the door swung open, I knew that bubble of happiness was about to pop.

"You, you bitch. Why are you still hanging around like a bad smell with my man?" Claire screeched. Ok I've had enough of this shit now. I stood up, arms crossed over my chest as I stared down at Claire.

"One, Tiff is not a bitch, two who the fuck do you think you are screaming at my girl, three I AM NOT AND WILL NEVER BE YOUR MAN NOR HAVE I EVER BEEN YOURS"

Claire stepped back and the look of shock on her face was priceless. Brad chuckled while Tiff held her hand over her mouth to stifle her giggles.

"Trav baby, you know we could be good together, you and me against the world. Think of how cute our babies would be".

"Please someone throw me a sick bucket" Tiff snorted.

"Claire honey, look I know this is really hard for you to understand but Travis doesn't like you" Tiff said in a patronising motherly way almost like Claire was a little kid.

"Only because you have turned him against me with some voodoo shit" Claire huffed at Tiff.

"Voodoo shit? Oh my god you really need to grow the fuck up honey and see what is clearly in front of you. Let me say it again for you. TRAVIS IS MINE NOT YOURS SO FUCK OFF" I watched as Tiff told Claire I was hers and felt that love bubble in my chest again. I am in love, no question about it. I love this girl, I fucking love this girl.

"Claire, I think it's best you leave" Brad grabbed Claire's arm and walked her back to the door.

"Don't worry Brad, we are leaving now anyway thanks for the burger and cake though" Tiff stood up and I watched as her face paled slightly and her hand went to her side. Quick as anything I dashed to her side to hide her pain from everyone else as I helped her walk back to the truck. Of course, Claire had to try and get the last word in as we left.

"I'm coming for you bitch".

"I'll be waiting," Tiff replied calmly.

I drove us back to Clint's. Tiff fell asleep in the car after taking some of her pain tablets. I carefully lifted her from her seat and carried her into our bedroom. Amber opened the doors for me as I walked past.

"Tough morning?" She asked as I stepped into the kitchen after tucking Tiff into bed.

"Emotional morning after seeing Mavis and Doris, she broke down at the cemetery. Broke my heart seeing her so upset and broken" I took the coffee Amber handed me as she sat down at the table opposite me.

"It will get easier for both of you over time. You have each other now and I can see that it's made it easier on you this time round".

"Yeah, I finally allowed myself to believe it's not my fault".

"About bloody time Trav."

"Claire showed up at the diner, kicking off at Tiff again. We need to watch her, she threatened Tiff as we left, and she had pure evil in her eyes".

"When will that girl learn and accept that you aren't interested in her?"

"Maybe we should set her up with Cole as they both seemed upset about me and Tiff being together" I joked but Amber's eyes sparkled with a plan.

"Amber whatever you're thinking, don't" I warned pointlessly because once Amber has an idea it is pointless trying to stop her.

"What time is everyone getting here?" I asked her in the hopes distracting her plan will make her forget about it.

"Around seven and Clint is picking the cake up now. Brad is picking Chance up and they will sleep in the guest room tonight. The car is loaded already for the morning, I packed Tiff's bag and noticed yours was already done".

"Yeah, I couldn't sleep last night so I packed my bag ready. We so need this holiday".

"We do. Clint sent that recording of to a local radio station by the way".

"What? Why?" I was shocked, Clint had never done this before.

"He said it was too spectacular to not share." Amber stood up and held out a pack of balloons to me. Guess I'm helping with the decorations then.

CHAPTER 25

TIFF

I knew today would be an emotional roller coaster for me but having Travis by my side helped me more than I think he will ever know. Mavis and Doris were amazing people and so cheerful. They loved Travis as a son and the relationship they had with each other was so heart-warmingly lovely. It was nice seeing Travis given so much love and attention as well as the ribbing and joking they did with him. The love and care that poured out of him at the cemetery helped me so much with dealing with all my emotions. I meant it when I told my dad that I was disappointed but not angry, and how could I ever hate my dad? Yes, he gambled me away, but he did try to hide me at one point. He was foolish and desperate, and he loved me in his own way. True, my opinion may well change as we learn more about who is after me and the real reason why. But for now, I stand by my words.

Brad made me laugh and again feel loved by a brother when we arrived at the burger joint or diner as Travis calls it. The look on both their faces when I ordered my food, I wish I had taken a picture as it was awesome. And then Claire walked in and ruined it with her screechy voice shouting about Travis being hers. I think we both made it very clear that she has never and will never be with Travis's though. Voodoo shit ha what planet or time zone is she living in? Her final words though and the evil look in her eyes told me that she is far from done with trying to destroy me and get Travis. Why do girls think that if you get rid of the girl that the guy will fall into your arms? Dumb asses, no guy who truly loves someone will fall into the arms of the girl who caused trouble, end of story.

"Hey you awake?" Travis's soft whisper sounded in my ear as his fingers gently stroked my hair back from my face.

"I am now" I giggled as I rolled on to my back and looked up at him. He was lying on his side propped up on his elbow, his hair tied back in a man bun on top of his head.

"You need to get cleaned up and dressed. We have guests. Brad and Chance will be here soon, and Frank will be popping in later as well."

"I need to pack as well" I stretched my arms above my head as I went to sit up.

"Amber packed for you already" Travis stroked a hand down my arm.

"Oh, ok then I guess I just need to get cleaned up and come find you guys in the living room then".

"Hurry up" Travis winked as he stood up from the bed and made his way back into the living room closing the door behind him. I quickly washed my face and put some clean jeans on with a pale blue jumper as my clothes from earlier had dirt on the knees from the cemetery. All refreshed and clean, I stepped out into the living room to see Clint, Brad, Chance, Cole, Mitch, Frank and Amber standing in front of me with a big banner stretched above them reading Happy Birthday and Travis standing next to me with a big smile on his face.

"Happy birthday" They all shouted together.

"You guys" I smiled as they all came in for a group hug. I admit I was surprised to see Cole among them and not fighting with Travis. I smiled at them all as we all pulled back from the hug.

"Thought you'd like a party for your eighteenth birthday, you know with it being a big one" Amber giggled at me.

"It's great, thank you. It's actually the first party I've ever had".

"Really? Please tell me you went to parties though" Chance asked a look of shock on his face.

"Nope never"

"Not even the college parties?" Brad added.

"I got invited to a couple but never went".

"That's sad. Why not?" Chance asked.

"Because she was a nerd, you, dickwad" Mitch elbowed Chance as he answered him.

"Hey, I find that offensive" I retorted with a small smile.

"Nerd" Mitch laughed.

"I hope you don't mind but we sort of invited a few friends along as Clint has a big announcement to make as well" Amber told me as the doorbell rang.

"No, that's fine by me, but what announcement?"

"You'll see or should I say here" Amber shouted back as she hurried to answer the door.

"Hey, TJ, I'm sorry for being a complete dick towards you and Trav. I can see how happy he makes you, so I'll back off. But if he ever hurts you, I will kill him" Cole told me as he looked at his shoes.

"He makes me happier than I've ever been Cole. And I'm glad you are backing off, but you will always be my friend" I patted his shoulder while Travis held his hand out to him. Cole took Travis's hand and shook it with a genuine smile. Thank God that little feud is over with.

The party got into full swing, everyone was laughing and talking, and a few people I'd never met before introduced themselves to me. A few girls told me I was a lucky bitch snapping Travis up. A few warned me to watch Claire but all in all everyone was friendly and welcomed me with open arms and smiles. I felt so lucky to have found a new family of friends to call my own. I always thought I was destined too always be alone. Frank's words about fate and soul mates came back to my mind as I looked across the room to Travis. Our eyes met and I couldn't help the smile that spread across my face. Yeah, I believe in it now as well and Travis is my soulmate.

"Guys can I have your attention please" Clint shouted making everyone go quiet and look at him.

"Today is a special day for two reasons. Firstly, it's Tiff's birthday, come here sis and show us where you are" I stepped up to stand next to Clint.

"When I first met Tiff, I knew she would hold a special place in my heart, but she captured all our hearts, especially our Travis. She has brought him back from the dark pit of despair he was drowning in. This girl is family from now until forever. Happy birthday Tiff my baby sister" Clint raised his glass and everyone else copied as they all shouted happy birthday to me making me blush.

"Turn on that radio Brad" Clint shouted.

"Radio?" Brad asked.

"Yes radio" Amber told him as she switched it on

"Secondly tonight we made the radio station playlist with a new song. Meet our new vocalist Tiff".

Just as Clint finished his speech Amber turned the radio up and we heard the broadcaster's words.

"Up next, we have a new song from a local band, this song will give you chills in a good way, the vocalist's voice is both haunting and beautiful. Here it is 'stronger than before' from the band Bloodlines" Then the music started, and I heard my voice come from the speakers playing the radio station. My heart rate increased as I listened to my song on the radio, holy shit my song was playing on the radio. The room was dead silent as everyone listened, I felt panic rise up inside me, they hated it. I felt so exposed and vulnerable right now. Why did Clint do this? Why didn't he warn me? Did Travis know? I needed to get out of here. I looked around the room and everyone was looking towards the radio like I was standing there, taking this opportunity I quickly ran out the back door into the garden and straight into Claire.

"There you are, I was looking all over for you. Listen before you start, I've done some thinking and I actually like Cole now so you can have Travis. Maybe we can be friends. I'm sorry if I was a bitch before" well I wasn't expecting that.

"Yeah, fine by me" I hurriedly replied wanting to get away from anyone and everyone right now. I needed space and to be on my own.

"T.J? You, ok?" Cole asked as he grabbed my arm.

"Yeah, no, I don't know" I suddenly felt hot and dizzy as a sharp scratchy feeling hit my neck. I turned to see Claire standing behind me with a syringe in her hand smiling.

"Now Cole before daddy gets mad at me" what the fuck is going on? Did she just drug me? Why was Cole helping her? The last thing I saw before everything went black was Cole picking me up and whispering "I'm sorry, I had no choice".

When I finally opened my eyes again, I was lying on a soft mattress, my head pounding with the worst headache I had ever had. I tried to move my hands so I could sit up only to find them tied together. Fuck what the hell is going on? Why would Claire and Cole do this to me? Well ok Claire I could totally see doing this as she is a crazy girl, but Cole?

"I see you are finally awake" A rough male voice sounded on my left. I turned to see where the voice was coming from. My eyes fell on a tall middle-aged man with dark probably dyed hair slicked back, he was clean shaven with dark eyes. He wore an expensive looking black suit and shiny shoes. He pushed himself from the wall and walked over to the bed before sitting down next to me.

"We haven't met before but I'm Henry your husband to be" what? Husband? I don't think so.

"You're crazy" I rasped at him, my throat dry and sore.

"No, you were promised to me in payment of a debt, your dad's debt to be precise" he raised his hand and went to brush my hair back over my shoulder, but I flinched away from him making him stop and sigh.

"I won't hurt you little one, in fact I will cherish you and take care of you".

"You call, drugging, kidnapping and tying me up taking care of me?" I snapped.

"That was all necessary as you wouldn't have come on your own accord, my daughter did try to warn you against being with Travis".

"Wait, daughter? As in Claire?"

"Well stepdaughter to be more correct, shame her mum died so soon after we married leaving me to bring up the spoilt brat. But she has her uses though, now back to you; you were supposed to be pure still when you came to me but obviously Travis took that from what I've heard. No matter though as I have the rest of our lives with you. Unfortunately, you will remain locked in this room until you accept your fate and agree to marry me. I will however undo the binds tying your hands together. There are clean clothes in the closet, and you have an En-suite with everything you should need in it. the maid will be up soon with some food for you, and I will be back shortly for bedtime".

"You are not sleeping with me, no way, not happening Mr. I will never accept you not now, not ever, now let me go" I struggled against the rope wrapped around my wrists.

"Stop this foolishness, you will accept me eventually and yes I will sleep with you, you are my betrothed" he stood up and walked towards the door. "As you still seem defiant, I will leave you bound for now. Maybe with some thinking time you will calm down and accept your fate" he slammed the door behind him, and I heard a lock click. Fuck my life!

How did they manage to get me out of the house without the security we had noticing? Is Travis looking for me? Will I get away from here? What part did Cole play in all this? I can't believe he would willingly help kidnap me for some sick pervert when he kicked off about me being with Travis like he did. I need to think, how can I get out of here? And without giving in to creepy Henry? My heart belongs to Travis, and I will never give it to another, especially some guy old enough to be my grandad. After what felt like hours the door opened and a young girl came in carrying a tray.

"Master said to make sure you eat the soup, but I have to feed you as your hands must remain tied. Please I beg you don't cause me any bother; master doesn't like it when we don't obey him" The fear was very clear in her eyes and as she rubbed her arm her sleeve rode up and bruising was evident on her arms. I knew I couldn't cause this girl any problems and would have to allow her to feed me to avoid her being hurt in any way.

"I'm Tiff, and your name is?"

"Maisie Miss"

"Maisie, call me Tiff, look I don't want to be here anymore than you do, I'll help you if you help me".

"I'll try Miss, but you need to be careful, eyes and ears everywhere" She looked at the door and whispered. I nodded my head in understanding.

"I'll eat the soup" I said loud enough for anyone listening to hear.

"Thank you, Miss," Maisie copied my loudness.

"Can you get a message to a man called Frank if I give you a number and an address?" I whispered so quietly I wasn't sure she would hear me.

"Here" Maisie slipped a phone into my hands in a way that I could type a number out quickly with my hands still bound.

Maisie quickly pocketed the phone and smiled at me as she spoon fed me the soup, as the bowl got emptier, I felt more and more tired, my eyes growing heavier. Did they drug my soup?

"I'm sorry Miss, I didn't know they would drug it" Maisie whispered in my ear as she carefully laid me back down and the world turned black again. Hopefully she would help me and get a message to Frank somehow. I knew asking her to get to Travis or the guys or even the police would be pointless as the guys and Travis would charge in without a plan and the police couldn't be trusted if me getting stabbed in the station and getting kidnapped while under their protection was anything to go by. Frank was my only hope of being rescued now. I miss Travis, I hope he is looking for me and hasn't given up on me already.

CHAPTER 26
TRAVIS

Looking around the room at everyone staring wide eyed at the radio as Tiff's voice filled the room, I couldn't help but feel proud of her. One last glance around and I lifted my head to look for Tiff stood at Clint's side, but she wasn't there, where was she? I quickly walked over to Clint grabbing his attention.

"Where did Tiff go?"

"She was just here a second ago" Clint looked around and then looked at me with worry in his eyes.

"Fuck, I should've known this might be too overwhelming for her" I ran my hands over my face as I tried to think. Garden, yes, she might have run outside. Clint was hot on my heels as we both ran out into the back garden only to find it empty, or almost, something shining in the grass from the light of a lantern caught my attention. I bent down to pick it up, a syringe? A fucking syringe. why? Who? Shit Tiff.

"Clint, I think someone took her" I showed him the syringe and watched his face pale.

"Shit, but how with all the police here?" He looked around and then my eye caught on someone who shouldn't be here. Claire and she was with the officer that Tiff said made her feel uncomfortable. Two people who shouldn't be here, and why were they here?

"Where is Wesley? Call him God damn it" I shouted at Clint as he pulled his phone from his pocket. Amber stepped out of the back door looking at our panicked faces.

"What's happened? Where is Tiff?" she asked as Clint held up the syringe and Amber turned back into the house shouting at everyone to remain in the house until further notice. Clever girl, she probably locked all the doors and windows as well knowing her. Wesley ran outside to us followed by two other men.

"Clint, Travis what's happened?"

"Tiff is missing, and Travis found this" Clint held up the syringe. Wes took it and handed it to one of the men behind him.

"Get it to the lab for testing, make it a priority" He ordered. "Have either of you seen anyone suspicious?"

"Yeah, that officer from the hospital was just inside the door with Claire" I answered as I gestured towards the door and Clint ran off towards it shouting that he would kill them if they hurt his new sister. Couldn't say I'd stop him either, hell if they had anything to do with Tiff's disappearance, I'd help him kill them. It didn't take long before I heard Claire screaming profanities at Clint.

"Guess I better go question our first suspect then" Wesley sighed running a hand through his hair.

"Mind if I watch? I know the bitch and will be able to tell if she is lying".

"Why not? It's your girlfriend that's missing after all".

I followed Wesley into the house and then we followed Clint who was pushing Claire into a side room in the hallway that was used as an office for Amber to do her paperwork for the pub.

"Sit" Clint ordered as he roughly shoved Claire into a chair.

"Why are you doing this?" She screamed at him.

"Where is Tiff?" Clint growled in her face.

"Tiff? Oh, you mean the bitch who stole Trav from me? How should I know?"

"Bitch please, how many times do I have to tell you I never have and never will be yours, now where is she?" I shouted at her; Wesley placed an arm in front of me stopping me from approaching Claire.

"Claire, if you know anything now would be the time to tell us." He spoke calmly to her as he sat in a chair opposite her his elbows resting on his knees as he leaned forward, his fist clenched together tightly in front of him.

"How should I know? Last time I saw her she was hanging off Clint like the whore she is. Trav baby you would be so much better off with me" She fluttered her eyes at me. Wesley turned a fraction to look at me.

"She's lying, she knows something" Claire always had a twitch in her eye and wrinkled her nose up slightly whenever she lied, something I picked up on in high school when she lied about homework or who she was with to her friends and teachers.

"I'll ask one more time before we head to the station with you under arrest. Where is Tiffany?" Wesley stared down at Claire as he stood back up and walked behind her chair gripping the back of it tightly tipping it slightly back making Claire look up at his face. She paled and stuttered.

"You're too late, you will never find her. He will have her hidden by now".

Anger boiled inside me as I gripped my fists tighter.

"Where did you take her? What did you inject into her? And who helped you?"

"Cole helped; I don't know what was in the syringe just that daddy said it would make her sleep".

"Daddy? You mean your fucking stepdad?" I interrupted her.

"He promised me I could have you once Tiff was out of the picture, he said you would finally see me and want me" Claire whimpered as Wesley let go of the chair sending it forcefully back to sit on all four legs causing Claire to tumble from it onto the floor in a heap.

"Amber, find Cole" Clint shouted out the door before turning to look at Claire.

"Your stepdad, he is the big gang boss? Henry Monroe?"

"Yes" she whimpered, crawling along the floor backing herself into a corner.

"Fuck, it's going to be impossible to find her, he's like some big hotshot CEO with multiple business and properties all over the country not just the town" I ripped my hair from the neat man bun it was in and tugged at it hard. Tiff was gone, I promised to keep her safe and I failed, I'm useless no one is safe around me.

"Travis, we will find her, it's only been an hour since we last saw her, he can't have gone far" Wesley tried to calm me down, but Tiff was gone I failed, anger coursed through my veins at myself for letting her down and at Claire for helping her get kidnapped.

"What does Henry want with her?" Clint asked.

"She was promised to him by her dad as a debt payment, Henry saw her years ago and decided he needed her for a true heir" Claire sobbed.

"A true heir, as in he wants her to carry his kid?" Wesley asked, his eyes wide with shock while my blood just boiled and boiled. If he laid a finger on my Tiff, I'd end him.

"I told him I could do it, but he said I wasn't made of the right stuff, that bitch gets every man wanting her and she is nothing special. A whore is all she will ever be, a breeding machine for the rich. Daddy said once she has given him his heir, he will sell her off to others for breeding" Claire sneered her face full of anger and hatred.

"Breed, she isn't a fucking animal" Clint roared as he paced the floor. The door slammed open, and Cole was thrown to the floor by a very angry looking Mitch.

"You are no brother of mine, no brother of mine would do what you did. How could you? I hope you rot in a cell for what you did. She didn't deserve that just because you couldn't have her" Mitch seethed at his brother who lay bloodied on the floor.

"What did he do?" I asked Mitch as Wesley cuffed Cole before he had a chance to strike out at any of us.

"He fucking helped that spoilt bitch take Tiff, he fucking helped them" Mitch broke down in front of us tears flowing freely from his eyes as his body shuddered and he fell to his knees.

"You better start talking Cole," Clint warned him.

"I had no choice, I owed Henry for some drugs that went missing that I was meant to be dealing. He said it was her life or mine".

"So, you chose hers? And drugs? What the fuck Cole, you said you had stopped all that stuff. You promised mum you would stay clean and on the right side of the law" Mitch questioned.

"I fucking know what I promised, but Henry wouldn't let me leave, once in the only way out is in a body bag. I owed him and he promised that if I got him Tiff then I could have the debt wiped clean and walk away with no consequence".

Without thinking my fist swung round and connected with Cole's face, the crunch of bone and the splatter of blood was satisfying but not enough, anger was beyond me now, I was a burning inferno of pure rage.

"Where did you take her?" Wesley asked as he pulled Cole back up to sit on a chair.

"He had a car waiting out front for us, he knew that once the song played, she would run either out the back or the front, he ordered us to wait in the garden and inject her if she went out there, if she went out the front then his men would grab her instead".

"Wait, the song? He knew about that. How? And how did he know how she would react?" Mitch asked again.

"He owns the radio station, and as soon as Clint dropped it off the D.J rang him as they needed his permission to play anything that doesn't make him money. Henry listened to it and knew from the words and her past trauma that she would react badly, he arranged to time for it to be played and he knew about the party because Claire was with me when you sent the text out".

Well damn Henry made a good plan, but how did he get past the police officers we had watching?

"How did he get past the police we have here?" I asked hoping that one of them would have an answer.

"Wayne helped us, he scrambled all the police radios and had a false alert sent to them so that they would be watching the wrong area" Cole sighed as Claire screamed at him.

"Shut up, you're telling them too much, daddy will kill you for this betrayal".

"Wayne? As in the guy who was giving Tiff that weird feeling at the hospital?" Clint asked.

"Yeah, he's on Henry's payroll, so are four other men in this house right now".

"Fuck" Wesley shouted as he paced running his hands through his hair.

"Claire, where would he have taken her? Your prison sentence will depend on your cooperation and answers, so I suggest you think long and hard about where he has Tiff right now" Wesley glared at Claire.

"If I tell you, will I stay out of prison?"

"Maybe, highly possible if you give us the information we need right now".

"Will you protect me from Henry? He will kill me".

"We can" Wesley promised.

"Cedar villa, it's a mile off the track out on the cliff edge forest. It's heavily guarded. Daddy has a meeting at Nola Corp early tomorrow morning that he has to attend in person. I'd say go after him then. Tiff is a smart girl and the staff who he will have looking after her don't owe him any loyalty if anything they would help her escape".

"Travis, where are you son?" Frank shouted as he crashed into the now very full room.

"Phone call, she can't talk for long, but she knows where Tiff is" Frank handed me the phone.

"Hello" I spoke as I placed the call on speaker so everyone could hear.

"Umm ..... hi.... Tiff is ok and safe for now, but they drugged her food and she fell asleep. Master is planning on forcing her to marry him tomorrow afternoon and then drugging her to make her sleep with him until she is pregnant with his child. She gave me this number. We are at his penthouse suite above Nola Corp as he has a meeting in the morning. He plans to stay in her room tonight and I fear it won't be good. Be quick" the timid voice spoke quickly on the other end of the phone.

"Try to keep him away from her. We will be there as soon as we can be. Drug him if needs be" Wesley answered as he pulled his phone from his pocket.

"Keep her safe" I begged as she hung up.

"What are we going to do? We can't trust any of the men you have here as they could be under Henry" Mitch asked.

"Do you need trustworthy men? Men not under anyone but themselves? Men who can infiltrate any building and get a job done?" Amber asked from her position leaning against the doorframe.

"Yeah, that's exactly what we need, but we don't have" Wesley answered. Amber gave Clint a look and Clint nodded his head.

"Make the call Babe," he told her.

Amber nodded and left the room.

"Mind telling me what the fuck you two are up to?" I asked Clint.

"Remember a few years ago Amber had that friend with the bikes? Well, he is now in a big bike group ... not a gang. They help people out in situations like this, they are good people trust us" Clint looked between me and Wesley.

"Are you talking about Xander's Mavericks?" Mitch asked.

"Yep, Amber knows most of the crew really well, in fact you all probably know a few of them as they come to the bar a lot" Clint smiled at us.

"I've heard about them, all good stuff as well, and I think it's our only option now" Wesley stuffed his hands into his pockets.

"What do we do with these two in the meantime?" Mitch asked glaring daggers at his brother,

"We keep them in here, locked up with no phones to stop them from informing anyone of our plan or knowledge" Wesley grabbed some zip ties from the desktop and quickly had Claire tied up.

"No, please you can't keep me here like this" She cried out.

"Really? We can't keep you locked up, but you can help daddy dearest to kidnap and keep Tiff prisoner? And rape her? Seriously?" I seethed at her my anger like a volcano about to erupt. If that happened, I doubt anyone would be able to hold me back from showing her and Cole just how much I wished them dead right now. They better hope they get a prison sentence as they would be much safer inside than let loose in the town, I'd make everyday a living hell for them.

"Xander is on his way with some men, I've cleared the rest of the people here to party. Xander's girl knows Tiff and said they will do everything they can to help us" Amber puffed out as she ran back into the room.

Xander and his men turned up twenty minutes later, filling the close with their bikes and a big van. Xander's girl walked in with him, she looked to be the same age as Tiff, her curly blonde hair tied back in a loose ponytail, leathers hugging her thin yet obviously toned body. She looked tiny compared to Xander who stood at over six feet tall and was a wall of pure leather clad muscle, his dark hair cut close to his scalp except for a thick strip that made a short mohawk look on the top of his head.

"Amber, long time no see" Xander pulled Amber into a side hug and ruffled her hair.

"This is Lara, my old lady" He introduced his girl to us. Bet she's happy to be called old lady. I knew from past experience in a bike club that an old lady meant girlfriend or wife, still seemed like an insult to me though.

"Hi, look I know Tiff from the care home, she kept to herself mostly, but she had a rough time of it. She didn't fit the mould so to speak. She's one-of-a-kind, heart of gold yet quiet and solemn. A fighter though and I know she will put up as much of a fight as she can. We are here to help get her back" Lara told us all as we sat around the kitchen table.

We filled the group in on all the information we had and started formulating a plan. We would strike in the morning while Henry is having his meeting. Hopefully Tiff will be safe from Henry for tonight and we can get to her before anything happens to her.

Frank's phone pinged with a text; he quickly showed us the screen.

Master is sleeping on the couch; I added his sleeping pills to his whiskey. I will try to keep him away for as long as I can.

A message from the girl earlier. Frank quickly replied.

Thank you, we will strike in the morning, do you know what time the meeting is? And which floor?

"8am third floor conference room, if you play it right you can destroy all his business in one sweep as it's with all his legitimate partners before he heads off on honeymoon.

Well shit we can take this arsehole down in many ways with that information. Brad, who was sitting with Chance, quickly pulled his laptop from his bag and started tapping away on it.

"Brad, what are you doing?" Clint asked him.

"Gathering intel on all Henry's partners good and bad, the more dirt we have the better".

"I'll help," Chance replied as he went to grab his laptop from the living room.

"Good plan, we can use any info we get against him, I need a suit and a car. Slug .... go grab me a suit and the Range rover from the lockup, time for me to become a fancy business tycoon" Xander chuckled. Some lanky older guy wearing black jeans and a leather jacket with long grey hair tied back nodded at Xander before leaving the house. Guess that was slug then. We talked more for hours before finally having a good solid plan in place.

We had a plan, we just needed to wait a few more hours before putting it into motion.

CHAPTER 27

TIFF

My head felt like it was being beaten by drumsticks from the inside, while my stomach rolled. A warm arm was slung over my waist holding me in place, but it didn't give me the usual feeling of warmth and safety that I normally got when Travis hugged me like this. Memories started to assault my mind, the party, my song, Claire and Cole, the bastard helped Claire drug me and then cart me off to some strange house where some deluded man claimed to be my future husband. I tried to move a hand to rub the sleep from my eyes but both arms came up. Ahh yeah, my hands are tied together still. I slowly opened my eyes to find Henry lying next to me, his arm was the one slung over my waist. I shivered with disgust as my stomach rolled, the bile rising in my throat. I tried to wriggle free from his clasp for two reasons, first being I didn't want this man touching me; the second I needed the bathroom. Though I was supposed to do the latter with my hands tied I was yet to figure it out, although I knew I would figure it out, no way was I asking for help on this matter, especially from this crazed man. I wiggled onto my side and scooted towards the edge of the bed slowly, his arm slowly dropping from my body. I sighed from the relief I felt that he was no longer touching me, but if he always slept this heavy then maybe just maybe I could escape while he sleeps. I swung my legs over the edge of the bed, the blanket falling away as I moved, then I realised with dread that my jeans I was wearing were now missing, how? When? And more importantly who? I moved my hands down and felt for my knickers sighing in relief at the fact that I was in fact still wearing them, albeit they were lacy and didn't cover much, but they covered enough for me to feel a little better about my state of undress. Using my core muscles, I stood up and ran towards the door that Maisie had used yesterday, gripping the handle I pulled only to find it locked. I looked around hoping to find the keys on the bedside table but nothing, shit where are the keys? I spotted a suit jacket slung on the armchair in the far corner. I need to check the pockets, but also my need for the bathroom was getting extreme. Looking at Henry still snoring on the bed I figured I had time to take care of my bladder and then search for the keys. I quickly dashed to the only other door in the room hoping it was a bathroom, thankfully it was. Stark white tiles covered every inch of wall, a shower big enough for a football team sat at the far end with a jet stream tub against the wall, his and hers sinks floated on the wall with the toilet just inside the door. All pristine white and clinical. I quickly took care of business in the bathroom and headed back towards the jacket I had spotted minutes before. Henry was still snoring thankfully. With my hands still bound together I felt the pockets of the jacket before almost crying out when I found a bunch of keys. I fumbled around trying to get the keys out of the pocket without making too much noise, but they fell into my hands as I lifted the jacket up and manoeuvred it around using my teeth. The keys now in my hands I ran across to the door fiddling with the keys one after another, but none fitted.

"Looking for this?" Henry called from the bed, making me jump. I spun around to see him holding up a single key, the key to my freedom.

"Come back to bed Tiffany" he patted the empty space next to him.

"No" I spat at him glaring daggers his way.

"You can come willingly or ......" I grinned as he stood from the bed in only his black silk boxers and started to stalk towards me.

"I will never willingly go anywhere with you much less your bed" I dived to the right as he lunged for me.

"There are many ways to make it seem you are willing my dear, so many things on the black market these days that I can procure, in fact I can use a few pills and liquids for the time being".

"Drugging someone to do what you want is not them being willing".

"Drugging will be a last resort if you do not comply with my needs and orders. You will submit to me and do as I say" Henry gritted his teeth and moved towards me again. I stepped back and then turned to run from him. I'd run around this room all day if it kept his grubby hands off me.

"You can run all you like, in fact I find it a bit of a turn on, however I have no time for childish games this morning. You will let my staff get you ready for our marriage. And you will do so without any arguing, or the consequences will be severe".

"I will never marry you".

"Ohh but you will. One way or another you will marry me today".

"Fuck you"

"Later" He fucking winked at me as he unlocked the door and stepped out into the hallway. I slumped down onto the floor, hitting my head back onto the wall. Think damn it think, there must be a way out of here. I looked around the room, curtains, curtains meaning a window which could mean people walking past. With my hands still firmly tied together I struggled and wobbled as I pushed myself to standing. I gripped the curtain in my hands and pulled hard bringing the rail down, but damn it, it was just a wall behind them, a fucking wall. Where the hell was I? I sat on the edge of the bed tears of frustration and fear rolled down my cheeks. My thoughts were of time with Travis that would never happen now. I imagined us on the beach, in the sea. Maybe getting married mini-Travis and Tiff running round our feet in the park. A future that looks impossible now. I knew that Henry would keep me locked up and most likely drugged up to keep me in line and at his side. The lock in the door clicked and I grabbed the sheet pulling it over my lower body. I sighed as the tension left my body when Maisie stepped into the room carrying a tray. She set it down on the bed next to me and slipped a napkin into my hands motioning with a slight nod for me to open it.

"Morning Miss, Master asked me to bring you breakfast" she said with her head bowed and glancing all around the room.

"It's ok he's not in here" I whispered as I opened the napkin to find a note written on it.

They are coming to rescue you soon.

Was all it read, but it was enough to give me hope.

"Don't smile Miss you will give the game up smiling too much" Maisie whispered as she poured tea from a teapot.

"Master asked me to add these pills to your breakfast routine, they are just vitamins, he said you need to take them to prepare your body for motherhood" Maisie held out a small cup with two tablets inside it, they looked like vitamins, but could I trust what I was told given he drugged my food last night?

"Tell Henry to shove them down his own throat" I pushed the tablets away and picked up the toast, that would be hard to drug right? How can you drug plain toast?

"Master won't be happy" Maisie sighed and rubbed her bruised arms again.

"Well, I'm not happy to be drugged and kept here against my will. I'll eat the toast and drink the tea, but I will not take any medicine that man offers me" I lifted the cup filled with tea and took a mouthful, my dry mouth savoured the fluid like it was a sponge absorbing water. I drank it in no time and held the cup out for a top up. Maisie smiled as she poured me another cup and set the now empty plate on the tray again. As I finished the last of the second cup my arms felt heavy and my mind fogged, I was not in control anymore, I felt numb to everything lost in a daydream.

"Miss, we have to wash you and get you ready for your wedding. I'm sorry. I only hope they get here in time. I drugged Master last night so he wouldn't be able to touch you, but I can't do that again" I heard Maisie, but I had no will or power to reply, it was like my head was detached from my body as she ushered me into the bathroom and turned on the taps to the oversized jet stream bath. I must have passed out or something as the next thing I know I am sat in front of a vanity unit in a fluffy bathrobe Maisie and another girl stood to either side of me with makeup and hair curlers in hand. Maisie whipped her head around to face me as I groaned, my mouth now felt like it was full of cotton wool.

"Miss, you must be thirsty, Sarah can you fetch a glass of water from the bathroom please" the other girl whose name I now knew to be Sarah nodded her head and walked towards the bathroom.

"They are here, they text me just now, not long now Miss" Maisie whispered in my ear as she ran a brush through my hair. Sarah placed the glass of water in my hand and like a fool I took a long gulp and carried on drinking until it was empty, the feeling of numbness spread quickly through me again as my mind became blank and my body heavy. I could hear everything going on around me but couldn't speak or move again. Damn it Sarah must have drugged the water without us knowing.

"Sarah, what have you done?"

"What Master told me to do" Sarah answered, sounding confused.

"I hope you didn't give her too much or Master will not be happy, he wants her compliant not comatose" Maisie snapped back.

"I gave her the dose Master told me to give her. Why are you trying to protect her? She can't help us you know".

"She can help us Sarah, she can help us escape this life of slavery. I want to get out of here and see the world far more than the garden and the high-rise buildings around us, I want to feel the wind in my hair as I watch the sunset on the beach. I want to kick leaves in the autumn as I run in the park, I want to be free, and she can help".

"You're more deluded than Master Maisie" Sarah snorted.

"We best get her ready for the wedding" Maisie sighed as she continued brushing then curling my hair as I sat like a robot watching through blurred vision, my mind foggy. Before I knew it my mind started to clear and I was standing in front of a full-length mirror in a white full ball gown style wedding dress, the corset top was adorned with diamonds glittering in the lights, the waist down billowed out like something a princess would wear, like Cinderella or sleeping beauty. My long black hair was curled and pinned in an intricate way so as to give the illusion of being tied back but yet still fell freely down my back. This look was so not me, not one little bit. I started to try and remove the pins from my hair with what little energy I had, then I saw Sarah behind me and saw the syringe in her hand, I spun round quickly grabbing her wrist firmly in my hand.

"Don't even think about it" I spoke between gritted teeth.

"Miss, Sarah didn't know what she was doing please forgive her" Maisie asked as she took the syringe from Sarah's hand and emptied it onto the carpet at my feet. I released Sarah's hand and faced Maisie.

"Why am I dressed up like my nan's toilet roll cover?" I asked, making both girl's chuckle.

"Master wanted you to look like the child bride full of innocence that he always dreamed you would be. He has also filled the wardrobe with clothes for you" Sarah answered as she gestured at the wardrobe.

"Please tell me it contains jeans and band t-shirts" I asked hopefully.

"No, it's full of dresses, not a single pair of jeans or trousers in site" Maisie answered.

"Fuck my life".

"Here, have a drink, it's a fresh bottle see the lid is still sealed" Sarah offered me the bottled water which I took gratefully from her. I unscrewed the cap and sure enough the seal broke with my twist.

No way could a sealed bottle be drugged right? I drank like I was dying for water on a desert in some far-off country, draining the bottle of all its contents. I swayed slightly as that same numb feeling spread through me again. How in the hell did they drug a sealed bottle? Of course, they had a back-up plan.

"I'm sorry" Sarah smiled at me as I stood staring at her blankly.

CHAPTER 28

TRAVIS

The sun was rising, and everyone was in position around the tall offices of Nola Corp. Xander had run over the plan again before we all left. I hardly recognised him this morning when he stepped into the living room wearing a black Armani suit with gold cufflinks, he even wore a wig to make himself look like he belonged in the business world. The plan should be flawless provided that Maisie's intel was correct. If it was then I would make sure to get her to safety too. Hopefully Tiff was still safe and unharmed.

The plan was that Xander would pose as a potential new business partner offering millions to invest in Nola Corp. Then one of his men, Adam I think he was called, would come into the room and hand Xander a tablet while whispering in his ear. The tablet would contain all of Henry's dodgy dealings and be linked to the projector in the conference room. While Henry would be busy dealing with that fallout, Xander would make his leave and head up to the penthouse with a few of his men posing as cleaning staff. Once in the elevator he would text us with the location of the stairs and we would storm the building and take down anyone who stood in our way without killing or injuring anyone. Xander said he had contacts in the FBI and MI5 that would be very interested in some of the dealings that Henry and a few of his business partners were doing. He had sent out emails with all the information attached but had been informed that no one could get here to join us until the evening. We couldn't wait for them, not if we wanted to save Tiff from a forced marriage and potential rape. We needed to act now. I just wanted to get to Tiff and make sure she was ok. I sat waiting in the shadows for Xander to send out the code word followed by directions, he said he would inform me which elevator to take to the penthouse as he felt that Tiff would need me there. For obvious reasons I couldn't go to the meeting with him or pose as a cleaner, so here I stood, hiding and waiting with my heart racing and my mind going crazy with the possible things that could have already happened to Tiff. Frank stood next to me as the only person capable of holding me back if shit hit the fan. His phone pinged and he showed me the text.

Master has another girl drugging Tiff. Have a doctor on standby as she may be overdosed.

My heart sank; the bastard was drugging my girl by using his maids to do the dirty work. Tiff wasn't stupid though, so it had to be being done carefully, in her food maybe? I would kill the bastard if Frank and Xander allowed it.

"Trav, keep a cool head. Whatever he has done to her he will pay for. Maisie will keep her safe until you get to her, but in order to do that she has to follow Henry's order's" I nodded my head at Frank's words. I knew he was right, but it still didn't stop my mind from overthinking everything.

My phone chirped as a text came in from Xander.

I'm in. Middle elevator from the left side of the lobby

That was all I needed to make my move. I quickly flashed my phone at Frank showing him the message before we both stepped out onto the street and as casually as we could while in a hurry, we walked towards the building holding my girl hostage. Security at the front desk was a bitch and needed some firm advice from a few of the Maverick's in order for us to pass and get into the elevator that would take me to Tiff. As the doors closed, we heard gunfire, shots had been fired. I knew it wasn't any of Xander's men as guns were forbidden, they lived by the rule that a life was never to be taken so guns and knives were never allowed as mistakes happen too easily with weapons. They used skill and stealth instead.

"Trav, keep your head in the game, Tiff needs you" Frank shook my shoulders but as I looked back at him, I saw the fear in his eyes. The gunfire had triggered his memories and PTSD from his days in the marines. He lost friends on his last day serving, a simple job went wrong when they were ambushed while collecting supplies. Frank took a bullet to his chest narrowly missing his heart that day.

"Frank, you with me old man?" I nudged him.

"Yeah, let's get your girl" Frank shook his head and smiled as he punched the button for the penthouse. My girl was only a few seconds away from me now. But what if the gunshots were from upstairs? What if she had been shot? What if we were ambushed as we stepped out of the lift?

"Trav, I can see your mind going overtime, Xander is up there, if there is any trouble, he will take care of it before we get there. Trust him" Frank gripped my shoulder as I nodded at him. I hoped he was right about Xander. I took what felt like forever to reach the penthouse floor and as the doors opened, I was met with fighting, at least four men were trying to hold Xander and Adam back, two more men I didn't recognise lay on the floor unconscious.

"The door is locked, check the pockets for keys" Xander shouted between grunts as he fought with two men. I bent to check the two lying on the floor as Frank jumped in to help Xander and Adam. I stood up empty handed as the door to the fire escape flew open and a few more of Xander's men spilled into the hallway. In just seconds the men had Henry's lackeys tied up with zip ties and sat in a row leaning against the wall.

"Now which one of you fuckers has the key? Xander growled out as I tried kicking the door down.

"None of us, boss, doesn't leave keys with anyone" One guy said as he spat blood onto the carpet.

"Is there an override switch?" Xander asked the same guy.

"I don't know, I'm new here".

"Why work for him?" I asked as I rounded on him.

"To save my sister from being sold by him to some rich bloke in Geneva" He hung his head. Fuck Henry was selling girls all over the world.

"Why your sister?" Frank asked.

"He saw her in town and said she looked perfect for his business. At first, we thought he meant as a secretary or something, but he meant for his business in forced marriage. We tried to keep her hidden, but Henry kept finding her and threatening us. She isn't of legal age yet, she just turned fourteen last week. He said if I proved loyal to him then he would spare her. He plans to take her next month to be programmed in preparation for her sale" the guy said as tears spilled from his eyes. I'm betting he thought his sister's life was over now.

"Your sister will be safe; Henry is in our custody and will be handed off to the correct authorities later today" Xander told him. The guy looked up at Xander with wide eyes.

"Who are you people to have that much power?" He asked.

"I'm Xander, president of the Maverick's. I help those who deserve helping and take down those who deserve justice to be served on them" Xander replied as he cut the guy's zip ties. "I'm undoing the ties as I believe you will be with us and not try anything funny or stupid. Ring your family and tell them to go to this address saying Xander authorised it, Peg will take care of them until we get you there" Xander gave the guy a business card and turned to look at the other men still tied up leaning against the wall.

"Does anyone have a reason to be here other than to be Henry's lackey?" Xander asked them as we all watched them flinch, a young guy or should I say boy sniffled and I pointed him out to Xander.

"You boy, how old are you?" Xander stood in front of him.

"Sixteen sir."

"What's your name and why are you here?" I asked him, feeling sick at the thought that Henry was using minors for security as well as selling them.

"Jake sir, Henry took me from my family and told me if I didn't do as he said then he would kill my baby brother".

The fucker was sick in the head, threatening to kill a child while forcing another child to do his dirty work was disgusting, Henry needed to die for what he was doing. But unfortunately, the laws in this country would mean he served the rest of his life in prison instead. Xander cut Jake's ties and pulled him to his feet.

"You're safe now and so are your family, do the same as I told the other guy and stay behind my men. Can you tell me if anyone else here deserves to be freed?"

"No, none of them deserve to be free, except for Niall the guy you just freed already, he's the only one who didn't hit or abuse me" Jake looked at the other guy and nodded.

"Again, does anyone know of a way into the suite?" Xander shouted at the men still sitting on the floor.

"Only from inside, Sarah the maid can open the door from inside" One guy grunted.

"And how do we get this maid to open the door?" I asked, desperate to see Tiff and make sure she was safe.

"Only if we text her, but if we do that, she will know that we are under attack and have orders to kill the girl" Well I'll be damned Henry had a failsafe plan too.

"Hold up, can all the maids open the door from inside?" Frank asked.

"Yeah, but I think only Sarah is inside" Another guy said.

"Maisie" I said as I saw where Frank was going with this question. Frank nodded and pulled his phone out typing a message to Maisie who I hoped was inside the suite still. A few seconds later we heard the sound of the lock click and the door swing open.

"Maisie?" Frank asked the small timid girl as she rubbed her arms and shuffled her feet. She nodded her head and pointed down the hallway towards a double door.

"Tiff is down there, hurry though before Sarah gets back from the kitchen" I ran past her heading straight for the door she pointed at and barrelled through it. The sight that greeted me froze me in the spot. Tiff was standing in the middle of the room, her white dress looked like something from every little girl's dream, her black hair curled and weaving down behind her. But what had me freeze was the girl stood behind her holding a knife to Tiff's throat.

"Don't take another step" She shouted at me, fear making her voice tremble.

"Just put the knife down and step back, I'm not here to hurt you" I held my hands up and took a small step forward, I could sense Frank and Xander at my back.

"Master said I had to kill her if anyone but him entered the suite" Her hand shook. Then I noticed how Tiff wasn't moving, I looked at her face, she had no emotions showing, her eyes glossed over. She was fucking drugged. As I watched her face, she swayed, then her eyes closed as she fell to the floor. I wasn't quick enough to catch her, but Sarah panicked, and the knife caught on Tiff's arm as Sarah went to stop her from falling. Blood flowed fast from the deep cut across Tiff's elbow. Maisie ran into the room knocking Sarah back and the knife flying across the floor towards Frank, Xander was next to me as we tried to stem the blood flow from Tiff's elbow.

"Doc, in here now" Xander shouted as a middle-aged man carrying a leather bag ran into the room, his blonde hair flipping over his eyes before he brushed it back. He pulled some powder out of a tub in his bag and spread it on to the cut.

"That will hold for now, but we need to get her back to base now" Doc said as he looked at Tiff's eyes lifting each eyelid one at a time.

"What drug did he give her?" Doc asked Sarah who was now sobbing in the corner being guarded by Maisie and two of Xander's men.

"We don't know, he had them in her food and drink, at least three times today he drugged her" Maisie replied.

"Please, I didn't want to. He made me, said if I didn't then he would make me his whore." Sarah cried.

"He can't get you anymore Sarah, I told you that she could help, but you wouldn't believe me" Maisie whispered to Sarah.

"How many of you are there that he uses like that? Like his own personal sex toy?" Adam asked the girls.

"Just me, and Sarah is new, but she has seen enough to know not to go against what Master says" Maisie looked down at her feet.

"Maisie, I promise you that Henry will never touch you again, you are free from him, you both are" I told them as I scooped Tiff into my arms ready to follow Doc and Xander.

"Come with us, you both need checking over" Adam held his hand out to both the girls who stood up to go with him, he grabbed Maisie by the hand and led them both out of the suite with us following close behind. In the elevator I watched as Adam wrapped his arm around Maisie in a protective way as she shivered with fear at leaving the building.

"How long since you last left the building?" I asked as panic set in on her face as we got closer to the ground floor.

"Too long, maybe a year since I saw the garden on the roof."

"That bastard" Adam seethed as he squeezed Maisie tighter making her yelp.

"Sorry, a beautiful girl like you should be allowed to see the sun and feel the wind" Adam gushed making Maisie blush and Sarah giggle.

"Looks like I have a couple of new members to my group" Xander chuckled as we both watched Maisie wrap a hand around Adam's arm.

"Wait, what? You mean you would take us both in?" Sarah asked with hope in her eyes.

"Yep, you both seem nice enough even with the drugging and accidental knife incident" Xander shrugged as Sarah smiled wide.

These girls had obviously gone through a lot in the last few years or in Sarah's case months. Xander offering them a home would seem like they had won the lottery.

I had Tiff in my arms and bleeding as well as drugged up with fuck knows what. I only hoped that whatever drug she had been given wouldn't cause any lasting damage and that Doc could somehow bring her around again. Tiff was limp in my arms, her arm bandaged up and held against her chest with a sling. The white dress she had been wearing was torn away as much as possible so that I could lift her up without tripping over the damn fabric. She looked stunning standing in the dress, but it wasn't my Tiff. My girl wasn't all puffy princess dresses and lace. No, my Tiff would rock up on her wedding day wearing her jeans and boots with a band t-shirt on if it was allowed. Although maybe for a wedding she would make an exception and wear something fancy.

Xander helped me put Tiff on the backseat of his Range Rover before we both jumped in the front and headed for the base as Doc called it. Apparently, the group used a base for all medical non-life-threatening injuries so as to avoid too many questions from the police. Because as we now know not all police officers are legit and if some bad ass wanted to find an injured person, then they check hospitals meaning the police get a tip off and then tip off whoever is looking for said person. No wonder people go missing never to be found again.

The base was an old club house on the outskirts of town, as we pulled up Doc was ready with a gurney and a few other people to take Tiff straight to the medical unit of the building. Xander had promised me that all the medical staff here had also worked at the hospital but were fed up with the bullshit that happened there. He said my girl would be safe and I believed him.

"I'll fetch you once we have her settled" Doc told me as I lay Tiff on the gurney kissing her forehead. I stood back and watched as they wheeled her into the club house. Xander patted my shoulder.

"Drink?"

"Yeah, I think I need it after the day we've had" I answered as I followed him into the club and up to a bar.

"Doc said he would get you, shouldn't be more than a couple of hours" Xander told me as he poured me a whiskey.

"Can I set up a room for the girls?" Adam asked as he walked over with Maisie still tucked into his side and Sarah trailing behind.

"Yeah, plenty of rooms up on the third floor, Peg sorted rooms out for the others yet?"

"Yeah, Jake's family got here ten minutes ago, Niall and his sister are ... oh, here they are" Adam grinned as Niall and a small teenage girl walked over to us.

"Thanks so much for this" Niall shook Xander's hand.

"It's nothing, as long as you and your sister are safe then I'm good" Xander replied.

"Niall? Deedee?"

"Dad?" Niall asked as he spun round to face the voice.

"Dad" Niall's sister said as she sobbed and ran into the arms of one of Xander's men.

"Dad, how? I thought you were dead" Niall sounded shocked, but the smile was happiness at seeing his dad alive.

"Xander here saved me, he found me by the bins at the back of Nola Corp a few years back. I came looking for you, but the house was empty, and no one knew where you had gone." Their dad said as Niall ran into his arms and the three of them hugged each other.

"Yeah, found him beaten to a bloody pulp and left for dead, he talked about his kids, didn't figure he was talking about those two though. Don't you just love family reunions like this" Xander smiled and raised his glass. I had to admit it was amazing seeing these kids reunited with their dad that they thought was dead. I just hope that I'm reunited with Tiff soon and that she is herself. I also hope he didn't get his fucking hands on her.

I sat back, drink in hand and watched as Niall and his sister sat in the corner talking about everything, they had missed with each other. I helped that happen, that I had actually helped save two people and reunite them with their dad. Maybe I wasn't a failure after all. Tiff was safe and so were Niall, Jake, Sarah, Maisie and Deedee and I helped with that.

CHAPTER 29
TIFF

My head throbbed as I tried to open my eyes, the light was too bright, and I immediately shut them again groaning at the pain I felt all over my body. What happened? The last thing I remember is drinking some water. Wait Sarah she drugged the water. Why? Where am I? Why do I hurt everywhere? Groaning again I tried to open my eyes again, I blinked a few times to adjust to the light before looking around me. Panic set in as I didn't recognise the room I was in, and two men sat by the door.

"Go get Travis and Xander tell them she is awake" A male voice sounded from the other side of the room, I whipped my head around and came face to face with another man I didn't recognise.

"Calm down Tiff, I'm the doc, I took care of you and your injuries. You need to calm down. Your heart is beating too fast right now."

"Where am I? "

"The base of Xander's Mavericks, we rescued you and a few others. Travis will be here soon, now please calm down" The doc told me, panic was still setting in though as I fought to breath, my chest tight and arms heavy. Had he drugged me like the others had? Where is Henry? Was he coming for me now?

"Travis get over here now, you need to calm her down before her heart gives out, with the amount of drugs they gave her and are still in her system a panic attack is not good" The doc yelled as I felt strong warm arms embrace me and heard Travis whisper in my ear.

"It's ok firefly, I'm here now, you're safe, I got you" his voice did calm me as my panic turned to tears and sobs of relief and joy. I was with Travis, I was safe.

"Cole, Claire" I sobbed trying to tell Travis not to trust them "They ... they ... drugged me" I managed to get out.

"I know babe I know" He picked me up and climbed onto the bed settling me back on his lap as he hugged me and kissed my head.

"The police are dealing with them now and Henry is in custody as well. We have people we can trust dealing with them. Your safe now" Travis reassured me.

"Tiff? We need to ask a few questions, so we know whether or not you need further treatment" A man with a funny mohawk hair style asked me. I nodded for him to continue.

"Did Henry or anyone do anything sexual to you?" he asked as Travis sucked in a breath. I shook my head before replying.

"No... I don't think so ... they drugged me a lot, so bits are missing but I feel fine and don't think they did anything".

"Maybe we should do a rape kit just to be sure" Doc said looking between Travis and the other man.

"I think that is the best idea, just to be sure. I'll get Melody down to do it though so as to not freak Tiff out anymore."

"Xander, I'm staying with Tiff" Travis growled at the funny looking man, who I now knew to be called Xander.

"I never said you couldn't, but shouldn't you ask your girl first? She might want privacy for this" Xander looked between me and Travis.

"I want him to stay" I whispered.

"As you wish, I'll go fetch Melody for you. Maisie is itching to see you as well, so I'll send her down when Melody comes back up".

"Maisie, she's here?" I sat upright looking around the room.

"Yeah, Maisie helped us get you out, I guess you gave her Franks number?" Travis asked me.

"Yeah, but she and Sarah drugged me".

"They had no choice, if they didn't then Henry would beat and rape them" Xander told me.

"Are they both safe?" I couldn't help but worry now about them both.

"Yes, they are both here and safe" Xander told me as he patted my shoulder and turned to leave. "Melody will be down in a few minutes" he told me before leaving with the doc following behind.

"I was so scared Tiff, I thought I'd lost you" Travis rubbed a thumb over my knuckles as he held me tight in his arms.

"You saved me" I whispered.

"We had help, Amber arranged for Xander's men to help us as the police couldn't be trusted given, they let you get kidnapped."

"How does Amber know Xander?" I was curious how Amber could know a man like Xander.

"Through a friend back when she was in care, talking of which Xander's girlfriend knows you and is eager to see you as well."

"Who? I don't know anyone" I answered with curiosity burning at me.

"Lara, she said her name was, tiny girl with long blonde curly hair".

"Lara? Lara is here? With Xander? "I couldn't believe it, Lara was the only person in the care home who didn't bother me.

"Yeah, she's upstairs in the bar with the others we rescued from Henry".

"Others? Who?"

"A guard called Niall, he was forced to work for Henry to save his sister Deedee, they found their dad when they came here. Xander saved their dad a few years back when he found him beaten to within an inch of his life. That was a family reunion that even had me shed a tear or two. Then Sarah and Maisie. Oh, Maisie seemed to be getting on well with Xander's right hand man Adam, thinking love might be in the air for those two. Then there is Jake, he's only sixteen, Henry threatened to kill his baby brother if he didn't work for him. He is upstairs with his family now and has got a lot of information on Henry and his business associates so he and his family will probably go into witness protection later on." Travis told me. This was information overload, but I was glad we helped save a few people.

"Hey, I'm Melody, I need to just do a rape kit on you, I'm sure Doc explained" A young lady probably in her late twenties stepped into the room locking the door behind her and walking towards me with a package in her hands. Her short black hair shaped her round face.

"I'll just pop you back on the bed Tiff, do you want me here or outside?" Travis moved and set me back on the bed as he stood next to it, I gripped his hand firmly.

"Stay, please" I begged as tears slipped from my eyes and ran down my cheeks. What if Henry had done something to me while I was drugged? Travis nodded and stood holding my hand as Melody set about doing her thing while I lay on the bed following her instructions but feeling numb.

"All done, I can tell you that you were not tampered with from what I can tell in any way while with that man" She shuddered while smiling at me. Thank God for that. I heard Travis let out a breath I didn't know he had been holding. Guess he was just as worried as I was.

"Lara and Maisie are dying to come down and see you, but I was thinking that if you're up to it maybe we could get you changed and head up there to them" Melody suggested. Getting changed out of this gown would be great, wait gown? I was wearing a wedding dress, who changed me?

"I changed you" Melody said as she must have seen the panic on my face.

"Thank you, are there clothes for me to change into?"

"Yeah, there are some sweatpants and a t-shirt on the chair in the corner, get changed and I'm sure Travis will show you the way up" She waved as she stepped out the room closing the door behind her.

"He didn't touch me Trav, am I really safe?"

"You're safe, I promise. Now let's get you changed and ready to meet the public" Travis chuckled.

After getting changed Travis led me up some stairs and into a large what seemed to be a pub bar area.

"Tiff, girl you scared the crap out of me" Amber grabbed me and hugged me before pulling back to look at me.

"Don't do that again, ever" She choked back a sob.

"Tiff? Lara stepped up behind Amber.

"Lara, I knew you liked bikes and the bad boy but wow" I laughed.

"Yeah, but Xander isn't a bad boy, he's sort of a superhero".

"He sure is," Travis laughed at my side.

Lara pulled me into a hug just the same as Amber had. In all the time Lara spent in the care home we never hugged, we occasionally spoke but never much more than a hello and maybe asking about her bike.

"Tiff, I'm so sorry for drugging you" Sarah stepped forward tears streaming down her face, her hands twisting together in front of her.

"Come here you" I held my arms out for her and she quickly ran into me sobbing as she hugged me. "I know you had no choice; I forgive you" I whispered in her ear.

"Tiff, I'm so glad you are ok, I was worried you had too many drugs" Maisie hugged my side as I still held Sarah.

"I'm all good thanks to Doc" I smiled at her.

"Let's go sit down, the erm MI5 guy needs to ask you a few questions Tiff" Xander said as he wrapped an arm around Lara's shoulder.

"I can't tell him much; I don't remember much" I shrugged as I followed them all to a seating area and sat down next to Travis. A tall older man in a grey suit sat down opposite me and started asking me questions. Questions I had no answers for. After he had finished, he shook my hand and pulled Travis and Xander to a corner and had a hushed conversation with them. I turned to Amber who was now sat with Clint and Mitch.

"Where are Cole and Claire?"

"Claire and Cole are both in custody, Claire had more involvement with Henry's business than we first thought and will be going to prison for a long, long time. Cole is also in custody and has been charged with, drug dealing, conspiracy to kidnap, and conspiracy to drugging, he's looking at a prison sentence too" Clint told me.

"Mitch, I'm sorry about Cole" I grabbed his hand.

"He made his own choices in life, he knew the punishment and he still did it, he's no brother of mine" Mitch stood up and stormed off slamming the door behind him.

"He's hurting, give him time to calm down and I'm sure he will be back to his usual self" Amber held my hand.

"Right guys we can all go home and back to a normal life" Travis said as he walked back over to us.

"Good because I need my bed" Clint yawned and stretched.

"I need a shower and hot chocolate" I laughed.

"Let's go then shall we" Travis held his arm out to me before sweeping me off my feet making me squeal.

"You don't have shoes on," He explained. Makes sense why he's carrying me then.

"What now though? Do I need to give a statement?"

"Nope, Xander and that man who questioned you have everything they need. Now let's get you home shall we" with that Travis carried me out to his car and drove us both back home, our home.

CHAPTER 30

TRAVIS

It has been three days since we rescued Tiff from Henry. Today was Cole's sentencing. Mitch was still struggling to cope with what his brother had done though, but had gone back to work, something Tiff kept asking to do. I agreed she could go back after today's hearing. Frank had taken her on properly at the garage so she wouldn't need to go to college anymore which she was more than happy about, apparently, she hated college more than she hated the smell of cabbage cooking. Her words not mine. Xander was having a get-together later today and had invited us all over. He had told me he planned to propose to Lara tonight so it would double as an engagement party.

"Are you ready Trav?"

"Yeah, are we still picking Mitch up or is Clint doing it?" I asked Tiff as I did my tie up. I hated wearing these damn suits and ties, but Tiff insisted that I wore it to the court each and every time. We still had Claire's trial and Henry's to go through but the solicitor dealing with it had told us that given the evidence the trials should be over quickly even though Claire and Henry are both pleading not guilty.

"You look super sexy in that get up" Tiff said in a sexy sultry way as she eyed me up and down biting on her lower lip.

"You look hot in that little black dress" I stalked towards her grabbing her round the waist as I rubbed my body against her so she could feel just how sexy I thought she looked.

"Stop that Mr, we need to get going, and Clint is getting Mitch" She slapped my hands away and backed out of the room with me following behind her grinning at how sexy she looked. I was one lucky man indeed.

The sentencing for Cole took all of ten minutes. He was sentenced to three years in prison. Mitch looked at his brother before telling him yet again that he was no brother of his and walking out of the courtroom. Amber chased after him.

"He's not taking it well at all is he?" Tiff asked.

"He blames himself, saying if he was a good brother he would've noticed and been able to stop Cole. He also says it's his failing as a brother that helped get you kidnapped" Clint told Tiff.

"Cole is a grown man, old enough to know right from wrong, he made mistakes not Mitch. I don't blame him for Cole's mistakes" Tiff told Clint.

"You need to tell Mitch that, not me," Clint shrugged as we all walked out the courthouse to find Amber and Mitch.

"Mitch, can we talk?" Tiff asked as she walked over to them.

"What about? Look I know it's my fault and I'm sorry".

"No, don't you dare. It's Cole's fault not yours. He is old enough to know what he did was wrong, yet he chose to do it anyway, that's on him not you. I will never blame you Mitch, not ever. Do you hear me?" Tiff took his arms in her small hands and gripped him tight. Mitch looked at her before he crumbled into her arms and cried into her shoulder. He was finally letting it all out, all those pent-up emotions came flooding out in his sobs and tears on Tiff's shoulder as we all wrapped around them both in a group hug.

"Come on you lot, let's get ready for Xander's party, I think Brad and Chance are meeting us there" Clint stepped back first.

"Yeah, I need to get out of this monkey suit" Mitch chuckled as he straightened his jacket then tugged his tie off. I followed his lead as did Clint. All of us men stood with our ties undone hanging around our necks, top buttons opened and hands in our pockets.

"Hold it right there" Amber shouted as she whipped her phone out Tiff copying her, and both started giggling as they snapped a few pictures of us.

"Hot damn girl, these men look hot" Amber pretended to fan herself as Tiff giggled.

"They sure do," she winked at me.

"I'll meet you all at Xander's place, Mitch you coming?" I asked as I headed towards Tiff.

"Yeah, I'll meet you all there. Tiff, love you" Mitch said as he ruffled her hair. I knew he meant he loved her as a sister, and I had nothing to worry about.

"Love ya too bro" She kicked his arse as he walked past her making us all laugh. It felt good to laugh after the shitstorm we had all been through these past few weeks.

Xander's place was decked out with banners and balloons, a disco was set up in the corner with a fancy light up floor taking up half the room, table after table of food was spread out along with tables for people to sit at. Xander walked in through the back door and smiled at us as he walked over.

"Hey, so glad you could make it" He hugged Tiff before clapping me on the shoulder.

"So how are you going to surprise Lara with the proposal with all these happy engagement banners up?" I asked with an eyebrow raised.

"Ahhh, she thinks this is for you two" Xander rubbed the back of his neck as he looked at me and then a laughing Tiff.

"Us? Seriously? Jeez she is going to be pissed when she finds out you lied, even with you proposing to her" Tiff laughed.

"What if it's not a lie?" I asked as I dropped to one knee and pulled a box out of my pocket opening it up for her.

"Tiffany Jade, I know we haven't been together long, and it's been a hurricane of sorts, but I feel like I've known you all my life. My heart beats stronger for you, my mind is clearer because of you. You brought light to my life when all I knew was darkness. Will you marry me and continue to be the light to my dark?" I watched as she looked down at me tears spilling from her eyes, and she nodded.

"Yes, yes Trav I'll marry you, but I'm not wearing a damn dress" Everyone cheered and laughed.

I never thought that I would fall in love yet alone want to get married but here we are, and I couldn't be any happier.

"My turn now" Xander whispered as he patted my shoulder.

"Lara, baby where are you?" He shouted across the room. Lara stepped off the dance floor and made her way over to us.

"Hey, I was so excited when Xander told me Trav was going to propose, hope you like the decorations" Lara hugged Tiff.

"It's perfect thank you".

"Lara, baby?" Xander dropped to one knee and Lara gasped trying to pull him back up.

"What are you doing you fool?" She whispers shouted at him as all his men gathered round with drinks in their hands.

"Lara, my ole lady, will you be my ole girl for life and ride bitch into the afterlife with me when we leave the roads when we are old and grey? Will you always be my ride or die? Will you take my name and be mine forever? Will you marry this fool?" Xander asked her as everyone laughed at his speech while Lara sobbed and nodded her head, unable to speak.

"I think she said yes" Tiff answered for her as Xander stood up and whirled Lara around, while everyone cheered and clinked glasses together. Tonight, was special for all of us and we got to share it with our friends.

We partied hard and late into the night or was it early the next day? Either way we had fun with those we were closest to. We had new friends and allies now and life was looking good. These past few weeks would finally be put behind us in the next few days after Claire and Henry were sentenced. I couldn't wait to get on with life and enjoy spending it with my girl. My phone rang in my pocket as we sat in Xander's kitchen area drinking coffee.

"Hello, Frank?"

"Yeah, Trav I just got a call from Wesley, Henry was found hanged in his cell about an hour ago".

"What? How?" I looked up at Tiff who looked at me wanting to know what was going on.

"Nobody is sure how, maybe he just couldn't face up to his crimes".

"Or maybe someone got to him?" I answered knowing were Frank was going with this.

"It's possible, he ripped a lot of families apart with his selling girls to be whores or as he put it breeders for the rich men, anyone of those families could've got at him if they knew the right person and had the money".

"Yeah true, look I gotta go and fill the others in, let me know if this will cause us any problems".

"Shouldn't do, if anything I'd say it's over now, just Claire to sentence and then you and Tiff can enjoy life. What did she say?"

"She said yes" I smiled.

"Congratulations son, I'll see you later".

I hung up and looked around the table. Xander, Lara, Tiff, Clint, Amber, Chance, Brad, Mitch, Maisie, Adam, Sarah, Jake, Niall and Deedee sat with us.

"What happened?" Tiff asked me as she took my hand.

"Henry was found hanged in his cell earlier, they don't know if it was suicide or murder but either way he's gone now".

"What a coward if he hung himself but if someone got to him then yay for them" Maisie shouted, and everyone seemed to agree.

"It's all over then?" Sarah asked me.

"Yeah, it's all over, none of you will ever have to face that man again".

"I say good riddance to another evil man" Xander raised his cup of coffee up "Here's to a brighter better future with new and old friends" He toasted as we all said his words and clinked our cups. He was right, the future was looking better and brighter.

A few weeks later Claire was sentenced to fifteen years in prison, and it seemed she had a hand in helping Henry take girls to be sold, as well as her involvement with kidnapping Tiff. We decided not to attend court that day and Clint went instead. The things that she did were disgusting and Clint said it was best for Tiff that we stayed away. Claire did put up a fight when she was led down to the cells after her sentencing and screamed at Clint `` It's all that bitchs fault, if she had just stayed away then daddy would've taken me instead and we would all be free and happy".

Her obsession with her stepdad was kind of sickening in reality but I suppose she was just desperate to be loved, and I could and would never be able to give her the love she craved, or any love if I'm honest. She was a crazy girl that's for sure.

Both Tiff and I had started back at the garage and Mitch was back to his usual funny charming self, we all got on better together and Mitch had even started hanging out with us at practice sessions giving us his thoughts and insight which was actually really helpful. Tiff was yet to sing in public, but no one wanted to push her after her little freak out when she heard herself on the radio.

You could say life was pretty fucking perfect.

EPILOGUE
2 YEARS LATER
TIFF

My wedding day was finally here, we put it off a few times as life had a way of throwing us a curveball, like the little bundle I was currently looking at. Xavier, our little boy. Finding out I was pregnant was a shock to us both. I collapsed at work and Trav rushed me straight to hospital as I fell breaking my arm when I collapsed. They did a pregnancy test before they did the x-ray. I was ten weeks gone and had no idea. Travis couldn't speak for a while after the doctor told us. I thought he was upset at first before a smile spread across his face.

"A baby, we are having a baby" he grabbed my face in his hands and kissed my hand then my lips.

Here we are a year later with our little boy lying on the bed next to me as we get ready for our wedding. Xavier looked up at me with his big blue eyes and gurgled with his little smile. He was the image of Travis with my eyes. Amber swept across the room scooping Xavier into her eyes.

"Hey little guy you need to stop distracting your mummy as she needs to get dressed ready to meet your daddy for their special day" She hugged him in her arms as she pointed to the dress hanging up.

"Get it on girl" She ordered me.

I know I said I wouldn't wear a dress for our wedding, but a girl can change her mind, can't she? I did after seeing Amber in hers when she married Clint six months ago and I sort of thought about it when Lara and Xander got married a year and a half ago. My dress was custom made by a friend of Lara's who was doing a dress making course in college, she used the dress as part of her final coursework, and I admit it is stunning. It had a racy navy-blue leather bodice with velvet piping around the edges and seams of the boning, the skirt part was a white satin material with navy blue detailing in it that looked like a marbled effect, it was perfect for me, not over the top flowy or puffy, a simple elegant straight skirt with a small train on the back. I stepped up to the dress and Lara appeared from nowhere making me jump.

"Here let me help you while Amber gets cutie over there changed" she took the dress from me and started to help me into it, pulling the laces on the bodice tight to fit me properly. She stepped back and stood next to Amber who was now holding Xavier dressed in his navy-blue romper.

"You look stunning, Travis isn't going to be able to hide his "Amber hit Lara in the chest to make her stop talking. Over the past couple years, we came to realise that Lara had no filter and a very dirty mind and mouth, probably what attracted Xander to her in the first place, they were very much a suited couple, and they were expecting their first baby in three months' time. Apparently seeing me pregnant made Lara broody. Both Xander and Lara were amazing with Xavier as were Amber and Clint.

A knock at the door interrupted us and Lara opened it to see Frank stood there waiting for me. He looked good in his navy-blue suit and tie.

"You look beautiful Tiff, shall we?" He held his arm out for me. As my parents were both dead Frank had become a father figure to me and would be walking me down the aisle today, but I had Frank, Clint, Mitch and Amber to give me away, it felt right as they had all helped me become the woman I am today.

Travis stood at the altar looking at me as Frank and I made our way to him. My heart was hammering in my chest, the look on Travis face was of pure love and lust, yeah, I looked hot in this dress.

Amber, Lara and Maisie walked behind me as my bridesmaids while Amber and Clint's adopted daughter threw confetti in front of us. She was adorable at four years old with her brown hair in ringlets and her princess Elsa dress on, she chose her own dress, and I was more than happy with her choice. Amber and Clint adopted her four months ago, she was the daughter of Clint's cousin who died from cancer. They did the right thing and took little Olive in and have loved her as a daughter ever since.

Travis took my hand as Frank handed me over to him and all the girls took their seats. Clint stood next to Travis with Mitch, Brad and Chance, yes, he had four best men as he couldn't pick between them. Mitch had become part of the family over the past couple years.

The ceremony passed in a blur and before I knew it, we were heading off on our honeymoon to a destination only Travis knew. Amber and Clint were looking after Xavier for us, I missed him as soon as we drove down the road, but I knew he was in good hands.

Life was perfect, I had love, a family and friends. I was happier than ever before.

TRAVIS

Our wedding day took a few attempts to get here but here we are. Tiff looks so beautiful in her dress, so sexy, shit I hope these trousers can hide my growing cock. Amber was holding Xavier in her arms as she walked behind Tiff. Did I tell you I'm a dad? Yeah, I'm a dad and Xavier is our boy, he's perfect just like his mum, although everyone says he looks like me with Tiff's eyes. The day we found out about him was a shock. Tiff collapsed at work landing on her arm awkwardly and breaking it, they did a test at the hospital before she could have an x-ray and then told us she was pregnant, they did a scan because she didn't know how far along, she was. Seeing our little man on the screen was amazing, she was ten weeks old, the doc said. I was speechless for a while before it sunk in, and I couldn't have been any happier. We postponed our wedding because Tiff didn't want to be a beachball when we got married. Now a year after and we are finally becoming Mr and Mrs Jones.

Clint and Amber adopted little Olive, Clint's cousin's girl after she died a few months back. She is adorable throwing confetti in front of Tiff as she walks towards me looking as gorgeous as ever. Lara walked behind with Amber and Maisie. Lara looked blooming with her pregnant belly showing in her Greek goddess style dress, her and Xander married fairly quickly after they got engaged and now, they were expecting their first baby. Maisie and Adam, yeah it didn't last. Maisie can't get over the trauma from her past and Adam lost patience and cheated on her. Xander told him to leave the club and has supported Maisie with her counselling and now she is in a relationship with Sarah.

The ceremony was over in a flash as we said our vows and then partied until we had to leave for our honeymoon. Leaving Xavier behind was going to be hard on us both but it was only for a week, and he was with Amber and Clint, so all is good. I'm surprising Tiff with a romantic weekend in Amsterdam. No, not a red-light district or drugs. Just windmills and fields full of tulips.

Life has definitely been chaotic for me, at one point I thought my life would always be full of darkness, but then this girl turned up at the garage and life changed. Life is brighter now. In fact, life is perfect.

THE END

Ingram Content Group UK Ltd.
Milton Keynes UK
UKHW040752210723
425555UK00001B/66